MW00676644

THE SACRED LAMP

THE SACRED LAMP

The healing power of a lamp through the gift of the Holy Spirit

DERWYN GOLDEN

To Chaplain Delora Ann
May God bless you and
your family with Grace,
Peace and Prosperity

Derwyn G.
04/23/2022

21st Century Storyteller Productions, Inc

CONTENTS

*"Wisdom is acquired through
thoughts of understanding,
but the thoughts of the unwise are filled with
perversions and confusion."*

---

*"Man captures the beauty of
nature in photographs and paintings;
God creates it."*

---

*"The Glory of a sunrise is due to the
Glory of its Creator."*

DEDICATION

First of all, to almighty God, through the power of the Holy Spirit, who inspired me to write this novel.

My deepest and sincere thanks to my aunt, Dr. Cledie Taylor. She has instructed and nurtured me throughout my life with tools of knowledge and gifts to enhance my abilities.

To my grandmother, Osie Collins-Matthews. She encouraged me and supported my ideas and projects until she made her transition to be with the Lord in 1996.

To Pamela McCants, who has always supported my ideas, whom I love dearly.

And to my cousin Larry Gaines and others too numerous to mention, who believed in me throughout my journey.

PROLOGUE

T his novel begins in the early 1990s, taking you through a past journey (The Gift) to the present (The Discovery). The book will inspire and give hope to a world that has become both autonomous in worshiping God and disobedient in obeying His commands. Man has established his own rules by redefining morality to satisfy his lewd and immoral behavior. Although this book is fictitious by definition of its content, it focuses on the real power and sanctifying grace that only the Holy Spirit can give to those who are believers in our Lord and Savior, Jesus Christ.

In Holy Scripture, King James Bible, Act 19, verses 11–12, Apostle Paul writes about preaching in Ephesus and working unusual miracles by his hands. Handkerchiefs and aprons were brought from his body and given to the sick and those possessed with evil spirits. The sick were healed, and the evil spirits came out of those who were possessed. God gave Paul the power to do these miracles through the Holy Spirit. In this novel, the Holy Spirit's healing power manifests itself through the light of a lamp, introduced by a young boy named Messenger Boy.

The first half of the book is entitled **The Gift**. In these chapters, people in possession of the lamp experience miraculous healings. The cause of these unexplained events is mysterious and unknown. The story begins in Detroit, Michigan, with two of the opening main characters, setting the stage for this mystical journey.

The second half of the book is entitled **The Discovery**. Several years have passed, and the unveiling power within the lamp reveals itself. As it is set in real-life scenarios, conniving people attempt to alter destiny in their favor for personal gain, which is the case here. But what God has put into place for His glory cannot be hidden, changed, or destroyed. With that said, sit back in your favorite chair, put on your reading glasses, and travel down the pathway leading to *The Sacred Lamp*.

Copyright © 2021 by Derwyn Golden

All rights reserved. No part of this book may be reproduced in any manner
whatsoever without written permission except in the case of brief quotations
embodied in critical articles and reviews.

First Printing, 2021

CHAPTER 1

The Gift

The year was 1992, and it was a cold, windy February evening as Ruben Polanski hurried to his car after finishing his twelve-hour shift. He drove a light blue 1987 Ford Taurus sedan and had worked at the Ford Motor Plant in Dearborn, Michigan, for eighteen years. Ruben, a Polish immigrant, came to America at twenty-three with his young son, Joey, in the early 1970s. Ruben's wife, Joanna, Joey's mother, died when she gave birth to Joey while living in Poland. His mother's brother, Uncle Benny, immigrated to America in the late '50s. He frequently wrote Ruben, telling him that in America, there was a better life. Ruben decided that America gave him a better opportunity for raising his son alone, so Ruben and his son came to America and stayed with his Uncle Benny in Hamtramck, Michigan. It was an area where numerous Polish immigrants lived, referred to as Poletown, named after the Polish immigrants who formerly lived there.

Now at the age of forty-three, Ruben's dark brown hair was beginning to thin, and his dark-brown-colored eyes appeared to sit deeper within his tan-colored face, emphasizing his high cheekbones and sharp nose. As Ruben merged onto eastbound Interstate 94, tears began to fill his eyes as he anticipated seeing Joey, his eighteen-year-old son. Ruben exited Interstate 94 and merged onto southbound John C. Lodge Freeway, Interstate 10, which led him to West Forest Street. It was six-thirty, and the night air seemed to hover around the Cass Corridor District, located on the west end of Detroit—known for drug trafficking and prostitution, giving the area a distinct eeriness as Ruben drove along the street, looking for his son. It wasn't comfortable traveling along the Cass

1

Corridor streets because it was a dangerous, unforgiving place to go at night. A familiar figure beckoned to him as one of the ladies standing on the street corner called out to Ruben.

"Hey, baby, are you ready for that date yet?"

As he drove past, he heard them sarcastically laughing and heard another one say, "Girl, he's looking for Poletown Boy, that dope head son of his again." Poletown Boy was a name local drug dealers had labeled his son, which circulated throughout the neighborhood. The Cass Corridor District also housed and fed the homeless, but it was a place where most people avoided. Joey strayed away from the foundation his father provided him by chasing after a girl he met in Poletown on Fat Tuesday, named Diana. Ruben had noticed that since Joey had been seeing Diana, he'd started staying out later and eventually dropped out of school. It escalated to the point where he stayed out all night and didn't care much for his appearance.

Diana had gotten addicted to coke—the street name for cocaine—from hanging around neighborhood girls where she lived in suburbia and easily persuaded Joey to join in on the mystical journey. Diana died from an overdose, and it left Joey spinning out of control, so he had to give up chasing Diana and started chasing drugs on the street. Ruben, a dedicated millwright worker, was committed to doing everything possible for his son's sake. He never remarried, so Joey and his job were his entire life, and canvassing the neighborhood, looking for his son, had become a weekly routine.

After he circled the block a few times, a tall, thin figure stepped out from behind a vacant house, wearing a shabby overcoat and hat with side flaps covering his ears. Ruben drove alongside the young man as he turned and looked toward Ruben. Joey was about six feet tall and looked like his father, with Slavic features and a medium-length beard. Ruben engaged the power window button and rolled down the window on the passenger side, and Joey walked over and leaned down toward the window's opening.

"Hello, Son, get in."

Joey got into the car and immediately placed his hands in front of the warm air vent.

"How are you doing, Son?"

"I'm doing okay, Dad."

Ruben hollered out, "Son, how can you be okay living on the streets of this godforsaken place!"

Joey looked up at his father with a boyish stare that Ruben remembered all too well. It's the look that they shared since Joey was a young lad, symbolizing their loving bond for one another. Still, Joey's appearance and street life attraction made Ruben feel he'd failed his son as a father. Hence, as they traveled toward Hamtramck, they silently sat and gazed at the familiar surroundings that provided access to Norwalk Street.

After a fifteen-minute ride, they drove up to a small wooden-framed house. Ruben pulled up into the driveway, and they both got out of the car. They entered through the front door and walked into the living room of the dwelling—a two-bedroom house moderately furnished with attractive colonial-style furnishings. Ruben headed for the dining room that led to the kitchen area as Joey walked over to the mantle above the fireplace. He picked up a five-by-seven-inch black-and-white photo of his mother and father. A neighborhood friend took the picture before Joey was born. They were standing together in front of the steps of the apartment where they lived in Poland. Joey always claimed that as his mother was dying during his birth, they passionately caught a glimpse of each other passing by. His father always laughed when he told him the story, claiming that he only met her in a dream, and that was all. His father's unbelief stirred up a little resentment in Joey, thinking that his father's unwillingness to believe him was because he wanted to minimize the pain of losing her by erasing her memory from his mind as well as Joey's. Regardless of what his father thought, it was unfair for his father to tell him to let go of his mother's only precious memory that he treasured. Despite that, Joey loved his father and regretted the day he met Diana, convinced that his naivety resulted from his father's strict discipline policies, which led him to pursue a rebellious Diana.

Next to his parents' picture was a photo of him at two years old, sitting on those same steps, dressed in a two-piece suit, and a third picture of his Great Uncle Benny and his wife, Aunt Rachel. They were dressed for a night out in Poletown to celebrate her forty-fifth birthday. Aunt Rachel died before Ruben and Joey came to America to live with Uncle Benny, and six years later, Uncle Benny passed away and left the house to his father. Joey's thoughts were interrupted by his father's voice calling him from the dining room.

"Joey, go and wash your hands and come and eat."

Joey walked past his father, made a left turn, and noticed two steaming hot bowls of stew that his father had placed onto the table. When Joey returned, he sat down at the table with his father. Ruben reached for his hand and blessed the food, and the two of them began eating.

"Well, Son, how does it taste?"

"It's delicious, Father."

"It's from a recipe Mrs. Kowalski gave me from the market down the street. She asked me how you were doing in school."

Joey quickly looked up at Ruben, "And what did you tell her?"

"What I tell her all the time. He's doing fine and will be graduating soon, but I don't know what to tell her when it's time for graduation."

Joey looked down at his meal and continued eating but didn't respond to his father's remarks.

"Well, Son, I'll figure something out by then. Ben told me you were at the shelter again last night. You know his wife, Eileen, is always keeping an eye out on you for me."

"I know Ms. Williams is watching out for me, and I do appreciate it, but I don't like it when she tries to talk to me. It makes me feel uncomfortable."

"Joey, she's only trying to help you. She's a social worker, and she knows how to help you. That's why she volunteers her time at the shelter, to help kids like you."

Joey became upset and lashed out at his father. "I don't need her help or anyone else's!"

"Okay, Son, calm down. I'm going to bed now, and here's some money. Maybe one day you'll use it to buy a set of new clothes instead of drugs."

Joey immediately stood up, took the money off the table, and walked over to his father. He kissed him on the cheek and headed for the front door. Ruben's eyes followed Joey as he closed the door and disappeared out of sight. Ruben rubbed the tears from his eyes, took the two bowls to the kitchen, and placed them into the sink.

CHAPTER 2

The Gift

It was seven-fifteen the following morning, and Ruben was arranging things in his tool bin. Ben Williams, the union rep, walked over to Ruben. Ben was a tall man, with a light brown complexion, in his mid-forties, and built like a linebacker.

"How's it going, Ruben?"

"Hi, Ben. Well, you know, nothing's changed."

"Eileen told me that when she saw Joey at the shelter a couple a days ago, he looked troubled."

"The only thing I can do at this point, Ben, is to keep praying for my son. He won't listen to me anymore. I pray that I don't get a phone call from the police telling me that something has happened to my boy."

"Eileen told me to tell you that she hasn't given up on him yet."

"Tell her I said thank you, and God bless the two of you."

"Not a problem, Ruben, and I'll talk with you later."

Ben stepped away as General Foreman, James Lucas Henning, walked up. James was medium height with dark brown hair and five years younger than Ruben. James, referred to as Jim, had known Ruben since 1974, the year they were both hired. Jim was familiar with the problems he had with his son and gave encouragement and moral support.

"Good morning, Ruben."

"Good morning, Jim."

"You look tired. Another long night?"

"Yes, but I'm okay. How's Ryan doing?"

"He's doing fine and growing like a weed. He'll be thirteen years old next week. Man how time flies. He said he wants to go to school to become a lawyer."

"He'll make a good attorney. Maybe one day, when he grows up and becomes a lawyer, he can represent my Joey."

"Ruben, I know Joey has issues, but I don't think it's that serious, is it?"

"Jim, the path my son is on, there are only three options: someone will kill him, he will kill himself, or he will get himself into a whole lot of trouble that will land him in prison."

"Let's hope not. Brenda and I will continue to keep you and Joey in our prayers."

"Thank you, Jim."

"Did those parts come in for the crane yet?"

"Not yet, but they should be in later this morning."

"Okay, good, I'll check back with you later."

As Jim walked off, Ruben stood up in front of the tool bin, slowly shaking his head from side to side.

———————

It was five o'clock Saturday late afternoon, and Joey had left his father's house over an hour ago. After taking the fifty dollars his father had given him, he returned to the Cass Corridor area. His father set aside this money four times a week to prevent Joey from stealing to sustain his drug habit, but it still wasn't enough. The money barely bridged the gap because of his high daily usage of drugs. To supplement his income, Joey roamed the neighborhood, breaking into cars searching for merchandise he could sell to unscrupulous buyers. Joey chose a different vacant house or building in the area each night to snort his coke to evade a drug dealer named Mike the Man who he owed money. Joey owed him $200 for a past drug debt but used the fifty dollars he got from his father to utilize the services of another drug dealer named Big Pinky.

He always paid cash for drugs he got from him because people who owed him money and didn't pay it back had a history of coming up missing. On the other hand, Mike the Man wouldn't come looking for you but waited for the opportunity to meet you on the street. Over the past three months, since Diana died, Joey had become extremely street-wise and had no trouble dodging Mike the Man at least up to this point. Joey knew that rival dope dealers kept their business to themselves, so his indebtedness to him was strictly confidential, and he was safe, as long as he continued to stay out of sight.

Joey had snorted his last bit of coke and was hurrying down the steps of an abandoned building to make it over to the Detroit Unity Center before seven o'clock curfew. The Detroit Unity Center, referred to as DU on the street, was an emergency homeless shelter that fed and housed men that needed an overnight place to stay. The men had to check into the facility by seven o'clock each evening and were required to leave the following morning by eight. The shelter accommodated as many as 125 men, all of whom had a heartbreaking story of how they ended up at DU. In most cases, it was drug-related, and Joey's situation was like so many men there. They started taking drugs, influenced by friends or acquaintances. In contrast, others were plagued by their family environment, filled with violence, physical and emotional abuse, which led them to use drugs as a way of escape. In either case, they found themselves homeless and destitute.

As Joey turned the corner and caught a glimpse of the open doorway that led into the shelter, he saw a group of men making a last-minute dash to get inside. Just as he stepped inside, he heard the supervisor tell the door attendant to close and secure the door. Joey had become a regular, and JK, known as Jerry Knockout, was the only person he became friends with while staying in the shelter. JK was thirty-four years old and a former light heavyweight boxing champion. He served ten years in prison for killing a man in self-defense. He had a dark brown complexion, medium weight and height, and had a physique and attitude that made it apparent to everyone that he wasn't a person who dealt with nonsense. He worked as a delivery man for a local office supply store during the day and saved his money to buy a house for his two-year-old son and his baby's mama. Since his baby's mama lived with her sister, he thought it best to wait until he could afford to buy a house before they lived together. Free sleepovers at the DU center allowed JK to save most of his earnings, and he was close to having enough money to bid on a HUD house.

He liked Joey because of his Slavic features that looked a little different from the other handful of Caucasian men who stayed in the shelter and because of his adolescent personality. Joey confided in JK about his attraction to Diana, which led him to a life of drugs and street life living. JK smiled and told him that most women enjoyed snaring the young and innocent like him into their web. That he must seek help and stop chasing drugs because his body would eventually shut down and he would die. That drugs only provided an illusion of escaping reality and was a Houdini magic trick that self-imprisoned one's body and mind, strangling it to death like a boa constrictor.

Joey carefully listened to JK as if he were given instructions from a classroom teacher about an upcoming exam. JK also didn't like the label given to him as Poletown Boy and called him PB instead. JK told Joey it wasn't wise to give out your real name on the streets, and it also was not good to have the dope dealers label you with a name. Joey nodded approvingly and lay back in his bed, looking up at the water-stained ceiling, and waited for the announcement to come for dinner. As he lay there pondering his thoughts, a familiar voice called out his name.

"Hello, Joey."

It was Eileen Williams, the wife of Ben Williams. Her husband worked with his father, and she volunteered her services, providing counseling to the homeless when needed. She was an attractive, light-brown-skinned woman in her early forties with hazel eyes and light brown hair and always checked up on Joey to see how he was doing.

"Hi, Ms. Williams."

"Have you seen your father lately?"

"I saw him today, and I'll see him again tomorrow."

"Good, you know I'm always here for you if you need me."

"Yes, Ms. Williams, I know that, and thank you."

Ms. Williams knew that Joey was uncomfortable speaking to adults in authoritative positions, so she always made her conversation short and to the point. When she walked away, JK looked at Joey with a wide grin.

"Man that's one fine-looking woman."

Joey looked over at JK and smiled. "Hey, JK, don't forget who you're saving money up to buy that house for."

"I won't, but she's reaching out to help you, and that would be a good place to start for getting the help you need. You wouldn't have no problem at all getting counseling two or three times a week while staring at a fine lady like that."

They both laughed and walked toward the back of the building to eat dinner. After dinner, Joey and JK made their way back to their area. JK was leading the way when a man stepped in front of Joey, preventing him from passing. He was a hard-looking, tall, dark-skinned man who frequently stayed in the shelter and was known for bullying other residents. His name was Tommy, and Joey had seen him before, demanding food, money, or anything else he could confiscate from residents, but this was his first time confronting Joey.

"Hey, white boy, it's your turn."

Joey nervously answered, "My turn for what?"

"Don't play dumb white boy"—Tommy smiled—"you know it's time to pay the piper, and I'm the piper."

"I don't have anything to give you."

"Well, you got about three seconds to come up with a satisfactory offer, or you're gonna have a broken jaw."

Joey looked terrified as Tommy started counting. "One, two—" Before he counted to three, JK stepped in front of Joey and stared Tommy in the eye.

"He ain't got shit to give you, and neither do I."

"I'm gonna break your jaw first, and then I'll deal with the white boy."

By this time, a group of men turned and looked in their direction. JK knew that fighting in the shelter wasn't allowed and would get them both put out on the streets.

JK replied, "Okay, Mr. Big Shot, we can meet out back in the morning and settle this."

"Bet, nigger. I hope you got your health insurance premiums paid up."

The commotion drew the attention of a staff member, Mr. Thomas, who started approaching the men.

"What's going on here?"

JK said, "Nothing, Mr. Thomas, just a couple of friends getting reacquainted."

"Well, you guys get back to your areas because it's time to shut down for the night."

JK and Tommy stared at each other before walking away as JK slowly moved his head up and down. "I'll see you in the morning, my brother."

"Bet."

CHAPTER 3

The Gift

The following morning was a cold and windy day with light snow falling. It was nine o'clock, and Joey stood on the corner of Alexandria and Cass Avenue, waiting for his father to pick him up. They attended Sunday mass service every week, the only requirement his father demanded of him if he wanted to continue receiving his weekly $200 allowance. Joey had a suit hanging up in his father's closet, along with a black cashmere coat that he wore to church each week. During that time, they spent quality time together, and after service, they visited a local restaurant and ate dinner together.

As Ruben pulled up, he examined his son's frail, unmuscular physique and thought how life could be a blessing to some, yet a curse to others. He prayed for his son every day, hoping that one day God would deliver him from the clutches of a dismal existence, an existence deprived of pride and humility. Joey got into the car and stared straight ahead, not allowing eye contact with his father. He wanted to avoid seeing his father's look of disgust, but regardless of his father's discontentment with him, Joey knew that they had a loving bond that would never end.

"Hello, Son."

"Hi, Dad, how are you?"

"I'm doing fine, Son, and you?"

"I'm doing okay, Dad." Joey paused for a moment. "I know you worry about me, and I want to stop the way I'm living my life. I've decided to talk with Ms. Williams about helping me."

Ruben smiled and looked at Joey with tears running down his face.

"That would make me happy, Son."

Joey looked over at his father and smiled back as they made their way to Poletown.

———————————

Joey thought about the day he'd spent with his father. Unlike most Sundays, this day had been an extraordinary one because he'd committed to himself and his father that he wanted to change his life. Joey knew that it would take time to turn away from his current lifestyle to one that didn't include drugs on the menu. That transition wasn't going to be easy, but he owed it to his father and himself to stop destroying his life, playing in a game that he could never win. If nothing else, it gave the promise to a future that could prove to be both fruitful and fulfilling, but his shivering body, due to the cold winter wind, brought into focus the reality that Joey wasn't there yet. So, for now, it was business as usual as he hurried through the streets of the Cass Corridor District, making his way to buy drugs from Big Pinky.

It was six forty-five, and Joey left the back door of a vacant house and had fifteen minutes to get to the DU Center before the seven o'clock curfew. He made his way through a maze of side streets and alleyways that he'd chosen as a safe route and heard the distinct rattling sound of a car engine. It was the sound that Mike the Man's maroon Cadillac made and became his car's signature sound, familiar to everyone who hung out in the Cass Corridor District. Joey hid between two vacant houses as the car suddenly stopped in front of a tall, heavyset black man. The man was wearing a dark corduroy jacket, and Joey recognized the man as Fat Boy. It was the name given to him by a drug dealer because of his massive body size. A loud voice pierced the cold night air as the driver got out and approached Fat Boy, standing on the corner.

"Hey, you fat mother...!" Mike the Man took a deep breath. "Where's my f... money?"

Fat Boy pleaded with Mike the Man. "I'm gonna pay you, Big Mike. I ain't got the money yet."

"Well, bitch, I'm collecting now!"

Fat Boy attempted to run away as Mike the Man fired two shots from a nine-millimeter revolver, and Fat Boy fell to the ground. Mike the Man got into his car and sped away as Joey, frightened and shaken, stood there watching. Joey turned around and ran toward the alley, between two other vacant houses, and across an open field until he saw the shelter's entranceway. It was a terrifying experience and reminded him of the fate that awaited him, if and when he met up with Mike the Man.

———————

Joey entered the shelter, looking around for JK. The facility provided beds on a first-come basis to overnight residents, and the quota of men allowed to stay overnight depended on the availability of beds. JK always arrived early, saving a bed for Joey. He waved his arms up in the air to get Joey's attention. Joey spotted JK in the last row and hurried to the back of the building. JK noticed a sense of uneasiness on the face of Joey and motioned for him to sit down.

"What in the hell is wrong with you? You look like you have just seen a ghost."

"JK"—his voice trembling—"I just saw a man get shot."

JK lay back on his bed and placed his hands behind his head.

"That shit happens around here all the time."

"I heard the man who shot him asked him for his money, and the man said he didn't have it and tried to run, and that's when he shot him."

"It probably was a drug dealer that he owed money to, and he sent a message to him and anybody else that owed him money. By the way, PB, that's rule number one, never buy drugs on credit."

Joey lay back on his bed with a feeling of hopelessness. He couldn't tell JK that Mike the Man shot him because he also owed the dope dealer, and the advice he gave to Joey was a little too late. As Joey and JK lay there, they heard footsteps approaching Joey's left. It was big bad Tommy with his left eye closed shut and his right eye badly swollen, looking like a monster out of a horror movie. He never looked in their direction and lay on the bed next to Joey and turned his back, facing the other way. Joey looked over at JK, who smiled and winked his eye.

"Well, PB, we got about ten more minutes before dinner, so I'll just lie here and rest."

Joey nodded his head, but his thoughts quickly changed to thinking about Mike the Man because that was a problem even JK couldn't resolve.

———————

It was Monday morning, and Ruben couldn't wait to see Ben at work to tell him that Joey wanted to talk with his wife about helping him with his drug problem. Eileen had told Ben that it was just a matter of time before Joey realized that he was fighting a losing battle. Ruben opened the cage to his tool bin and sat down, sipping on a hot cup of coffee, waiting for Ben to arrive. After about ten minutes, he saw Ben walking up the aisleway in his direction.

"Ben! Ben!"

"Hey, Ruben, what's all the excitement about?"

"My Joey, he wants to talk with Eileen so he can get help. He told me yesterday when I picked him up to attend mass service."

"That's good news. Eileen has been waiting for the chance to talk with Joey. She'll be glad to hear about this."

"Yes, yes. So please inform her so she can meet with my Joey."

"I'll tell her this evening."

"Thank you, Ben. Thank you, and God bless you."

Ben walked back down the aisleway, and Ruben began singing an old song from his country as he jumped up and down, dancing joyfully around.

———————

It was ten after eight, and the residents had finished eating dinner. The word had circulated throughout the shelter that Peggy Weber was back from her winter vacation. Ms. Weber was the assistant director of the shelter and took two weeks off in February each year to visit with her daughter in Florida. The men in the shelter called her Old Lady Weber. Gregory Tillman, the director, stayed cooped up in his office watching old movies on the company's VCR and only made an appearance when needed. That left Ms. Weber in charge of managing the operation.

She was a tall, dark-skin woman in her late fifties with grayish black hair. Ms. Weber had a stern, hard-core disposition and ran the facility as if the warden of a state prison. Her feelings were void of kindness and compassion and she would let everyone know that if you broke any of the rules, you were out the door. It was hard to tell if her cold-hearted personality was necessary to keep control of the men or whether she was just a mean-spirited person. About four or five days a week, a dozen or more of the men were escorted out the front door for facility violations, no matter how minor the infraction, and never given a second chance. For those unfortunate men, a thirty-day probationary period was imposed before they could return to the facility, requiring them to reregister—placing their application at the bottom of the list.

This transitioning cycle provided a daily mix of familiar and unfamiliar faces, causing staff members to watch for unusual and suspicious activity. It wasn't long before one man was spotted sneaking a cigarette to another man. Possession of cigarettes in the facility was prohibited, whether you were smoking them or not, a rule initiated by Old Lady Weber, so both men had to leave the building. The temperature outside was about ten degrees Fahrenheit, so they were in for a long, cold night. Joey and JK watched them reluctantly escorted out of the building, and JK looked over at Joey, shaking his head while sitting on his cot.

"PB, you got to wonder why some people just don't think. Playing by the rules may not be what you want to do, but when you're playing on somebody else's turf, you better abide by their rules. Imagine being outdoors on a cold night like this, trying to find shelter in a vacant house with no heat."

Joey looked at JK with a distressed face because it seemed like everything JK was saying over the last couple of days was like a sword thrusting deep into his heart, but it wasn't JK that he envisioned on the other end of the blade; it was Mike the Man.

CHAPTER 4

The Gift

It was another cold night, and Joey broke into a car and stole a cell phone left on the front seat. There was always an opportunity to steal merchandise out of a car because people were careless about leaving things, mostly unintentionally, and in plain sight. Breaking into vehicles was also the safest option for avoiding aggressive interactions with people. However, on a couple of occasions, Joey was caught in the act but escaped by outrunning his angry victims. His fleet-of-foot agility was his most significant asset, allowing him to escape apprehension easily. Joey operated alone and relied on his father's money and his thievery to get the money he needed to buy drugs and quickly hurried along the side streets, avoiding anyone who might recognize him.

Two or more addicts formed alliances, sharing their drugs with members within their group. It assured them a daily supply of coke for satisfying their daily habits. But you were only allowed to stay in the group if you contributed when it was your time to produce. This relationship came with enormous consequences because occasionally, a body or two were found in dumpsters with their throats slit—the penalty for those who didn't comply. Although Joey didn't associate with other users, it was safer to avoid seeing them on the streets. They were aware of who owed the dope boys money and would snitch to them about his whereabouts to stay in their good grace. But for the moment, a drug-free life consumed his thoughts, and he wanted to honor the promise he had made to his father.

He had to find a way to resolve his debt issue with Mike the Man. That wasn't going to be easy because even if he had the money to pay him, it was no guarantee that he'd spare his life. The debt had been out-standing for three months, so at this point, his reputation was worth more than the money. Mike the Man was probably going to prove a point with Joey whenever he saw him, and there was a good chance his fate would end up the same as Fat Boy's. He made his way along his route, and his coughing from a cold he'd contracted from a resident in the shelter the night before had become more pronounced, and his throat was getting sorer. People were frequently sick with an illness, con-taminating nearly everyone else in the facility, despite Old Lady Weber's policy of not allowing anyone into the shelter who showed evidence of colds or other illnesses. If an intake staff member identified him as be-ing ill, he wouldn't be allowed access into the shelter and directed to go to the free clinic for treatment. That wasn't an option because the clinic was closed, and walking to the hospital for treatment was more than an hour away. The only other option was to have his father pick him up and take him for treatment, but he'd worried his father enough and dis-missed that idea altogether. Joey thought about how he'd complicated his life being a drug addict, putting his health and life in jeopardy while compromising his relationship with his father. Cold tears began flowing down his face as he looked up toward the heavens and cried out.

"Lord, please help me!"

Suddenly, there was the sound of a car engine. The engine had that familiar rattling sound, and fear came across Joey's entire body. Joey started thinking, *Surely he didn't spot me because I wasn't walking along the main streets. Mike the Man must have driven up on someone else that owed him money.* Joey stood quietly alongside a vacant building, waiting for Mike the Man to take care of his business before running off, but the rattling stopped because the engine quit running. Joey's body started to tremble, not because of the cold winter air that chilled his body, but be-cause he felt like he was dreaming the worst nightmare of his life. Only it wasn't a nightmare; it was a reality. He wanted to peek around the corner of the building to see what was happening, but too frightened to move, he waited as it remained quiet. After a few more seconds of silence, Joey felt a jabbing into the small of his back, and a voice began silently speaking.

"What's up, Poletown Boy? You knew that sooner or later, I'd catch up with you. You thought you were going to continue to hide from me? I could have tracked you down like a bloodhound anytime I wanted to. You addicts are all alike. You might disappear for a while, but eventually, you must come home to roost. I know you've been staying at the DU Center and been in and out of vacant houses doing your thing, but I was in no hurry to collect. I also saw you walking behind the old mission building a couple of days ago, but you didn't see me because I was riding with someone else. You know what the f... pisses me off about you? I gave you drugs on credit, and you avoided me to go and spend your money with Big Pinky. I guess there is no loyalty among thieves and drug addicts. I hope you told your daddy goodbye because I know you heard about what happened to Fat Boy. Well, you getting ready to join him, so you got any last words to say mother...?"

He placed the gun to the back of Joey's head. Joey closed his eyes and stood motionless as tears rolled down his face. He thought about his father and how sad and hurt he'd be when he got the news of his death. He thought about the pictures on his father's mantle, him as a little boy, and his Uncle Benny and Aunt Rachel. He thought about Diana. She lit the fuse that started the fire burning, leading to his demise and this tragic moment. He also thought about JK, but unfortunately for Joey, his words of wisdom came too late to save him. There was just nothing that Joey had to say in his final moments; he just wanted it to end. He braced himself for the bullet's impact as Mike the Man spoke softly into his ear.

"Tell that mother... Fat Boy I said hello."

But through the cold blowing sound of the wind, a voice echoed out behind Mike the Man that froze him in his tracks.

"Let him go!"

As Mike slowly turned around, a young boy about the age of twelve stood there, staring him straight in the eye. Joey cautiously turned around and couldn't believe it when he saw the boy standing face-to-face with Mike the Man. He was about five feet, two inches tall, with a medium brown complexion and black hair. The streetlight illuminated his black eyes, which shined like black pearls, and his attire consisted of a light-colored waist-length jacket with dark pants and shoes. Mike the Man, a tall, medium-built, dark-skinned man wearing a Gucci jacket and a Panama hat, appeared twice as tall as the boy. The young lad stood undaunted as he continued staring Mike the Man in the eye. Mike the Man pointed the gun at the boy and took a deep breath.

"I don't know who in the f... you are, little boy, but your ass is about to die along with Poletown Boy."

Mike the Man's hand began to shake, and he couldn't stabilize it as his arm went limp. His speech became slurred, and he was losing his balance. He gathered himself and slowly staggered past Joey toward his car and immediately got into his vehicle, started the engine, and drove away. Joey was astonished and incredibly grateful to the boy who just saved his life, but he thought to himself, *This is like something straight out of The Twilight Zone.*

"I can't believe what just happened. Who are you? Why are you walking around in this area at night and in the cold?"

"I was just walking along and heard an ungodly voice and thought you needed help."

"Where do you live?"

"I have no place to stay. I have no mother, and my father lives far away."

Joey grabbed the boy by the arm, shaking his head, still amazed by what had just happened.

"Come on, let's get out of here. Mike the Man has added you to his list as well."

Joey ran behind the boy, pushing him in his back while applying pressure to his left or right side, depending on the direction he wanted him to run. He thought about how the young boy stopped him from getting killed but didn't take any chances, so he avoided major intersections and thoroughfares.

CHAPTER 5

The Gift

J oey started coughing and had forgotten about his cold and sore throat, which worsened his situation. It would be difficult to get into the shelter because of his illness, and how would he get the little boy into the facility for the night? The boy wasn't registered, and minor children weren't allowed to be in the shelter with adult males. Joey's only option was to get to the facility and worry about that when he got there. When they arrived, Ms. Weber was standing next to the intake table and stared sternly at Joey.

"Young man, why have you brought this child into the shelter?"

"Ms. Weber, I found him wandering in the Cass Corridor District, and he said he had no place to stay."

She directed her attention to the young boy.

"Is that correct, young man?"

"Yes, ma'am."

"Where are your parents?"

"I don't have a mother, and my father lives extremely far away."

Joey was unable to hold back his cough and began coughing uncontrollably for about three seconds.

Ms. Weber looked over at Joey. "The boy must leave and go over to the family shelter in the morning, and you cannot stay here until you get treated by the clinic."

"But, Ms. Weber, it's freezing outside, and we have nowhere else to go."

"That isn't my problem; you're going to have to figure that one out for yourself."

Joey and the young boy stood there as Ms. Weber motioned to him to take the boy and leave, but just as they were leaving, Mr. Tillman walked up. Mr. Tillman, in his late fifties, was a tall, dark-skinned distinguished-looking man with thick gray hair, long sideburns, and a bushy mustache. He'd been the facility director for fifteen years, and unlike Ms. Weber, he was stern but kind and compassionate.

"What's the problem, Ms. Weber?"

"This young man has a cold, and I told him to go to the clinic for treatment. His name is Joey, and he's a regular here, but I don't know who the young boy is. I've never seen him before. He told me that he didn't have a mother and that his father was nowhere around. I told Joey that he couldn't stay here tonight because of his illness, and neither can the boy because he is a minor. He'd have to take the boy to the family shelter in the morning."

Mr. Tillman directed his attention to the young boy.

"What is your name, Son?"

"Everyone just calls me MB."

"MB, surely you must have a first and last name. What does the MB stand for?"

"Messenger Boy, sir."

"Messenger Boy!"

The two men sitting at the intake table started laughing, and Joey and Ms. Weber looked confused when he told Mr. Tillman his name. Joey looked at Mr. Tillman and pointed to MB.

"Mr. Tillman, this boy saved my life."

Mr. Tillman looked over at the boy, then at Joey, and finally over at Ms. Weber.

"Ms. Weber, I'm going to let them stay in the emergency shelter room tonight, and this young man can take"—he hesitated for a moment—"MB to the family shelter in the morning."

It was apparent that Ms. Weber disapproved, but she directed a staff member to check them into the room. The room had four double bunk beds, separated to form eight single beds. On the side of each bed stood a small cabinet for storing personal belongings. A two-foot rectangular window in the middle of the door provided the means for monitoring residents by staff personnel. Joey and MB sat across from each other on opposite beds, with Joey still confused about MB's name and origin.

"Messenger Boy, so that's your real name?"

"As far as I know."

"When was the last time you saw or spoke with your father?"

"It's been a while since I saw him, but I talk to him every day."

"Every day, so have you spoken with him on the phone?"

"No, I get on my knees and pray to him."

"Does he answer you back?"

MB looked over at Joey with an honest and sincere expression.

"Always."

Joey, still confused but satisfied with his answers, lay on his bed and closed his eyes. MB looked over at Joey and said goodnight, and they both fell asleep.

———————————

Early the next morning, MB stood over Joey, and Joey opened his eyes.

"Good morning, Joey, I must leave you now, but I'll return this evening."

Joey sat straight up and began coughing, gently rubbing his sore throat. "Where are you going, and what about me getting you into the family shelter?"

"I won't need it because I'll be leaving this evening."

"What do you mean? Where are you going?"

"I'm going to bring a gift to the shelter for allowing me to stay here last night before I continue on my journey."

"A gift, but, MB, that's what they do. It's their job."

"Always remember, Joey, it's better to give than to receive. Just meet me at six forty-five this evening at the shelter entrance."

Joey nodded approvingly, and MB went on his way. Joey left the shelter and made his way along a maze of side streets, still concerned about Mike the Man. The free clinic was about ten blocks away, and it wasn't his first visit. He remembered taking Diana there when she came down with the flu, and although it was only three months ago, to Joey, it seemed like a lifetime. His thoughts began to reflect on his dad because if it weren't for MB, his father would have been filled with grief that morning if he had received the news of his death.

He remembered asking God to help him right before Mike the Man pulled up and confronted him. At that time, he thought that it was God's denial of his plea and payback for breaking his father's heart. But now he felt that God, in His grace and mercy, sent MB, the Messenger Boy—His angel—to save him. Joey was committed to changing his life, but now, he was also committed to serving the Lord.

Joey spent most of his days selling stolen merchandise that he received from breaking into cars the night before. He had a special hiding place where he stashed his goods and returned the following morning to sell them. His specialty was stealing car stereos and secured a buyer from a local chop shop that bought all his merchandise. He targeted cars that had the best stereo units because he received more money for higher-end merchandise.

Joey had become highly proficient in getting in and out of vehicles, using a slim jim or lockout tool, allowing him to snatch out a stereo system—usually within two minutes. But today, he had a different outlook on things. He'd made his mind up to speak with Ms. Williams when he got back to the shelter. She'd been out with the flu for a couple of weeks and was due to return this evening.

Joey's thoughts then turned to MB, the mystery boy. *Where did he come from, and why is he leaving tonight? What type of gift is he bringing to the shelter?* These were questions that Joey asked himself, but his primary concern was dealing with Mike the Man without him. That was a question he'd planned to discuss with MB that evening.

With the meeting still three hours away, he headed over to the Main Library on Woodward Avenue. Joey was a travel enthusiast, and although he never ventured more than five miles away from his father's house, he loved to read about the places he wanted to visit.

CHAPTER 6

The Gift

It was six-thirty and already dark as Joey made his way from the library to the DU Center. Unlike yesterday, the cold night air was calm, not blowing into his face, allowing him to focus more on what he had to do. His first order of business was to clear things up with MB. MB had become the X-factor and a significant part of Joey's life over the past twenty-four hours. He wondered what fate had in store for him. Was he beginning to climb out of a hole of despair, or were these things the calm before the tsunami took complete control of his life? He continued walking, avoiding open areas, and heard sirens not too far away. He poked his head out from behind the building that he used as cover to see what the commotion was all about. There was a trio of police vehicles and an emergency vehicle blocking the street, and a police officer directing traffic away from the scene. It was almost time to meet MB, so Joey picked up the pace and headed to the DU Center. His meeting with MB took priority, and he wasn't going to be late.

Joey arrived at the shelter at exactly six forty-five and waited for MB to arrive. He stood outside and saw a group of men lined up to get inside the facility, including Tommy. Joey felt his heart beating rapidly within his chest and began wondering if maybe MB had no intention of showing up at all. A feeling of disappointment came over his body, as time was running out to get inside before the door was closed, but just six minutes before seven, Joey heard MB's voice calling his name from behind.

"Joey."

Joey turned around with a big smile and embraced MB.

"MB! Boy, am I glad to see you. I thought you weren't going to make it."

"This is the gift I'm going to give to the shelter."

He raised his left arm and showed Joey a small, beautiful, custom-made lamp. The wood-grain finish was unusual but elegant looking, with an engraved image of an angel carved out on the front. Joey, stunned by seeing such a magnificent-looking lamp, had no words to describe its beauty.

"MB, where did you get such a lamp?"

"I made it."

"You made it? How did you learn how to make a lamp this incredible?"

"I appreciate it when people show me love and compassion like Mr. Tillman did, and I wanted to show my appreciation by giving a special gift, a gift that comes from the heart. I've always had a talent for creating unique items."

"Well, I'm sure he'll be happy and surprised to get this gift."

"Come on, Joey, we better get inside before they close the door."

As Joey and MB walked inside, Joey's coughing started again. The man sitting at the table looked up at Joey but didn't comment. Joey looked around for Ms. Weber but didn't see her. The man looked over at Joey and smiled.

"If you're looking for Old Lady Weber, she took the day off."

Joey gave a big sigh of relief as the man directed his attention to MB.

"I heard Mr. Tillman tell you yesterday that you were supposed to take the boy over to the family shelter this morning."

Joey replied, "He's not staying here tonight. He only came to give a gift to Mr. Tillman for the shelter. MB, show him the lamp you made."

The stocky Caucasian man in his mid-thirties stood up when he saw the lamp, not believing his eyes.

"Man, you got to be kidding me. Where in the hell did you get a lamp like this?"

MB replied, "I made it."

"Come on, kid. You're pulling my leg, right?"

Joey looked at the man and smiled. "No, he's not kidding; he made it."

The man looked around until he saw Mr. Tillman, and motioned for him to come over. When Mr. Tillman arrived, he took the lamp from MB and showed it to Mr. Tillman.

"Mr. Tillman, take a look at this."

Mr. Tillman's eyes widened as if they were going to pop out of his head. "Wow! This lamp is magnificent! Where did you get this from, Jerry?"

"The kid made it."

"Yes, sir, I did, and I made it for you to keep in your office for letting me sleep here last night."

Mr. Tillman was at a loss for words and shook MB's hand as a gesture of his gratitude for the gift.

"Well, young man, thank you for this lamp."

"You're welcome, sir, but now I must be leaving."

"But, young man, I thought you were going to check in with the family shelter down the street this morning?"

Joey quickly replied to Mr. Tillman's comment. "He told me this morning that he wasn't going to stay there and that he'd be leaving this evening."

"But where will you go to tonight? I'll let you stay here another night."

"Thank you, sir, but I must go tonight."

Mr. Tillman scratched his head and looked over at Joey, who shrugged his shoulders.

"You know, young man, you're a minor. I could have you picked up by the juvenile authorities, and they'd transport you to the family shelter in the morning."

He looked at MB, waiting for a response, but MB remained silent.

"Very well, I guess you must have it all figured out. Good luck, young man." Mr. Tillman turned around and walked down the aisleway toward his office, with the lamp tightly secured under his left arm. MB looked up at Joey and motioned to him, and they walked over to the corner by the front door.

"Well, Joey, I really must be going, and you'll be all right. Don't worry about the man who wanted to hurt you. He won't bother you anymore."

Joey looked at MB and smiled. "I want to thank you again for saving my life. I'm putting all of my faith and trust in the Lord, Jesus Christ, from here on out."

"If you do that, Joey, you're going to be okay."

Joey and MB hugged one another, and Joey opened the door for MB and waved goodbye. Joey walked back toward the row of beds, and JK waved his arms, getting his attention. Joey walked over to JK, and they shook hands and both sat down.

"Man, where you been? I've been worried about you, and who was that kid you were with?"

"JK, it's a long story, but I'm okay."

"PB, did you hear what happen tonight?"

"No, what do you mean?"

"Two of the dope boys got into an argument, and one dealer got killed. I think I heard someone say that his name was Mike the Man."

Joey jumped straight up to his feet. "Mike the Man! Are you sure?"

A man to JK's right looked over at JK and Joey. "Yeah, that's right. His name was Mike the Man."

"JK, I saw police cars and an emergency vehicle on my way over here, so that must have been when it happened."

"Yeah, PB, it happened about six-thirty this evening."

Joey fell back onto his bed and felt like he'd just gotten a new lease on life. Joey certainly didn't want to wish for the death of anyone, not even Mike the Man, but it sure was going to make his life a lot easier.

Mr. Tillman sat at his desk, admiring the lamp he'd just received from MB. He had memories of a hundred or more stories stored in his head of the things he experienced and saw over the past fifteen years as director of the DU Center, but never anything quite like this. He wondered how a boy so young could have created such a jewel. Michelangelo himself couldn't have designed such a masterpiece as this lamp, but as beautiful as it was, Mr. Tillman knew that it was against state policy to accept gifts from residents.

He planned to return it in a couple of days but just wanted to admire it for the moment. Besides, the office needed a significant upgrade, and the lamp was a big improvement. It was made like a desk lamp and only needed a light bulb and complimenting lampshade to accent its beauty. He opened his desk drawer, took out a sixty-watt light bulb, screwed it into the socket, and turned it on. After examining the angel's image on the front, he used his table tent on his desk to shield his eyes from the direct light.

He headed back out into the main shelter area to speak with Joey. He wanted to find out more information about MB and if Joey knew where he'd gone. When he arrived back, a barrage of coughing bellowed throughout the room, which was a concern to Mr. Tillman. He walked over to Joey and found him covered up to his neck with his blanket and sweating profusely. It was apparent that a virus had spread throughout the facility, requiring the Mobile Medical Unit's services.

The Mobile Medical Unit was dispatched to emergency shelter facilities when a potential virus outbreak was suspected. Virus outbreaks usually occurred about once or twice a quarter, and mobile medical care provided an effective method in containing and treating viruses. Mr. Tillman told his staff members and security guards that the medical unit would be there in the morning and that Ms. Weber would manage the operation. He walked back to his office and prepared to leave for the evening. The overhead lights were usually kept on but weren't necessary since the lamp's illumination added a sense of vitality to an otherwise dull and dismal-looking room.

CHAPTER 7

The Gift

E arly the following morning, Ms. Weber parked her car in her usual spot where a sign read, Reserved for Staff Members Only. She had to prepare herself mentally and physically to deal with a group of men who'd be short-tempered and irritable because of the virus epidemic. It was nothing new to her, but when this type of situation occurred, it required her to exercise a bit more compassion and concern for the men, which she wasn't going to do. She felt that most of the men had put themselves into their current predicament through drug addiction or were rehabilitated criminals unable to find work. Hence, leniency wasn't part of her program. Ms. Weber got out of her car and hurried inside to coordinate with her staff before the medical unit arrived. When she opened the door, the entire team stood at the entrance and greeted her. Ms. Weber, surprised to see them standing around the door, became irritated because they weren't in their assigned areas.

"What's going on here? Why is everyone standing around upfront instead of manning your work areas?"

Jerry quickly replied, "Ms. Weber, the men are all well. Whatever illness they had last night has cleared up."

"What do you mean, Jerry, cleared up? Mr. Tillman told me on the phone last night that everyone in the facility had come down with an illness, and he'd contacted the clinic to have the medical unit dispatched this morning."

Darnell, a twenty-seven-year-old security guard, tall with a light brown complexion, said, "Go and see for yourself, Ms. Weber. It's true; no one is sick."

Ms. Weber walked up and down the aisleways, carefully inspecting each resident as she passed by them. There wasn't anyone coughing, and no one appeared to be ill. Most of them were sitting up as others stood and waited for her to pass. Ms. Weber focused her attention on Joey because Mr. Tillman told her that he'd broken out into a sweat and could have had a fever.

"Joey, I understand from Mr. Tillman that you weren't feeling well last night. Is that correct?"

"Yes, Ms. Weber."

"How do you feel now?"

"I feel fine."

She looked across the room and addressed the entire group.

"How many of you were ill last night?"

Everyone raised their hands.

"And how many of you are feeling better this morning?"

Everyone raised their hands again.

"Okay, everyone, I know you might be feeling all right this morning, but the medical unit will be here in a minute. Everyone still needs to be examined before leaving. The staff is preparing breakfast, so you'll be able to eat before being released."

Ms. Weber stood in her office and noticed the lamp on Mr. Tillman's desk, which provided the light that illuminated the room. Her desk was adjacent to his, and documents were neatly placed, unlike his, which had papers scattered. She became mesmerized by the sheer elegance of the lamp and wondered how Mr. Tillman had acquired such a gem and why he didn't provide it with a suitable lampshade. She compared the shadeless lamp to a man wearing a new tailored suit while wearing a pair of shoes with the heels badly worn. Ms. Weber walked over to the door and turned the overhead lights on and went over to Mr. Tillman's desk, and turned the lamp off while bending down to take a closer look. Her office phone began ringing, and she walked over and picked it up. It was Mr. Tillman, checking with her to see how things were going.

"Hello, Ms. Weber."

"Yes, Mr. Tillman, good morning."

"How are things going? Did the medical unit get there yet?"

"Yes, they're here, but strangely enough, everyone is fine, and all of the illnesses seemed to have disappeared."

"You're kidding. Wow, I'm glad to hear that."

"I'll know more after I've spoken with Dr. Purifoy. By the way, Mr. Tillman, where did you get that beautiful lamp?"

"The little boy that Joey brought in the other day gave it to me as a gift."

Ms. Weber remained silent for a few seconds, and Mr. Tillman knew what she was thinking.

"Ms. Weber, I have no intention of keeping it. I know it's against state policy to receive gifts from residents. I'm planning on returning it. I just wanted to admire it for a couple of days. I'm sure you'll agree that it's a magnificent piece of craftsmanship?"

"Yes, Mr. Tillman"—pausing and speaking slower than she usually does—"it's an exceptional piece of work."

"Ms. Weber, I can sense concern in your tone of voice about my decision to accept it, even though I told you I was giving it back. Is there more you'd like to say?"

"Well, Mr. Tillman, to be honest with you, I think you should give it back to the boy today. The state housing director is visiting on Monday, and it wouldn't look good for us to have this lamp displayed."

"Giving it back could present a small problem since the boy told me last night that he wasn't returning."

"Then how were you planning to return it if you knew that was the case, Mr. Tillman?"

"I guess I just wasn't thinking."

"I'll give it to Joey to return to the boy. If anyone sees him again, it will be him."

Mr. Tillman hesitated before speaking and gave a big sigh. "Okay, Ms. Weber, give it to Joey and tell him to return it to MB."

"Yes, Mr. Tillman. I'll make sure Joey gives it back to him."

"Fine, Ms. Weber, and I'll see you this afternoon."

They ended their conversation, and Ms. Weber shook her head.

"Messenger Boy, what total nonsense."

———————

Dr. Purifoy, the doctor in charge of the medical unit, walked up and stood in the doorway. Dr. Purifoy, a middle-aged stocky-built man, medium height, with a dark brown complexion and a short Afro, gave a big smile.

"Ms. Weber, you'll be glad to know that everyone is doing fine, and this is the first time that we've responded to a false alarm."

"This wasn't my call, Dr. Purifoy. Mr. Tillman initiated it. I was just following instructions."

"I understand, Ms. Weber. I'll be finishing up my report, and we'll be on our way. Take care."

"You, too, Dr. Purifoy."

Ms. Weber sat back in her chair and thought about the number of times the medical unit had been dispatched to the facility over the past five years. It had to be over fifteen times or more and never a false alarm. That was unusual, and what about this exceptional-looking lamp given to Mr. Tillman by a boy named Messenger Boy, who had no mother, an unknown father, and unknown origin. It just didn't add up, but it didn't matter to Ms. Weber, because the lamp had to go, and it had to go today. She walked over to the storage cabinet, took out a black trash bag, and placed the lamp inside. Ms. Weber saw Joey standing next to the door, getting ready to go out, when she stopped him.

"Joey, I need for you to return this lamp to the little boy. Staff members are not allowed to receive gifts from residents."

"But I can't, Ms. Weber, I don't know where he went, and he told me he wasn't going to return."

Ms. Weber stood there, staring at Joey for a moment.

"Okay, Joey, I'll handle it."

She turned and walked away, and a few minutes later returned wearing her coat and hat. Joey had left the shelter and walked down the alley when he looked back and saw Ms. Weber walking toward the dumpster. She tossed a black bag over the open dumpster's top and went back inside the facility. Joey couldn't believe what he'd just seen and thought, *How could Old Lady Weber throw away the lamp*? He rushed over to the dumpster, unlatched the hinge on the front door, and opened it. Fortunately, the bag with the lamp was lying on top and within reach. He grabbed it and hurried across the facility parking lot, when a car horn started blowing, which got his attention. It was Ms. Williams. She rolled down her window and waved to Joey to come over. Joey's heart, beating rapidly from the excitement of retrieving the lamp, ran over to her car and stood by the window.

"Hello, Ms. Williams."

"Hi, Joey, have you got a minute?"

"Sure, Ms. Williams."

"Come on and get inside."

Joey ran to the other side of the car and got in.

"How are you doing, Ms. Williams? I heard you've been out with the flu."

"That's right, Joey. I'd planned to return last night, but I was told that a virus had infected the facility, so I stayed away."

"Everyone had been sick, Ms. Williams, but when we woke up this morning, we all felt okay. The medical unit came out this morning, but no one required treatment."

"Is that so? Maybe I was given incorrect information?"

"No, Ms. Williams, we really were sick."

"I saw you take a plastic bag out of the dumpster. What was it?"

Joey took the lamp out of the bag and showed it to her.

"Oh my God! What a beautiful-looking lamp. Why was that in the dumpster?"

"Ms. Weber threw it away. It was given to Mr. Tillman from a little boy who stayed overnight. Mr. Tillman allowed him to stay in the shelter, and he gave it to him in appreciation of his kindness. Ms. Weber brought it to me this morning to give it back to the boy because she said they weren't allowed to receive anything from residents. I told her he left and wasn't returning, so I guess that's when she decided to get rid of it."

"What a heartless woman. I can see why they call her Old Lady Weber. She could have given it to someone else instead of throwing it away."

Ms. Williams shook her head from side to side in disbelief and then turned her attention to Joey.

"Joey, I've been trying to catch up with you for two reasons. First, I heard you're ready to talk to me about getting you help. Is that correct?"

"Yes, Ms. Williams. I do want help."

"I'm glad to hear that, and so was your father when he told my husband. The second reason I came to speak to you is about your father. He's been sick and hasn't been to work, and he won't go to the doctor."

"Oh no! I was on my way to see him, to give him this lamp."

"Your father needs more than a lamp right now, Joey. He needs you to be there with him, and he's been asking for you."

Joey started crying and asked Ms. Williams to take him home.

"Joey, if you're sincere about stopping what you're doing, I'll help you get the proper assistance."

"Thank you, Ms. Williams. I appreciate your support."

CHAPTER 8

The Gift

Ms. Williams drove up and stopped in the driveway of the Polanski home. Still feeling a little stunned about hearing the news of his father's illness, Joey took a deep breath.

"Ms. Williams, I hope my father is well enough to open the door."

"I'll wait to make sure everything is okay before I leave."

Joey walked up and firmly knocked on the door, and after about two minutes, the curtains in the window slowly opened.

"Hey, Dad, it's me."

Joey heard his father struggling to open the door and became impatient.

"Dad, are you okay? Please open the door!"

Ruben finally gathered up enough strength to turn the lock, and the door opened. Ruben stood there, shaking and unsteadied, as Joey led him to the couch. He took the lamp from under his left arm and placed it on the sofa next to his father.

"Dad, I have Ms. Williams waiting outside. She brought me home, and I must let her know that she can leave, now that I'm inside."

Ruben glanced up at Joey and nodded his head, and Joey walked back outside to the car.

"Thanks, Ms. Williams. I can tell my dad isn't feeling well."

"Does your father have a primary care doctor you can contact?"

"Yes, and I have his phone number."

"Give his office a call and tell them that your father needs an immediate appointment to see a doctor, and he might even need emergency treatment. Take my card and call me if you need help with anything, and let me know how things are going. We'll get together toward the latter part of the week to start working on your situation."

"I'll keep you informed, Ms. Williams, and thanks again for all of your help."

"You're quite welcome, Joey. Just remember the promise you made to yourself and to your father."

Joey smiled. "I won't forget."

Joey entered the house, helped his father to his feet, and led him into the bedroom. He pulled the covers back and adjusted his father's pillow, tucking him in tightly.

"Dad, I'm going to call the doctor's office and make an appointment for today."

Ruben nodded his head in agreement. Joey heard a slight knock on the front door. He walked into the living room, looked out of the front door's peephole, and saw Jim Henning standing outside. He quickly opened the door and greeted him with a smile.

"Come in, Mr. Henning."

Jim stepped in as Joey closed the door.

"How are you, Mr. Henning?"

"I'm doing fine, Joey. I came here to check on your father, and thank God you're here."

"Ms. Williams told me my father was sick, and she brought me home. I just got here about twenty minutes ago."

"I've been checking on him to see if I could convince him to go see a doctor."

"My father's stubborn, Mr. Henning"—Joey smiled—"I guess that's where I get my stubbornness. Come on back. He's in the bedroom."

Ruben opened his eyes and smiled when he saw Jim.

"Hey, Ruben, how are you doing?"

Ruben, remaining silent to this point, spoke softly to Jim. "Hello, Jim, I'm doing better."

"I don't see any improvement from yesterday, Ruben, and I think you need to see a doctor."

Ruben looked over at Joey. "I mean, I'm doing better since my Joey is here."

Joey looked over at Jim, and his expression showed a feeling of disloyalty and distrust toward Joey, which made Joey turn away in embarrassment.

"Ruben, I'll stay here with you so we can get you to a doctor."

"No, no, Jim, I'll have Joey call the doctor, and, thanks."

"Okay, Ruben, but don't wait another day."

Jim turned and looked at Joey.

"Please keep me informed."

Joey avoided direct eye contact with Jim as he answered.

"I will, Mr. Henning."

"I'll see myself out, Joey."

Jim walked out of the bedroom and exited out of the front door. Joey stood over his father with his eyes filled with tears.

"Dad, I've changed, and I'm not going back to the Cass Corridor. I'm going to stay here and take care of you."

Ruben's face lit up but quickly turned to a sad look of concern.

"I know you don't believe me, Dad, but you'll see. There's been a lot of things that have happened to me these last couple of days. I love you, Father, and I want you to be proud of me. I'll be back. I'm going to call the doctor's office."

Joey left the room as Ruben lay there feeling weak and feverish. Joey thumbed through his father's handwritten phone book, located the number for Dr. Corvinski, and called his office. Jill, the receptionist, answered the phone, and Joey explained to her his father's condition. She advised Joey to have him taken to emergency at the Henry Ford Hospital because it appeared that Ruben required immediate attention. She offered her assistance, but Joey said he'd take care of it himself and ended the conversation.

Ruben had heard the conversation but wanted Joey to warm up the soup in the refrigerator and make him a hot cup of tea before making the phone call. Joey hesitated for a moment and then headed to the kitchen. Ten minutes later, Joey returned and sat his father up in the bed and began feeding him the spicy chicken noodle soup. After five spoon-fuls, Ruben motioned to Joey that he had enough and wanted the tea. Hot cinnamon tea was Ruben's favorite, and Joey held the cup up to his mouth so Ruben could slowly sip it down.

A sudden urge came over Joey, and his internal clock was sounding the alarm that it was time for a quick fix, causing his hands to start shaking. Joey managed to sit the cup on the table next to the bed, and Ruben stared wearily into his son's eyes because he'd seen this behavior before. Joey jumped up, walked out of the room, and stood looking out of the dining room window. Sweat began running down his face, and he clenched his hands together, grabbing hold of the dining room table to keep his balance.

Joey knew that to leave his father now would be the final blow that would permanently separate the bond between them. Ruben wouldn't get the medical assistance he needed, seriously putting his life in jeop-ardy, and it would be Joey's fault if Ruben were to die because of his negligence. He heard his father's weak voice call out to him as he stood there, fighting with the urge to flee.

Fortunately, after several minutes of battling with his conscience, Joey fought off the desire to leave and slowly walked back into the bed-room. Ruben extended his hands toward Joey, and they held hands as Ruben recited the Lord's Prayer. The prayer seemed to ease both Ruben's and Joey's anxieties for the moment, but Ruben felt that this wouldn't be the end of Joey's battles. Joey went and got a damp, cool face cloth and gently wiped his father's face. Ruben smiled and nodded his head, indicating that it felt good, and drifted off to sleep.

Weary from the stress of worrying about his father and resisting the temptation to leave, Joey walked into the dining room and sat back in one of the chairs. He stretched his legs out and rested them on another chair across from him. It was similar to sleeping on a hard mattress pro-vided to shelter residents, so he closed his eyes and immediately went to sleep. A few hours later, Joey woke up and ran into the bedroom to check on his father. Ruben was still sleeping, and Joey placed his hand on his father's forehead to see if the fever had broken. The sweat on his father's face had dissipated, but his body felt quite warm. Ruben opened his eyes and smiled at Joey.

"Hello, Son."

"Dad, how do you feel?"

"I'm feeling better, and thank you for not leaving me here alone."

"I told you, Dad, I'm not leaving, but that's not important right now. I must get you to the hospital."

"Joey, I told you that I'm feeling better. Please wait until tomorrow morning, and if you think that I still need to go to the hospital, I'll go then."

Joey decided to honor his father's wishes but thought about what Ms. Williams and Mr. Henning would say if they found out that his father hadn't received any medical attention, and what if his condition worsened? Joey wasn't about to let that happen and wouldn't hesitate to call for emergency assistance if necessary.

CHAPTER 9

The Gift

T he sun was setting, so Joey turned on the ceiling light, but the room still needed additional lighting. Joey went and got the lamp off the couch and placed it on the table next to the bed. The light bulb was still in the lamp socket, so Joey turned the switch, and the lamp came on. The light's glare was too bright and needed a lampshade, so Joey turned it off until he found a suitable covering.

He went into the closet and grabbed a few clothes hangers, bending two of them into circular shapes, having the same circumference. Joey made four metal strips, connecting them to the circular piece's top and bottom, forming a cylinder shape. He attached the metal strips across the top, securing it into place, leaving a small circular opening at the top. Joey used a brown paper bag as shading by taping it around the perimeter of the object. It was a perfect solution, and it shielded his eyes from the glaring light. Just as Joey finished, Ruben opened his eyes and turned his head toward the lamp.

"Joey, what a beautiful-looking lamp."

"You like it, Dad? A little boy who stayed in the shelter made it. He said his name was MB, and he saved my life."

"Your life, from what, Son?"

"It's a long story, Dad. One day I'll tell you about it."

"Such a beautiful lamp. I pray you didn't steal it, Son."

Joey, offended by his dad's remark, answered abruptly. "No, Dad! The manager of the facility, Ms. Weber, disposed of the lamp in the dumpster behind the building, and I took it out. The boy gave it to the facility as a gift, and because Ms. Weber didn't like the boy, she threw it out."

"She obviously has no eye for beauty."

"The guys in the shelter call her Old Lady Weber. She's mean and heartless, but who cares about her now because I'm never going back to the shelter. You can ask Ms. Williams; she saw me take the lamp out of the dumpster."

Ruben looked up at his son, hoping that Joey's eyes would affirm the statement he'd just made. Joey sensing what his father thought, gave his father a big smile.

"Don't worry, Dad, I'm never going back to the shelter. That I promise you and I didn't steal the lamp. Are you hungry?"

"No, Son, just still a little tired."

Joey straightened out the covers on the bed and kissed Ruben on the forehead before turning off the overhead light and the lamp.

"I'm going to lie down in the living room. You get some rest."

Tonight had been a defining moment that reestablished their relationship, and the only thing left to do was for Joey to prove it to his father, but first, he had to make sure his father received medical attention. If Ruben's condition turned for the worst, it could set Joey on a life-long journey without a mother or father. Joey lay on the couch, closed his eyes, and silently prayed before falling off to sleep. A few hours later, Joey woke up and heard his father coughing. He leaped off the couch, ran into the bedroom, and turned on the lamp. Ruben's coughing began to diminish, and he motioned for Joey to sit down in the chair next to the bed. Ruben looked over at Joey with a slight smile on his face.

"I had you worried for a moment, didn't I, Son?"

"Yes, Father, you did."

"I'm okay. What time is it?"

Joey glanced over at the clock on the table.

"It's half past midnight."

"Please, Son, go make me a cup of tea."

After a few minutes, Joey got up and headed for the kitchen. He returned with a piping hot cup of tea. He sat his father up against the headboard, and Ruben took a couple of small sips.

"Ahh, that tastes good, Son."

"You must also eat, Dad, to regain your strength."

"I'm not hungry, and I'll probably need to go to the hospital in the morning if my condition doesn't improve."

"I would have already called for emergency transportation if you hadn't stopped me, Dad."

"I know, Son; I just wanted you here with me for a little while. If something were to happen, at least I had spent my last moments—"

Joey quickly lashed out at his father. "Don't say that, Dad! Maybe I should call 911 now!"

"No! No Joey! I didn't mean anything by that. You don't know how much I missed you being here with me. I need you, Joey. You're all I have."

Joey lay his head on the bed next to his father and started crying. "I'm sorry, Dad, I'm sorry, please forgive me."

"I already have, my son, and I do believe that you won't leave me alone again. Now you get some sleep, and we'll go to the hospital in the morning. I'm a stubborn man, Joey, but it's time for me to start taking better care of myself." Reuben started laughing. "For crying out loud, I want to see my grandkids someday. So I must live!"

They embraced each other, and Joey sat back down in the chair and watched his father fall off to sleep. He left the room, leaving the lamp on, and made his way back to the living room and stretched out across the couch. The cold winter wind pushed against the living room window and sent a slight rattling sound echoing throughout the house. It had been a challenging day for the Polanski household, filled with anxieties and high expectations for the future, and it was about to be solidified with a miraculous event that would impact their lives forever.

———————

It was two in the morning, and the wind had increased in strength, causing the window to rattle even louder as Joey lay motionless across the couch. Ruben was lying on his left side facing the doorway in his bedroom, sound asleep, when the lamp's light went out. Seconds later, Joey lifted his head because he thought he heard voices coming from his father's bedroom. He noticed the lamp's light wasn't illuminating the wall opposite to where he was lying. Joey quickly dismissed the phantom voices as the wind made strange sounds and continued pushing against the window. He concluded that the lamp's bulb had burned out, so Joey lay his head back down on the sofa's armrest, trying to go back to sleep. Suddenly, a bright flash of light filled the dining room and momentarily brightened the entire living room. Fear came across his face, and Joey became incapacitated, unable to move or speak.

He wondered if the house was on fire, and he had to find the strength to get to his feet and save his father, but the light quickly dissipated, and Joey felt a comforting sense of peace and calmness. He looked over at the wall and saw that the reflection from the lamp had returned. Joey thought, *Have I been dreaming?* He was able to stand and slowly made his way toward the bedroom to check on his father. Ruben was sleeping peacefully.

Joey sat down in the chair next to the bed, reached over, turned off the lamp, and fell asleep. Later that morning, the sun shined brightly between the bedroom window's blinds when Joey woke to the sound of footsteps moving briskly across the floor. To his amazement, Ruben was getting dressed and whistling a memorable tune that Joey remembered his father singing to him as a young lad.

"Dad, what are you doing?"

"What do you mean, what am I doing? I'm putting my clothes on so I can get my day started."

"But, Dad, you must go back to bed so I can fix you breakfast, and then we can go to the hospital."

Ruben pulled his pants up and placed his arms under his suspenders, and looked over at Joey.

"The hospital? Why in the world do I need to go to the hospital?"

By this time, Joey, perplexed and convinced that something strange was going on, stood up from the chair, walked over to his father, and placed his hand on Ruben's forehead. Ruben had no sign of fever and stood smiling at his son.

"Joey, what in the heck are you doing? Are you feeling okay, Son?"

Joey stepped back a couple of feet and stretched his arms out.

"Dad, don't you remember anything? You've been ill and had a terrible fever last night."

"All I know, Son, is that I feel perfectly fine, and I'm going to have my Saturday morning coffee with Mrs. Kowalski down the street. It's Saturday, isn't it?"

Ruben saw the concern and confusion on Joey's face, so he told him about a dream he had.

"Son, last night, I had this wonderful dream, and I was in a place of sheer comfort, joy, and peace. I heard this voice speaking to me. The voice said, 'Because of your faith in the Lord, Jesus Christ, you have been restored.' There was also this bright light. It was fantastic!"

Joey stood there, thinking about the light that had filled the room and the voices he heard. His father may have recalled it as a dream, but to Joey, it wasn't a dream. Joey watched his father put on his coat and hat as Ruben walked over and gave him a big hug.

"Welcome home, Son. It's good we're together again. I'll be back shortly, so just stay relaxed until I return."

Ruben exited the front door as Joey stood there speechless. It had been a night of bitter and sweet occurrences that wouldn't be clearly understood either by Joey or his father. Joey watched his father get into the car and drive off.

CHAPTER 10

The Gift

T he telephone rang and Joey made his way to the table to answer the phone. Joey cradled the receiver in his right hand and placed it up to his ear.

"Hello."

"Hello Joey, this is Mr. Henning. I was calling to check up on your father. How's he doing?"

Joey hesitated before replying because although his father appeared to be okay, he was negligent in not deciding to get him any medical attention. Hence, the remarkable turnaround in his father's condition had nothing to do with any action on his part.

"He's doing better, Mr. Henning. He felt well enough to go have his Saturday-morning coffee with Mrs. Kowalski this morning."

There was a brief moment of silence before Mr. Henning replied, "You're kidding? Did the doctor give him the approval to go out of the house?"

Feeling pressured by Mr. Henning's questions, Joey politely made an excuse to get off the phone. "Mr. Henning, someone is at the door. I'll have my father call you later."

Joey quickly ended the conversation and walked over to the couch, and sat down. He closed his eyes and tried making sense of the things that had occurred over the past twelve hours.

Joey had fallen asleep and woke up to the sound of the front door opening. Ruben briskly walked toward the kitchen, carrying a brown shopping bag. Joey quickly stood up and followed him. Ruben placed food items he'd purchased onto the kitchen table as Joey stood watching, still amazed at how his father had miraculously recovered.

"Son, we're going to have a great dinner tonight. How does homemade lasagna sound?"

"That will be just fine, Dad, just fine."

"Good. Guess who I met while I was in the market?"

"Who, Dad?"

"Ms. Williams. She was on her way over here to check on me and couldn't believe it when she saw me walking around. She said, 'Mr. Polanski is that you?' I said, 'Of course, my dear Ms. Williams, it's me.'"

Ruben laughed, almost out of control, which made Joey laugh along with his father.

"I can say, one thing, Son, everyone I met today, including Mrs. Kowalski, was happy to see me. Oh, by the way, Ms. Williams told me that she did see you take the lamp out of the dumpster, and she agrees with you that Ms. Weber is not a nice lady." They both chuckled.

"Dad, Mr. Henning called you while you were out, and I told him that you'd return his call."

"My dear friend Jim. He's also been worried about me." Ruben turned and looked Joey in the eye. "Son, never forget to treat people fairly and always keep your word. There were times after Uncle Benny died when we faced plenty of rough challenges. You were too young to know that, but because I always stood by my word to people, they put their trust in me and helped us, and I'll always be grateful."

Ruben reached over and hugged Joey. "I'll give Jim a call after I take a good hot bath and finish preparing dinner. Is there anything you need? Are you okay, Son?"

Joey looked at his father and smiled. "No, Dad, I'm fine."

Ruben made his way toward the bathroom, and Joey walked into the living room, turned on the TV, and sat down on the couch. Joey dismissed all the unexplainable events that had taken place and just wanted to enjoy the moment and looked forward to a promising future between him and his father.

It was a mild March morning, and Ruben was anxious to get to work. He'd been off for just over a week because of his illness, but today he felt healthy and full of energy. Ruben passed by the gate guard, waving cheerfully to him, and hurriedly walked up the five steps that led to the main entrance. Familiar faces greeted him when he entered through the doorway as he made his way to the elevators. The elevator stopped on the fifth floor, and Ruben darted out and smiled when he caught a glimpse of his tool bin about two hundred feet away. It felt more like a month than a week since his last workday. Jim, Ben, and a host of other coworkers walked over to acknowledge his return.

They were glad to see him back, which delighted Ruben. Ruben remembered that tomorrow was the day they planned a thirty-ninth surprise birthday party for Jim in the cafeteria. He decided that the lamp would make a perfect gift because Jim was good at making things, and he'd appreciate receiving a custom-made gem as the lamp. Ruben left just before lunch to go up to the school with Joey, and Eileen Williams arranged to meet with them for a meeting scheduled with Joey's counselor, Ms. Greene.

Eileen met them in front of the school, and they exchanged greetings.

"Hello, Mr. Polanski, and hello, Joey."

Ruben responded with a nod and a big smile, as Joey said, "Hello, Ms. Williams."

"Well, Joey, this is the next step to getting you back on track. Are you ready to go?"

"Yes, Ms. Williams, I'm ready."

"What do you think, Mr. Polanski? Do you believe that your son is ready to turn his life around?"

Ruben smiled. "Yes, Ms. Williams, my Joey is ready to go."

Ruben opened the school door, and the three of them walked in together. The meeting lasted about an hour and had been productive. Ms. Greene facilitated a plan manageable for Joey, requiring extra assignments with little time for lollygagging. During the meeting, Ms. Greene acknowledged that Joey was the brightest student in his class before falling off in school.

She informed them that Joey represented the school in the city chess tournament the previous year and won the first-place title, and if he got back on track, he could compete in next month's competition. That put a smile on everyone's faces, knowing that Joey's success or failure relied solely upon his efforts. When they walked outside the building, Ruben and Joey said goodbye to Ms. Williams. Ruben couldn't thank her enough for all her help, and Joey made his mind up that he wasn't going to disappoint his father, Ms. Williams, or himself.

———————

Joey couldn't stop talking to his father during the ride home from the meeting. He was excited and ready to make a fresh start, beginning tomorrow morning, with his first day back at school in three months. Joey's enthusiasm made Ruben laugh and sing. It was the happiest day of their lives.

"Well, Son, it certainly has been a good day."

"Yes, Dad, and it's only going to get better."

"I'm going to stop over at the thrift store on the way home. I saw a nice wooden box that I'm going to put the lamp into and give it as a birthday gift to Jim tomorrow."

Joey hesitated and looked over at his father.

"You're going to give it away? I know my homemade lampshade doesn't look good, but I'm going to buy an appropriate one."

"No, no, Son, that's not it. Jim likes making things with his hands, and he'd appreciate receiving a handcrafted gem such as that one. It's the most remarkable lamp I've ever seen, and the image of the angel is magnificent. You don't mind if I give it to him, do you, Son?"

Joey hesitated for a moment. "No, Dad, of course not. It will be a special gift, and I'm sure he'll be pleasantly surprised."

"Now, Son, tell me about this boy who made the lamp and saved your life."

Joey was embarrassed to talk about it but knew that he'd eventually need to explain what had happened.

"I owed this dope dealer money for drugs I received on credit. I avoided him and didn't pay the money. He caught up with me one night and was getting ready to shoot me in the head, and that's when MB showed up out of nowhere and stopped Mike the Man from killing me."

Tears filled Ruben's eyes as he carefully listened.

"Mike the Man just froze in his tracks and couldn't even speak but just muttered, and he got into his car and drove away. He was later shot and killed by another dope dealer."

"What happened to the little boy?"

"He told me that his name, MB, stood for Messenger Boy, and he stayed with me in the shelter for only one night. He left the following morning and told me to meet him that evening at the homeless shelter. When we met, he had the lamp with him and gave it to Mr. Tillman, the facility director, for allowing him to stay there. It was the last time I saw MB."

"I know that God has answered my prayers, Son. He may have sent this little boy to protect you. Maybe he was an angel?"

"He could have been because it's strange how and when he showed up and just disappeared."

"Well, my son, let's just be thankful that you're safe, and we have only God to thank."

CHAPTER 11

The Gift

The following morning, Ruben arrived an hour earlier to work. It was his responsibility to lure Jim into the lunchroom for his surprise birthday party. Jim avoided eating in the cafeteria most of the time, jokingly saying that the food wasn't fit for human consumption. Ruben told Jim the day before that he'd put in for a transfer to go to another plant and wanted to discuss it with him tomorrow during lunch. The pending relocation got Jim's attention, which made him eager to discuss this surprise decision. Ruben was the best millwright that he had, and this move would complicate fulfilling the current workloads. Jim avoided seeing Ruben the entire morning, clearly indicating that Jim was upset with Ruben's decision. At five minutes to noon, Jim walked up.

"Let's get this over with, Ruben."

They walked together to the other end of the building to the cafeteria. It was on the same level, so there was no need to take the elevators or steps. Jim walked faster than his usual pace, never saying a word, another indication of his disapproval. When they walked through the double doors entering the cafeteria, a small gathering of coworkers jumped up with loud echoing voices.

"Happy birthday, Jim!"

Jim glanced over at Ruben with frowning raised eyebrows. "Ruben, you devil you."

Everyone shook Jim's hand, including Ben, a few other men and women, and the kitchen staff. Jim thanked everyone and blew out the candles on his cake, and received several gift cards and homemade baked goods from the women. Ruben walked behind the serving counter, picked up a small wooden box, and gave it to Jim.

"Happy birthday, Jim."

When Jim opened the box and pulled out the lamp, everyone, including Jim, bellowed out various harmonious sounds of shock and approval.

"Wow, Ruben, what a surprise. This lamp is beautiful!"

"I'm glad you like it, Jim."

"Ruben, you know how I feel about custom-made craftsmanship, and this one takes the cake." He graciously pointed at his birthday cake. "Except for this one, of course."

Everyone started laughing, and Jim looked over sternly at Ruben. "Does this mean you're not going anywhere?"

Ruben smiled. "Yes, sir, that's exactly what it means. I'll be here until they put me out."

Jim smiled back. "I'm certainly glad to hear that."

The celebration ended, and everyone went back to work. Jim placed the box next to his desk and couldn't wait to take it home.

––––––––––––––

Jim drove up into the driveway, glancing at his two-story ranch-style home. It had been his family's dwelling for eight years. He sat there, surveying all the improvements made over the past two years. A new roof, gutters, awnings, and high-grade siding—making it the best-looking house on the block. He reached into the back of the seat and picked up the wooden box containing the lamp. Jim walked up the steps, onto the porch, and up to the front door. Ryan, his thirteen-year-old son, greeted him when he entered through the doorway. Ryan was about five feet, four inches tall, medium-built, with light brown hair and dark brown eyes.

"Hello, Dad!"

"Hi, Son. How did things go today in school?"

"Everything went fine. What's that you got in the box?"

Jim placed the box onto the floor, took out the lamp, and placed it onto the coffee table.

"Wow, that's a neat-looking lamp, Dad. Where did you get it?"

"Ruben gave it to me as a birthday present. A group of people at work surprised me with a birthday party in the cafeteria today. It was completely unexpected. Where's your mother?"

"She's in the basement washing clothes. Do you want me to tell her to come up?"

Jim smiled. "Yes, Son, tell your mother to get up here."

Ryan called down to his mother, and she rushed up the stairs. Brenda was in her mid-thirties, medium build, and height, with light brown hair and light brown eyes.

"Ryan, it sounded urgent. What do you need?"

"Dad's in the living room and told me to call you up."

"Oh, your father. He thinks everyone must rise to attention when he gets home from work. But it is his birthday, and I should show more consideration for your father's request."

Brenda walked into the living room, wrapped her arms around Jim's neck, and gave him a big kiss.

"Honey, I must apologize. I was fussing at Ryan because you told him to call me up from the basement. I was doing the laundry and wanted to finish before I came up. How selfish of me." Brenda gave Jim a second kiss. "Will you forgive me, dear, after all, it is your birthday?"

"Of course, my love. I know how you can get when you want to finish your chores. They gave me a surprise birthday party at work today."

"That was thoughtful of them."

"Look at this lamp Ruben gave to me as a birthday present."

"Oh, how nice. This lamp is splendid!"

"Yes, honey, it's quite remarkable, and it's custom-made."

"Where on earth did Ruben find a lamp like this?"

"I don't know, honey. You can't just ask a person where they purchased a gift that they gave to you as a birthday present. He'll probably get around to telling me later."

"What do you plan on doing with it?"

"I'm not sure, but I'll shop around and find a suitable lampshade. I'll leave it here on the coffee table for now."

"By the way, sweetheart, Kevin and Marcy said they'd be joining us for your birthday dinner this Saturday at the restaurant. That completes the final fifteen reservations that we had booked."

"Good, I'm looking forward to my birthday celebration with our friends."

"You and Ryan get ready for dinner, honey, while I set the table."

Brenda exited the room, and Jim picked up the empty box and walked down the stairs to the basement.

The following morning Jim was sitting at his desk when Tim Riley, the fifth-floor supervisor and an attendee at his surprise party, walked into his office. Tim was a tall, thin man in his mid-forties with light blonde hair and was the kind of a guy concerned about everyone's business except his own.

"Hello, Jim, how's it going? That was a great surprise party that the girls planned for you. Man, you should have seen your face light up."

"Yes, I was surprised, and I thanked everyone for their participation."

"You know the word's been getting around the plant about that lamp Ruben gave you."

"I can imagine. It's quite an extraordinary gift."

"I mean, people are talking about how Ruben got the lamp."

"What are you talking about, Tim? Didn't Ruben pay someone to have it made? It looks to be an expensive lamp."

"The word is that his son Joey gave it to him."

"And where did you hear that from?"

"I was up on the sixth floor getting supplies and heard two women walking by me talking about it. I mean, it doesn't matter to me, Jim, where Ruben got it from, but they said that Joey had a drug problem, and maybe they thought the lamp was stolen."

Jim turned his head and looked Tim in the eye. "And what do you think?"

Tim began acting a bit nervous. "It doesn't matter to me, Jim."

Tim tried to downplay the conversation like it was no big deal, but he'd accomplished his intent by informing Jim of how Ruben acquired the lamp. Jim knew that was the only reason he came down to visit: to see his reaction and the expression on his face once he found out. It was a petty move on Tim's part; nevertheless, it had Jim fuming inside to think that Ruben had given him stolen merchandise. Jim didn't let Tim know that he was upset; instead, he questioned Tim's motive.

"What's your point, Tim?"

"No, no, Jim, don't take it the wrong way. I was just mentioning it in case someone at the party wanted to buy one for themselves, because it's a fine-looking lamp. There would be no sense in asking Ruben where he bought it from because he wouldn't be able to tell them."

"Have you thought that since Joey gave him the lamp, he'd be able to tell Ruben where he purchased it from?"

"Oh, yeah, sure, Jim. Joey would know since he gave it to his father, but I never saw a lamp like that before. It looks to be custom-made."

"Yes, it's exceptionally eye-catching, but I suggest you let Ruben answer that question for anyone who may be interested, because it's neither your business nor mine as to how he acquired the lamp. Ruben has always been a man of honesty and integrity, and I'll leave it at that."

"Okay, Jim, you're absolutely right, and I'll talk at you later."

Tim walked out of the office, and Jim stood up from his desk and headed to Ruben's work area.

CHAPTER 12

The Gift

W hen Jim arrived, Ruben was getting back from completing a job and was putting away his tools. Ruben looked up and saw Jim standing there and could tell by his facial expression that this was more than a job-related visit.

"Good morning, Jim!"

Jim didn't acknowledge his greeting but got right to the point. "The lamp you gave me yesterday, where did you buy it?"

Ruben's face quickly changed from a pleasant smile to a look of uneasiness. "Why do you ask, Jim?"

"Answer me one question, and that will be all I need to know."

"Sure, Jim, what is it?"

"Did Joey give you the lamp?"

Ruben knew what this question was leading up to because he'd spoken with Tim a couple of hours before the birthday party and realized that he'd committed an unpardonable act. Tim's intentions would have been evident to anyone else, but Ruben's naivety had surrendered him to the serpent's tongue.

"Yes, Jim, Joey gave the lamp to me, but I wanted you to have it because of its superb craftsmanship. I knew that you'd appreciate it because you're good at making things."

"Do you really expect me to accept the lamp that you received from Joey? Sorry, Ruben, I don't accept stolen property, so I'll be bringing the lamp back to you tomorrow."

Ruben attempted to plead his case. "Jim, it's not what you think. Joey didn't steal the lamp. A young boy gave it to the homeless shelter, and the manager discarded it into the dumpster. Joey retrieved it and brought it home to me. The boy was Joey's friend, and he said the boy was extremely gifted."

"Ruben, it sounds like nonsense to me, and you think you can rely on Joey to tell you the truth?"

Ruben became visibly upset because Jim never considered that he might be telling him the truth.

"Okay, Jim, if that's the way you feel, but you can ask Ben's wife. She knows where Joey got the lamp."

Ruben, saddened by Jim's comments, slowly walked away and headed to the cafeteria.

Later that afternoon, Ben spotted Jim standing next to the vending machine and walked over to him. Jim appeared to be in a hurry and not in the mood for a conversation, but Ben blocked his pathway when Jim tried to scurry away.

"Hey, hey, Jim, what's the hurry? You got a plane to catch?"

Jim knew that trying to sidestep Ben was an impossibility because of his height and size.

"What do you want, Ben? I need to get back to my office."

"Listen, Jim, I heard what happen between you and Ruben, and frankly, I'm surprised that you didn't have more faith in Ruben. Eileen confirmed Ruben's story. She saw Joey take the lamp out of the dumpster. It's the same morning that you checked in on Ruben and Joey was at the house. Eileen had just dropped him off."

Jim settled down and apologized to Ben for his rudeness.

"I apologize, Ben. I had no reason to take it out on you, and I do remember Joey telling me that your wife had just dropped him off when he opened the door."

"Apology accepted, my friend, but I don't think it's me you should be apologizing to."

Jim looked at Ben and smiled while patting him on the shoulder.

"I guess you're right. I owe Ruben an apology."

Jim made his way back to Ruben's work area, feeling embarrassed about how he'd been such a jerk. When Ruben saw Jim coming, he sat in front of his tool bin and turned his back toward Jim.

"Ruben, I came to apologize."

Ruben slowly turned around and stared Jim in the face. Jim had the look of a ten-year-old who'd snuck his hand in the cookie jar and gotten caught.

Jim continued speaking. "Ben told me that Eileen confirmed Joey's story. I hope you can forgive me, Ruben."

Ruben stood up and placed his hand on Jim's shoulders. "Of course I can, Jim. We all make mistakes, and God knows I've made my share."

They embraced each other and shook hands as Jim replied, "Thank you, my friend, thank you."

———————

Jim was in his car, headed home, and felt relieved that he had reconciled his relationship with Ruben, but now he felt uncomfortable about keeping the lamp. He began thinking to himself, *Who was this mysterious little boy, and where did he get such a magnificent-looking lamp? And what happened to him?* These questions continued ringing in his head as he drove up into his driveway.

He thought about the stories his grandfather told his dad about receiving gifts from strangers. His grandfather said that where he grew up in England, witches and sorcerers would put a spell on objects and pass them on as gifts to unsuspecting strangers. It was worth considering, but he had to keep the lamp because it was a birthday present, so he decided to store it away for a while and planned to dispose of it later. When he walked into the house, Brenda was in the kitchen finishing up dinner, and Ryan was in his room. Brenda, busy cooking dinner, didn't hear Jim come in, so he snuck up on her and wrapped his arms around her shoulders.

"Hey, honey, you about scared me to death."

Brenda wrapped her arms around his neck and kissed him.

"Now, isn't that much better than sneaking up on me?"

"I agree with you, dear, one hundred percent. Where's Ryan?"

"He's upstairs in his room doing his homework."

"Good. Hey, what's for dinner? It sure smells good."

"Baked chicken, broccoli casserole, scalloped potatoes, candied yams, and peach cobbler."

"Sweetheart, you certainly know how to make a man come straight home. Do not stop at go; do not collect two hundred dollars but go straight home."

"Okay, you Monopoly guru, get out of the kitchen so I can finish up dinner."

While Jim entertained his wife, his mind focused on storing away the lamp, so he went down into the basement and returned with the wooden box under his arm. Jim placed the lamp into the box and hurried up the steps to the attic. The attic was extremely congested with tables and chairs he'd made and boxes filled with papers and clothing. Jim managed to clear a pathway and placed the box onto the floor against the back wall. Brenda and Ryan were waiting for him when he came back downstairs.

"Oh, Jim, there you are. Dinner's ready."

Ryan looked over at the table and noticed the lamp missing.

"Hey, Dad, what did you do with the lamp?"

Brenda was also standing there, waiting to hear Jim's response.

"I, hmm"—he hesitated—"stored it away until I can find a unique lampshade. A lamp like that requires more than an ordinary one, so I figured that storing it away in a safe place would be the best place for it."

Brenda said, "Okay, dear, but it's a shame to hide away such a beautiful gift."

Ryan momentarily stared at his dad before the three of them walked into the dining area.

———————

The following two years proved to be favorable for the Polanski family. Joey finished high school, and Ruben got him hired at the Ford Plant as an assembly-line worker. It wasn't a job that Joey wanted to end up at, but it was a start, and at the age of twenty, he planned to attend night school and acquire an engineering degree. He'd been drug-free for over two years, taking more responsibility for his life, unlike the irresponsible Joey of the past.

The Hennings and the Polanski family had become closer, and Ryan, Jim's fifteen-year-old son, became more like a younger brother to Joey. Ryan's mother, Brenda, was quite fond of Ruben because he was a man of integrity and never uttered a single profanity.

She also felt comfort in the relationship Joey provided to Ryan as a big brother role model. Occasionally the two families celebrated summer holidays together, usually in the Hennings' backyard. Ruben and Joey had no other relatives to share with during the holidays, so Jim always included them in their family gatherings. Another became an honorary member of the Henning household: a six-week-old German shepherd that Ryan named Teddy. Teddy, looking like a K-9 police dog, was given to Ryan the previous Christmas by his father.

CHAPTER 13

The Gift

It was the Fourth of July holiday, and the temperature was hovering around ninety-five degrees Fahrenheit with high humidity, and local swimming pools and public beaches were filled to capacity. Jim had planned a backyard barbeque for a few friends, which included Ruben and Joey. The Hennings' backyard featured a large, shaded patio area and a custom-built Gazebo, which seated ten to twelve adults. It had always been the perfect place to enjoy summer festivities. While Jim operated the gas grill, Ruben and Brenda were sitting in the gazebo, drinking a glass of ice-cold lemonade. During his last two years in high school, Joey had been the city's chess champion and was in the den with Ryan giving him a few lessons.

"Checkmate, Joey."

"Hey, wait a minute, it can't be."

"You can look at it a hundred times, Joey, but my rook has your king at my mercy."

Joey smiled. "I guess you could say that the student has become the teacher."

"Let me go and tell Dad and your father that I, Ryan the Great, have defeated the master."

As Ryan dashed outside, with Joey following behind, a couple of the neighbors arrived. Kevin and Marcy Kettering walked into the yard, waving at everyone. Jim turned and greeted the couple. Marcy was a short, thin, blonde-haired woman in her mid-thirties, and Kevin, a short, stocky, forty-three-year-old man with black hair.

"Hey, you two, how's it going?"

Kevin replied, "I'm doing fine, Jim, but I'd be doing a lot better if this heat lightened up a bit."

"Well, go up there with Ruben and Brenda and get a glass of that cold lemonade."

Jim motioned toward Ruben, sitting in the gazebo.

"You remember Ruben and his son, Joey."

Ruben waved and said hello, and Brenda walked down and greeted Marcy.

"Come on up here, Marcy, and get out of the sun. Where are your boys?"

"They're spending the weekend with my brother and his kids."

Ryan, excited about beating Joey, interrupted the conversation between his father and Kevin. "Excuse me, Dad."

Jim and Kevin directed their attention to Ryan.

"What is it, Son?"

"I just put Joey in checkmate, winning the game."

Jim called out to Ruben. "Did you hear that, Ruben?"

"Yes, I did, Jim. He might become the next city champion."

Ryan looked over at Ruben. "No, Mr. Polanski, I'm going to be the next state champion."

Everyone chuckled as Kevin looked over at Joey.

"So, you were the city chess champion?"

"Yes, sir, two years in a row."

"That's quite impressive, and you were able to beat him, Ryan?"

"Sure did, Mr. Kettering."

"Good job." Kevin looked around at the group. "People, we may have another Einstein on our hands."

Everyone laughed as Jim announced that the food was ready.

"Come and get it. We have hot dogs, hamburgers, and Polish sausages."

Teddy ran up to Ryan with a ball in his mouth and was ready to play. Ryan tossed the ball across the yard a couple of times, and Teddy quickly retrieved it and brought it back to him. Ryan led Teddy to the back door and motioned for him to go in.

"Come on in, boy, so I can feed you, and I can get back out here and eat."

They went into the house as everyone else sat around the table in the gazebo and started eating. Kevin took a bite of his Polish sausage and pointed at Jim.

"These sausages are delicious, Jim."

"Ruben brought them over, specially made by Mrs. Kowalski herself, from the Kowalski Market in Hamtramck."

Ruben said, "That's right, the best sausages in the world."

Kevin looked up at the big red maple tree in Jim's yard and gave a big sigh. "Well, everyone, I'm not trying to be a party pooper, but there's one more summer holiday left, and fall will be upon us."

Marcy replied, "Okay, Mr. Grim Reaper, no one is thinking about fall except you." Marcy turned and addressed the group. "Sorry for my husband's inability to enjoy the moment; that's just the way he is."

Jim said, "That's okay, Marcy; cooler fall air would feel pretty good about now. Besides this is the year that my family and I spend Christmas in England with my brother."

Marcy turned toward Jim. "England, how wonderful. He lives there?"

"Yes, he graduated from Cambridge University, got married, and became a supreme court justice."

"Wow, how nice. Will that be your first time going, Brenda?"

"No, Marcy, I won't be going. My sister and her daughter will be coming here for Christmas. I haven't seen her and my niece for three years. I went with the family four years ago to England, and we had a wonderful time."

Jim replied, "Ryan and I will be going along with my parents. The two of us will be flying down to Orlando, Florida, on Monday the 21st, to meet with them. The following day the four of us will be leaving for England."

Kevin said, "I remember your parents, Mr. and Mrs. Henning. They were here a couple of years ago; that's when Marcy and I met them. How are your parents doing?"

"They're doing fine. My dad plays golf three or four times a week, and my mother is always busy with her social events."

"Good for them."

Ruben motioned to Jim and stood up. "Jim, I need to go to the bathroom. This lemonade is delicious, but it makes you want to go."

"Sure, Ruben, you know where the bathroom is. Make yourself at home."

Ruben stepped out of the gazebo and made his way to the back door. When he walked into the living room toward the back of the house, his eyes wandered around, looking for the lamp he'd given Jim two years ago. It was the third time Ruben had visited Jim's home without seeing it or Jim mentioning its whereabouts. Ruben had been apprehensive about inquiring about it, hoping that Jim would eventually bring it up, but that never happened. When Ruben walked back out into the yard, he saw Jim standing in front of the grill and decided that this was the best opportunity to question him about the lamp. Jim turned around and faced Ruben when he approached.

"Find everything okay, Ruben?"

"Yes, yes, Jim, I did. Jim, I'd like to ask you a question."

"Well, speak up, old man. What is it?"

"Do you still have the lamp I gave to you?"

Brenda walked up in the middle of the conversation and could sense that it was more than a casual discussion.

"Oh, excuse me, guys. I didn't mean to interrupt anything."

Ruben replied, "No, Brenda, you didn't. I was just asking Jim if he still had the lamp I gave to him."

Jim glanced over at Brenda—who stared him in the face before answering. "Of course, Ruben, I still have it. I just never found an appropriate lampshade for it and stored it away in a safe place."

Ruben looked over at Brenda and then at Jim. "That's good to hear."

Jim sensed that Ruben was uncomfortable with his answer and volunteered to show him the lamp.

"Look, Ruben, if you'd like, I'll go and bring it down?"

Ruben smiled at Jim, looking him directly in the eye. "No, my friend, your word is good enough for me."

Jim knew that Ruben had baited him with his initial question and answer. He'd accused Ruben of giving him stolen merchandise when he found out that Joey had given the lamp to Ruben, who, in return, gave it to him as a birthday gift. Ruben's word hadn't been good enough when he told Jim that Joey didn't steal it until Eileen confirmed that it was true, so Ruben's acceptance of his explanation only added insult to injury and made Jim feel even worse.

CHAPTER 14

The Gift

I t was the morning of December 21st, and Ryan had just finished loading up their luggage into the trunk of Kevin's car. Kevin had volunteered to take them to the airport to catch their flight out to Florida. There was a slight winter breeze, and the sky was cloudy and gray, with light snow falling. Ryan hurried up the steps to give his mother one final hug as Jim embraced Brenda with a kiss.

"I'll call you, honey, when we arrive in Florida."

"Okay, dear, you two have a safe flight."

Teddy, standing next to Brenda in the doorway, barked at Ryan and wagged his tail. Ryan bent down and hugged him around the neck.

"You take care of mom while I'm gone, boy, and I'll see you when I get back."

Ryan ran to the car and got into the back seat as Jim waved goodbye and sat in the front next to Kevin.

The following morning, Brenda had finished warming up the car and drove out of the driveway. Her sister, Clara, and niece Tiffany were due to arrive at Detroit Metropolitan Airport in an hour and a half. Brenda had plenty of time to get there, so it made the ride to the airport stress-free and enjoyable. The airport traffic was congested, and Brenda had to circle the airport three times before spotting them. The security guard motioned at her to pull up to make room for other vehicles, and she stopped the car just feet away from Clara.

Brenda pushed the trunk release button on the dashboard, and the trunk popped open. She jumped out of the car, ran to the back, and hugged both Clara and Tiffany as the baggage handler loaded up their luggage. Clara, the older of the two, was in her late thirties, with a medium build and height and dark brown hair, wearing a dark brown wool coat with a matching beanie cap and gloves. Tiffany was six years old, had long, dark brown hair pulled back into a ponytail, tied with a yellow ribbon, and wore a wool blue-and-yellow checkerboard pattern coat.

"Clara, it's so good to see you," Brenda said as they embraced. "And look at my beautiful niece."

"Good to see you, too, Brenda."

"Hello, Aunt Brenda."

Brenda reached down and grabbed Tiffany by the shoulders, and kissed her on the cheek.

"Hello, sweetheart. Look at how you've grown."

Clara tipped the baggage handler after he shut the trunk, the three got into the car, and Brenda drove off. The ride back from the airport gave them time to catch up on the latest events and activities as home-makers and mothers. Tiffany sat quietly in the back, playing with her Pretty Ballerina Doll that she'd named Jennifer.

"Well, my dear sister, how are Jim and Ryan? Have they made it to England yet?"

"No, they won't arrive until tomorrow. Jim and Ryan flew out yesterday and met Jim's parents in Florida. How's Melvin doing?"

"Speaking of flying, other than piloting all around the country for United Airlines, he's doing okay. He chose to work during the Christmas holiday so our families could spend the New Year holiday together. He'll be flying out here on the 30th to join us."

"That will be wonderful. Jim and Ryan are so excited about us spending the holiday together. By the way, Clara, Jim bought Ryan a dog. He's a year-old German shepherd that Ryan named Teddy."

Tiffany laid her doll on the seat and commented. "Ryan has a dog?"

"Yes, sweetheart, but he's friendly, and you're going to like him."

"Tiffany loves dogs. Melvin promised to get her one next year."

"Yes, Aunt Brenda, I'm going to get a poodle."

"Good for you, sweetheart."

Brenda moved to the right lane and exited the freeway. They made it to the house, and Clara had unpacked their luggage and sat in the living room, talking with Brenda, as Tiffany stood across from them, getting acquainted with Teddy. He wagged his tail, allowing her to rub him up and down his back. The fireplace provided most of the illumination in the room, creating a warm, comfortable environment.

"It looks like Teddy has found a new friend, Clara."

"She just loves dogs."

"How's her asthma doing? Teddy's presence won't trigger anything, will it?"

"No, the dog will be okay. That's why Melvin waited on getting her one. He had to check with her doctor first, and he said it was okay. She's had her problems during the damp winter months, but I have her inhalers with me."

It was Christmas Eve morning, and Brenda had just prepared breakfast. The three of them were sitting down at the kitchen table when the telephone rang.

"You and Tiffany get started, and I'll be right back."

Brenda got up from the table and answered the phone. "Hello."

"Hi, honey, it's me."

"Oh, hello, dear, how's everyone?"

"We're all fine. We're going to do a little sightseeing today."

"That sounds exciting."

"I heard that there's a snowstorm headed your way?"

"That's what they said. Maybe eight to twelve inches is expected. It started snowing at about five o'clock this morning." Brenda hesitated before continuing. "Don't worry, dear, I know what you're thinking. I have plenty of everything."

"Good, I knew you did. I just wanted to hear you say it."

Brenda chuckled. "Okay, Mr. Worrywart, let me go and eat my breakfast before it gets cold."

"Okay, dear, I'll be in touch."

Brenda walked back into the kitchen and sat down.

"That was Jim, checking up on us. He's concerned about the snowstorm headed our way."

"Oh boy, Aunt Brenda, I get to see snow." Brenda and Clara chuckled.

"Yes, you will, dear, but maybe a little bit more than you bargained for."

The phone rang, and Brenda stood up from the table.

"Clara, I know this can't be Jim again. Excuse me." Brenda walked over to the table in the living room and quickly answered the telephone.

"Hello."

"Hello, Brenda, this is Marcy."

"Oh, hi, Marcy, are you all ready for Christmas?"

"About as ready as I'm going to get. My two boys are all set. Kevin went all out for them this year."

"How old are your boys now?"

"Alan's nine, and Bruce will be seven next month."

"Boy, how time flies."

"I was calling to wish you and your sister a Merry Christmas. I was also calling to let you know that they're predicting another four to five additional inches of snow on top of the twelve inches they already predicted."

"Oh really? I better turn on the news so we can keep up with this weather front. Thanks for the heads-up, and a Merry Christmas to you and your family."

"Thanks, and I'll talk with you later."

Brenda hung up and walked back into the kitchen.

"Hey, Clara, when we finish eating breakfast, let's go into the living room. Marcy just called and said they're expecting an additional five inches of snow. I'll turn on the TV so we can watch the news."

They finished eating and walked into the living room, and Tiffany went chasing after Teddy into the den. The local news coverage was tracking the movement of the storm, informing viewers to stay indoors.

"Clara, if they're right, it will blanket the city with snow, immobilizing travel of any kind."

"It doesn't look good, Brenda. We might be snowed in for a couple of days."

"You're right, Clara, but let's not worry about it. I went shopping yesterday, so we have everything we need."

"Good, I think I'll go upstairs and lie down for a while. Keep an eye on Tiffany for me."

"Sure, Clara."

Later that evening, Brenda walked over to the Christmas tree standing in front of the large living room window and plugged up the lights. Red, green, and white flashes of light began flickering alternately throughout the room, making Tiffany jump up and down in excitement.

"Look, Teddy, at the pretty lights on the tree."

Teddy ran over to Tiffany and started barking as Brenda and Clara stood there laughing.

"Okay, Tiffany, it's time to take your bath and get ready for bed, because Santa will be coming here tonight."

"Did you hear that, Teddy? Santa Claus will be coming here tonight, hurrah!"

Brenda turned, looking over at Clara. "Isn't it wonderful being a child, so sweet and innocent, and she's so precious."

Clara smiled and nodded her head approvingly. She gripped Tiffany by the hand and led her up the stairs as Brenda walked over to the couch and sat down.

CHAPTER 15

The Gift

I t was eight-thirty that evening, and Tiffany was asleep in the guest bedroom upstairs. Brenda and Clara were sitting in the living room watching TV, monitoring the latest weather developments, while Teddy was lying on the floor next to the coffee table. Clara turned around and pulled the curtains back, and commented to Brenda while looking out of the window, "Brenda, the snow is piling up. I hope it doesn't affect the fellas' travel plans in getting back here."

"No, it shouldn't. Jim and Ryan will be back on the 29th. They predict that the snowfall should end tomorrow morning, and there are no other storms in the forecast over the next two weeks. It might be a little rough traveling on side streets, but major roads and highways won't be affected. They should be clear."

"Good. Melvin will be arriving on the 30th, so he won't have to alter his travel itinerary."

Clara motioned to Brenda while leaning her head sideways toward the stairway.

"Brenda, could you turn the TV down for a moment?"

Brenda picked up the remote and muted the sound. Tiffany had begun coughing, and Clara quickly took an inhaler out of her purse and ran up the steps. She hit the light switch, walked over to the bed, and sat Tiffany up, who was still slightly wheezing. Brenda stood in the doorway, watching as Clara administered the medication.

"Okay, sweetheart, you know the routine. Inhale quickly."

The wheezing diminished, and Clara lay her back down on the bed with Jennifer cradled in her left arm.

"Clara, is everything all right?"

"She's had a minor asthma attack. She'll be okay. Brenda, I think I'm going to take my shower and lie down with my baby. We've got a big dinner to cook tomorrow, and we'll need to get started early."

"You're right about that. I think I'm going to turn in myself."

Clara took her shower and lay down next to Tiffany, and Brenda retired to the master bedroom. Teddy had bedded down on the floor in Ryan's bedroom next to his bed. It was midnight, and the snow was still falling. The city streets were silent, indicating that the roads had restricted travel due to the severe weather conditions.

Tiffany's wheezing and coughing started again, and Clara quickly sat up and reached for the inhaler on the table next to the bed. After giving her another dose of the medication, she tucked her in tightly, walked downstairs, and prepared a hot cup of tea. The hot tea usually helped to open the air passages to Tiffany's lungs. When she came back upstairs, Tiffany was breathing heavily, leaning back against the headboard. Clara held her up around the shoulders and placed the cup up to her lips.

"Here, honey, try to take a couple of sips."

Brenda walked out of her bedroom and stood in the doorway. "What, another attack, Clara?"

"Yes, but this one appears to be getting worse. I need more light; the room is too dim. I want to watch her eye movement."

"Let me go and get a flashlight."

"That might work."

As Brenda started walking downstairs to the basement, Teddy started barking and scratching underneath the door leading up to the attic.

"What is it, Teddy?"

Teddy looked around at her and started yelping while continuing to claw beneath the door. Brenda opened the door, and Teddy dashed up the steps. She turned on the light switch and walked up the stairs to see what was troubling him. Teddy made his way to the back of the attic and started pushing his nose against a wooden box. Brenda bent down and opened it and was surprised to see the lamp Ruben had given to Jim two years ago. It was the first time she'd seen it since he had it stored away.

She took it out of the box and hurried downstairs with Teddy following behind her. Brenda continued walking downstairs to the basement and pulled the string hanging over Jim's workbench, turning on the light. There was an old broken lamp on the basement floor, leaning against the wall. Brenda removed the old lampshade, took a bulb out of the workbench table's drawer, and ran upstairs. She hurried into the bedroom and placed the lamp on the table next to the bed. Then she plugged it into the wall socket and turned the switch.

"Thanks, Brenda, that will work perfectly."

Tiffany was breathing heavier, and Clara started massaging her chest.

"Come on, sweetheart, breathe deeply."

Tiffany began breathing rapidly, and then her body became limp, and she stopped breathing.

"Oh my God, Brenda, she has stopped breathing!"

Brenda burst out in tears and started screaming. "No! Clara, no!"

Brenda pushed Clara away from Tiffany and started administering CPR as Clara stood in the middle of the floor in shock. Teddy began running around the room, barking, and yelping. It was total pandemonium. After about five minutes, Brenda stood up from the bed and embraced her sister, and they cried uncontrollably.

"Come on, Clara, we must call 911!"

Brenda ran to her bedroom, picked up the phone next to her bed, and dialed 911.

"911, what's your emergency?"

"My niece had an asthma attack and has stop breathing!"

"Have you tried applying CPR?"

"Yes, but she didn't respond!"

"What is your address, ma'am?"

Brenda gave her address to the 911 operator.

"Ma'am, stay calm and continue to administer CPR. Due to the winter storm we're experiencing, it may take up to three or four hours before assistance can arrive."

Brenda hung up the phone and ran back to the bedroom, still crying. "Clara, they'll never get here in time to save her because the weather's too bad. Besides, I've already tried to resuscitate her, and it didn't work!"

They both stood there, embracing each other, and stared at Tiffany's lifeless body. Clara lay in the bed next to her daughter and hugged her while still weeping.

"Oh, God! Oh, God! What am I going to do?"

Brenda lay in the bed next to Clara and placed her left arm around her waist, and they continued weeping. Brenda stood up and grabbed Clara by the hand.

They held hands and walked toward the doorway, and Brenda turned off the overhead light before slowly closing the door. Clara followed her sister to the den, and Brenda reached behind the bar and placed a bottle of brandy on the counter. She poured a shot of brandy into two glasses and gave one to her sister.

"Drink this; it will calm us both down."

They consumed the shots of brandy and walked over to the leather couch recliner, and sat down next to each other. Brenda pulled down the handle on the side of the couch, and the leg rest opened out. They lay back, holding hands, and cried themselves to sleep.

At 2:00 a.m., they awoke to the sound of Teddy barking. They sat up and heard voices coming from upstairs and ran up to investigate. Teddy was scratching at Tiffany's bedroom door in the same manner that he did at the attic door, and light was shining underneath the door. Brenda hurried to open the door, but not before the light had dissipated. Teddy ran up to the bed and started barking as Tiffany lay motionless.

"My God, Clara," she said, speaking hysterically, "what just happened?"

Clara, not hysterical at all, spoke nervously, "I'm not sure, but I suddenly feel a sense of calmness and peacefulness in the room."

Teddy ran around barking and wagging his tail.

"Clara, we heard voices, and what about the light we saw? Look at how Teddy's acting, Clara. He feels it too!"

"Let's go back downstairs, Brenda. This is just a little bit too much for me to handle."

They gazed over at Tiffany's lifeless body and began crying uncontrollably, then walked back down the steps with Teddy following behind them. Brenda poured a second shot of brandy and drank it down as Clara sat on the couch with her head draped in between her hands.

"Oh, Brenda! How do I tell Melvin?"

Brenda sat next to her and placed her arm around Clara's shoulders, and they lay back against the couch.

"I don't know, Clara. I just don't know. Let's get a couple of hours of sleep and then start making phone calls. I don't know what else to do."

They both closed their eyes and went to sleep.

The sun started to rise, and both were still sound asleep. Teddy began barking just as he did earlier that morning, but this time things were going to be a lot different. Brenda woke up when she heard Teddy barking and nudged her sister.

"Clara, get up, honey. We have a lot of things to do."

Clara sat up and started crying. "I know, Brenda; I just don't want to face it."

They stood up, and a familiar voice echoed throughout the house. They ran up the steps to the bedroom, and to their amazement, Tiffany sat on the side of the bed playing with Teddy. Brenda fainted and fell to the floor as Clara stood there in a state of shock, unable to move or speak. After about fifteen seconds, Clara let out a scream. "Oh my God! My baby is alive!"

She grabbed Tiffany into her arms and kissed her continuously up and down her face. Brenda managed to stagger to her feet, snatched Tiffany out of Clara's arms, and began kissing and caressing her.

"Oh, Tiffany, Tiffany, I love you so much. Thank God for hearing our prayers."

Teddy had become so excited that he jumped onto the bed, started barking, and ran around in circles. Tiffany looked at her mother and her aunt and smiled, amused at their outburst of emotions. They both managed to calm down, including Teddy, and Brenda sat Tiffany on the bed between the two of them. Clara started talking while placing her left arm around Tiffany's shoulder.

"Brenda was Tiffany really—" she hesitated and then quickly said "—or did we make an unpardonable assumption?"

"No, Clara, she was what we thought."

"Then how do we explain her recovery?"

"We don't. We just thank God and move on because He's the only explanation we need to know."

Clara started crying, and for the first time since her revival, Tiffany spoke. "Mommy, why are you crying?"

Tiffany's statement started Brenda crying, and they both gripped Tiffany by the hand, and their crying turned into tears of joy.

CHAPTER 16

The Gift

The snow had stopped falling, and the roaring sound of a loud noise drowned out the conversation that Brenda and Clara were having in the living room. It was Kevin with his snowblower clearing the walkway of Brenda's house. Tiffany sat on the living room floor, playing with the new dollhouse that Santa had brought her for Christmas. The phone rang, which was sitting on the coffee table, and Brenda picked it up and spoke loud enough to overcome the noise of the snowblower.

"Merry Christmas!"

"Merry Christmas, Sweetheart. What is that terrible noise in the background?"

"It's Kevin with his snowblower!" The noise stopped, and Brenda spoke in a normal tone. "Okay, honey, that's better. Kevin must have finished."

"Good, how are you ladies doing?"

Brenda took a deep breath. "Oh, we're doing okay, and we survived the snowstorm. How's everyone there?"

"Everyone's fine, dear. Ryan wants to speak with you."

"Merry Christmas, Mom, and how are Aunt Clara, Tiffany, and Teddy doing?"

"Merry Christmas to you, Sweetheart. We're all doing quite well."

Brenda heard voices in the background hollering out Merry Christmas.

"Oh, Mom, that's Uncle Fred, Aunt Pauline, and the boys wishing you a Merry Christmas."

"Tell them Merry Christmas as well, Son, and tell your Aunt Pauline I'll talk with her later."

"Okay, Mom, and I'll see you later this week. Wait, Mom, here's Dad."

"You take care, honey, and I'll see you on Thursday."

"Sounds good, dear, goodbye."

Brenda walked over and sat on the love seat and watched Tiffany play with her dollhouse. Teddy was upstairs and started barking, and Clara volunteered to check on him.

"Stay seated, Brenda, and I'll go and see what Teddy is into now."

When Clara got upstairs, she saw Teddy standing next to the bed, barking at the lamp.

"What's wrong, Teddy?"

She looked down at it and became mesmerized by its beauty.

"This lamp is absolutely stunning."

She examined it for a little while longer and then led Teddy downstairs.

"Brenda, I had no idea how beautiful that lamp was."

"Oh my God, the lamp! Clara, I must put it back. If Jim found out that I took it out of the box, he'd never forgive me!"

"What are you talking about, Brenda?"

"It was a gift from a coworker as a birthday present. The origin of the lamp is somewhat sketchy. Something about a strange little boy making it and giving it to a homeless shelter. I don't know all the details, but Jim's superstitious and kept it stored away. You must not say anything to him about us using it. You must promise, Clara!"

"You seem to be serious. I promise I won't say a word."

"Thank you."

Brenda hurried upstairs, unplugged the lamp, and took it up to the attic. After removing the lampshade and light bulb, she placed the lamp into the box and took the lampshade back down to the basement. Brenda placed it onto the broken lamp and put the bulb back into the drawer. She returned to the den and stared Clara in the face. "You know Clara the EMS vehicle never arrived."

Clara smiled and said, "Oh yes it did sister and the paramedic on board was Jesus Christ and He brought Tiffany back to us."

Brenda said, "I'll drink to that." And picked up the brandy bottle, poured another shot, and drank it down.

Clara watched her and shouted out. "Slow down sister! You're going to pass out. Are you sure you're okay?"

Brenda looked over at Clara and started chucking. "I'm doing fine, sister. I couldn't be better; besides, we got Tiffany back."

"I guess I'll have to drink to that."

Clara walked over to the bar. "Pour me one, sister."

Brenda filled up a shot glass, handed it to Clara, and poured herself another one. They tapped their glasses together and drank it down.

———

It was a sunny but cold Thursday, December 29th, and Kevin had telephoned Brenda to tell her he was on his way to the airport to pick up Jim and Ryan. Kevin, a faithful and reliable neighbor, frequently volunteered to transport family members and friends to and from various places. He injured himself at work a few years ago and came out on disability. His transportation commitment was his contribution as a good Samaritan and neighbor, and except for the snow piles accumulated by the city's snowplows, the streets were relatively clear for travel.

They had a late afternoon arrival, so Brenda had finished cooking and planned for everyone to eat dinner together. Clara sat in the den reading a book, and Tiffany stared out the living room window, impatiently waiting for Ryan. Brenda went upstairs to lie down until her husband and son's arrival, while Teddy walked back and forth from the den to the living room as if he knew that this was the day Ryan would return home. At 5:15 p.m., the front door opened, and everyone hurried to the door to greet Jim and Ryan. Ryan closed the door, and they sat their luggage on the floor.

Ryan replied, "Hello, Mom, Aunt Clara"—he gave them both a hug—"and look at my little cousin, Tiffany."

Clara said, "Hello, Jim and Ryan."

Jim replied, "Clara, how are you?"

Jim hugged Clara and reached down and picked up Tiffany, and kissed her on the cheek.

"Tiffany, you're just a sweetheart."

Jim put Tiffany down, Ryan picked her up, and Tiffany wrapped her arms around his neck.

"Hey, little cousin, how have you been?"

"I'm doing fine, Ryan. I've been waiting all day for you to come home."

Everyone chuckled as Teddy jumped up on Ryan and started barking.

Ryan replied, "Hey, boy, I missed you."

Jim turned and embraced Brenda.

"Oh, Sweetheart, I'm so glad to be back. Let Ryan and I put away our things, and we can all meet up in the den."

The group dispersed as Ryan and Jim headed upstairs.

The following morning, Jim drove Clara to the airport to pick up Melvin. He was visiting the Detroit metropolitan area for the first time, other than his stops at DTW as a commercial airline pilot. Traffic was moderate, so they had no trouble finding a place to stand in front of the United Airlines terminal. It wasn't long before Clara spotted her husband and ran out of the car to meet him. Melvin Stein was a tall, distinguished-looking man in his late thirties with thick black hair, stylishly cut, and a neatly trimmed beard and mustache. Jim had met Melvin three years ago when his family visited them in Atlanta. Jim got out when they walked up to the car, shook Melvin's hand, and placed his luggage into the trunk. Clara sat in the back, and Melvin sat upfront with Jim. Jim drove out of the arrival terminal and merged onto the freeway.

"How was your flight, Melvin?"

"It was quite nice, Jim. I always enjoy the times when I can be a passenger for a change."

"I can imagine. Well, you and your family can sit back and relax for the next few days as our honored guest."

"I'm looking forward to that, and thanks, Jim."

Jim drove up into the driveway and instructed Melvin and Clara to get out so he could park the car into the garage.

"Well, we made it, people. Clara, you and Melvin can go inside the house while I park the car in the garage. I left the front door unlocked. Melvin, we have a German shepherd, but don't be alarmed. Teddy will know that you belong with us and are a family member. Unless you're afraid of dogs, and if so, I'll go in and put him up."

"No, I'll be all right. I've never had a fear of dogs."

Melvin and Clara got out of the car and walked up to the house. Clara led the way, and when she opened the door, Teddy came charging over. Clara called out Teddy's name and stood in between the two.

"Hey, Teddy, I've got someone with me."

She bent over and rubbed Teddy down his back as he stared at Melvin.

"Hey, big guy. How are you doing?"

Melvin slowly raised his left arm and attempted to rub Teddy along the back. Teddy growled and then wagged his tail and walked up to Melvin, allowing him to pet him. Melvin rubbed him along the back a couple of times, and Teddy turned and headed in the opposite direction.

"I guess, honey, Teddy had to check you out first."

Tiffany heard her mother's voice and ran out of the den to the front door. When she saw her father standing there, she dropped Jennifer onto the floor and ran into the arms of her father.

"Daddy! Daddy!"

"How's daddy's baby girl doing?"

Brenda and Ryan came up from the basement and greeted him with a hug.

"Hi, Uncle Melvin!"

"Hello there, Ryan. You've grown a bit."

"Yes, about two inches since you last saw me."

"Brenda, you're looking well."

"Thanks, and so are you."

Jim walked in from the back and led everyone into the den. "Have a seat, Melvin. Care for a brandy?"

"That sounds good."

Jim picked up the ice bucket on the bar and handed it to Ryan.

"Son, go to the refrigerator and fill it up with ice."

Clara sat next to Melvin on the couch while Tiffany sat on his lap. Ryan came back and handed the ice bucket to his father. Jim placed the bucket onto the bar countertop and turned over two glasses, standing face down. He put two ice cubes in each glass and reached down for the brandy bottle, only to find it almost empty.

"Hey, what gives?"

He looked over at Brenda, seated on the La-Z-Boy recliner adjacent to where Melvin and Clara were sitting.

"When the cat's away, the mice will drink up all of your brandy. I see you girls had a good time while I was gone."

Brenda looked over at Clara before replying, "Oh, sweetheart, Clara and I just did a little pre–New Year's Eve celebration."

Jim looked over at Melvin. "Well, Melvin, I guess while you were flying the friendly skies, our wives were also flying. They just didn't have an airplane as you did."

Melvin smiled. "Clara's not much of a drinker."

He turned his head, looking at Clara. "Honey, what made you overindulge?"

Clara looked down at her lap and avoided eye contact with Melvin.

"Well, honey, I guess I was a little uptight and wanted to unwind."

Melvin placed his index finger under her chin and turned her face toward him. "Are you sure everything's okay?"

Clara took a glance over at Brenda before speaking. "Yes, sweetheart, everything is fine."

It was New Year's Eve, five minutes before midnight, and the entire family waited for the clock to strike twelve. They were standing around the fireplace, illuminated by the fire and the lights from the Christmas tree. The adults were holding glasses of champagne, while Ryan and Tiffany had glasses of sparkling grape juice. One minute away from the new year, Jim lifted his glass.

"I propose a toast to our family. It gives me great pleasure to have the opportunity to bring in the new year with my beautiful wife, my son, Ryan, my lovely sister-in-law and niece, and her husband, Melvin. God bless us all!"

Everyone broke out into cheer and laughter, which started Teddy barking. Jim looked down at Teddy.

"Oh, and let's not forget to acknowledge our illustrious watchdog, Teddy."

The clock started chiming, and everyone shouted out, "Happy New Year!"

They toasted and drank from their glasses and extended hugs and kisses to one another. It was 1995, a new year, and a new beginning for everyone.

Clara was setting the dining room table, and Brenda had just taken the ham out of the oven. It was New Year's Day, and the delightful smells of a holiday feast filled the air. Brenda brought the ham out on a large platter and placed it in the center of the table. Clara followed with bowls of candied yams, string beans, mashed potatoes, macaroni and cheese, potato salad, and homemade rolls. Brenda placed a pumpkin pie and apple pie on top of the buffet table and announced to everyone to take a seat at the dining room table. Jim sat at the head, and to his right were Brenda and Ryan; to his left sat Melvin, Clara, and Tiffany—holding Jennifer in her hand.

Clara said, "Sweetheart, give Jennifer to me. You'll get her back after you finish your dinner."

Clara took the doll and placed her onto the buffet table behind them as Jim looked around the table.

"Anyone care to lead us in prayer?"

To everyone's surprise, Melvin volunteered. "Sure, Jim, I'll be glad to."

They stretched out their arms and gripped the person's hand next to them.

"Dear Heavenly Father, we thank thee for allowing us to see another year. Bless this food with your sanctifying grace. Keep us safe, healthy, prosperous, and wise, wise enough to do the things that meet your approval. For thine is the kingdom, the power, and the glory. In our Lord and Savior and your son, Jesus Christ's name, we pray. Amen."

The group responded by saying amen, followed by a response from Jim.

"Melvin, that was an excellent prayer. Are you flying passengers around, or is it your church ministry that you have seated on your aircraft?"

Clara smiled. "Jim, Melvin is quite active in our church; we both are dedicated members."

Melvin replied, "Jim, when you fly around the country as much as I do, you better have faith in a power greater than your piloting skills to keep that plane up in the air."

Clara said, "Amen to that, sweetheart."

The group continued eating until Tiffany made a statement. "Guess what, Daddy?"

"What, sweetheart?"

"I saw an angel."

Brenda and Clara quickly looked over at one another as Ryan chuckled.

Melvin replied, "An angel, where did you see an angel, sweetheart?"

"It was in my room standing next to my bed."

Clara replied, "She probably had a dream; you know how kids can imagine things."

Tiffany quickly folded her arms together and started pouting. "I didn't imagine it. Jennifer saw it too." She looked back at her doll. "Didn't you, Jennifer?"

Brenda attempted to calm her down by changing the subject. "Okay, Tiffany, we believe you. Why don't we finish up—"

"I'm not finished! Guess what else, Daddy?"

"What, honey?"

"The angel spoke to me."

Clara said, "Now, now, Tiffany, that's enough."

Melvin said, "No, let her speak. What did the angel say, honey?"

"The angel said, 'Hello, little one, don't be afraid. Go back to sleep. You have been made whole.'"

Melvin continued, "Okay, sweetheart, that's good."

Jim smiled. "It looks like my niece has a vivid—" he paused "—well, had a lot to say."

Everyone chuckled as Jim continued. "I guess that's the end, right, Tiffany?"

"Yes, Uncle Jim, because when the angel finished talking, he jumped back into the lamp, and it came back on."

Brenda and Clara looked terrified as Jim stood up and shouted out, "Lamp! What lamp! Excuse me."

Jim hurried from the table and made his way up the attic steps. Melvin and Ryan looked around, wondering what was going on. After a couple of minutes, Jim calmly walked into the room and sat back down at the table as Melvin looked over at Jim.

"Are you okay, Jim?"

Jim looked over at Brenda and spoke softly.

"Yes, Melvin, everything is fine."

———————

Jim sat in the car parked in the driveway, and Ryan had put everyone's luggage into the trunk. Ryan walked over to Melvin and hugged his uncle.

"Well, nephew, I've enjoyed you."

"I've enjoyed you, too, Uncle Melvin, and I'll see you next time."

Melvin replied, "You take care, Ryan."

Brenda, Clara, and Tiffany were standing on the porch.

"Take care, Clara."

Brenda bent down and kissed Tiffany on the cheek. "You be good, Tiffany, and Aunt Brenda will see you soon."

"Okay, Aunt Brenda."

Clara reached out and hugged her sister. "Brenda, we'll remember these days for the rest of our lives."

"How can we forget, but it's our secret. We must continue to give God all the glory for what happened."

"I agree, Brenda, because it was by His divine providence that Tiffany is still with us. Brenda, Tiffany talked about that lamp. You think it had a hand in any of this?"

"I don't see how, but who knows, and we'd never be able to convince my husband of that, even if we believed it. That's why he must never know that we used it."

They hugged each other for a second time. Clara turned and walked toward the car with Tiffany, who looked over at Ryan.

"Bye, Ryan."

Ryan picked up Tiffany and gave her a big hug. "Bye, little cousin. I'll see you next time." He turned toward Clara. "I'll see you next time, too, Aunt Clara." They hugged one another.

"Okay, Nephew, you take care of your mom and dad."

"I will, Auntie."

Melvin got into the car and sat up front with Jim; Clara and Tiffany sat in the back. Jim pulled out of the driveway and drove off as Brenda and Ryan waved goodbye.

CHAPTER 17

The Gift

Ryan had just finished his criminal justice class and headed over to the cafeteria to meet with Sarah. They were students at the University of Michigan, and Ryan was in his second year of law school. Sarah pursued a teaching degree in children's education and met Ryan a year ago on campus at a book fair. Since that time, they started dating and were inseparable and even talked about marrying after college.

Sarah was twenty-two, a couple of years younger than Ryan, with long, dark brown hair and medium height and built. It was Friday afternoon and a warm mid-summer day. Sarah and her parents had invited Ryan to dinner that evening, which had butterflies spinning around in his stomach. It would be Ryan's first time meeting her parents, and he wanted their first impression of him to be favorable. Ryan had a red Ford Mustang that his father bought him when he went to college, and he had it sparkling, cleaned, and ready to go. Sarah's parents' home was in an expensive, upscale property in Bloomfield Hills in Oakland County.

They drove up through a gated two-acre property featuring a beautiful colonial-style home that included a circle driveway and a three-car garage. The landscape featured a small pond with a waterfall structure. Ryan drove up into the driveway, and they got out of the car. As they walked up to the house, the front door swung open, and Sarah's mother walked out and stood there smiling.

"Hello, Mother." Sarah and Thelma embraced.

Thelma was in her mid-fifties, medium height and build, and had light silver-brownish hair. She'd worked as a seamstress for thirty years and retired when the industry became more technologically advanced, requiring an upgrade of her skills.

"Hello, sweetheart."

Thelma stretched her arms out and hugged Ryan. "And you must be Ryan. It's a pleasure meeting you."

"Yes, Mrs. Jones, I'm happy to meet you."

"Come on in with me to the family room. Your father is watching the ballgame."

They walked into the family room and saw Sarah's father lying back in his recliner, watching TV.

"Honey, here's your daughter and her boyfriend, Ryan."

Steven stood up, hugged Sarah, and reached over and shook Ryan's hand. "Hello, Ryan, I've been looking forward to meeting you."

"Hello, Mr. Jones. It's a pleasure meeting you as well, sir."

Sarah's father, Steven Christopher Jones, had retired as a criminal justice attorney and had financial success in real estate, buying and selling blue-chip properties. He was a tall, stocky-built man in his late fifties with black, grayish hair and a thin mustache.

"Have a seat, Ryan, over there on the couch," Steven said as he sat in his recliner.

Thelma took Sarah by the hand. "Come on, Sarah, help me set the table and bring the food out so we can eat."

"I'm a big Detroit Tigers fan. What about you, Ryan, are you a base-ball fan?"

Sarah had informed Ryan of her father's obsession with baseball and with the Detroit Tigers.

"Oh, yes, sir, and so is my father. I think the Tigers will make the playoffs this year."

"They're a good team but still need help in the bullpen. Not like those '68 Tigers: Al Kaline, Willie Horton, Bill Freehan, Mickey Lolich, Norman Cash, and Denny McClain. Sarah tells me you're in law school studying to become a criminal defense attorney?"

"Yes, sir. Next year is my last year. Sarah told me you were a criminal lawyer, Mr. Jones?"

"Yes, that's right, fifteen years as a corporate attorney and seventeen years specializing in criminal defense. Now I strictly work in real estate. When you graduate and pass the bar, I'll connect you with a few of my contacts."

"Thank you, Mr. Jones. I'd appreciate that."

Sarah walked in and announced that dinner was ready. Ryan and Steven got up and followed her into the dining room.

———————————

The following weekend was Sarah's turn to have dinner with Ryan's parents, and unlike the Joneses, the Hennings lived a more modest lifestyle. Nevertheless, Sarah, nervous about meeting his parents, asked Ryan numerous times how she looked.

"Do I look okay, Ryan?"

"Sarah, for the sixth time, you look splendid."

As Ryan placed his key into the lock and opened the door, a familiar sound of footsteps ran to greet him. It was Teddy, and although he'd lost a step or two, his enthusiasm to see Ryan was always a Kodak moment. Ryan bent down and grabbed him around the neck—their signature greeting.

"Hello, boy, how you doing? Sarah, this is Teddy, who I told you about, he always seems to know when I'm coming home."

Sarah replied, "Hi, Teddy." She bent over and rubbed him down his back as he wagged his tail and barked. "He's a beautiful-looking dog Ryan."

Jim and Brenda walked in as Ryan shut the door, and Brenda immediately embraced Sarah.

"Sarah, so glad to meet you. Besides Ryan's studies, you're at the beginning and end of all his conversations."

"It's a pleasure meeting you, Mrs. Henning."

Jim said, "Hey, hey, it's my turn."

Jim hugged Sarah and stood back and smiled. "Son, she's a beautiful-looking young lady."

"Thank you, Mr. Henning. I'm glad you approve."

Jim replied, "Let's go into the den and get comfortable."

They headed for the den, with Teddy bringing up the rear.

It had been three weeks since Ryan had Sarah over for dinner, and Brenda thought about how pleased she was with Ryan's choice. There was a slight mist in the air as she prepared to go to the Southfield Library to meet with her group. The library provided free private meeting rooms that she and her book club members utilized once a month to review and discuss their favorite books. It was a convenient, comfortable place to visit and less than a twenty-minute drive away from her home. It was mid-afternoon on a Monday, and traffic was flowing moderately on the Southfield Freeway.

Brenda had been on the freeway for a couple of minutes when she heard the screeching sound of car tires. In her rearview mirror, she saw a vehicle spinning out of control directly behind her. The rear end of the pickup truck struck her from behind, causing her to lose control. Her car turned to the left, positioning itself perpendicular to the median strip and right into the path of an oncoming semitrailer. The impact imploded her vehicle, killing her instantly.

Traffic was delayed for about two hours as law enforcement personnel closed all northbound lanes. The police report concluded that the pickup truck driver was driving too fast for the wet road conditions and lost control of his vehicle. He was twenty-seven years old and taken to a local hospital in critical condition.

Jim had just walked into the house about fifteen minutes before the state trooper arrived. Jim heard a knock on the door, and when he opened it, a state police officer wearing a blue uniform stood at the door. It was the first time a police officer had ever stepped on the porch of his home, and a feeling of utter shock and despair came over Jim.

"Yes, Officer, how may I help you?"

"Are you Mr. James Henning?"

"Yes, I am."

"May I come in?"

"Of course."

When the officer walked in and removed his hat, Jim knew that the next words out of his mouth would be distressing. Teddy ran up and started barking, and Jim told him to go into the den.

"Mr. Henning, I'm Officer Cook. Your wife, Mrs. Brenda Henning, has been in an accident and sustained injuries she was unable to survive."

It was the worst feeling Jim had ever felt, and tears rolled down his face.

"Mr. Henning, I'm sorry for your loss, would you like me to assist you in contacting someone?"

"No, Officer. I'll take it from here."

"Here's my card, Mr. Henning, and feel free to contact me if you require further assistance."

Officer Cook left, and Jim walked over to the couch, sat down, and cried. It took Jim about half an hour to compose himself, and he stood up and walked into the kitchen and made himself a cup of tea. It was four forty-five p.m., and Ryan routinely checked in with a phone call at five. At five minutes after five, the phone rang, and Jim answered. "Hello, Ryan!"

"Yes, Dad, it's me."

Ryan could tell the difference in his father's tone of voice. "Dad, what's going on?"

"I just need you to get into your car and get here right away!"

"Dad! What's this—" Jim quickly hung up before Ryan could say another word, and called Kevin.

———

An hour later, Ryan pulled up into the driveway and recognized Ruben's car parked on the street. He hurried up the steps and didn't bother using his key but turned the handle, and the door opened. When he walked in, there stood his father, Kevin, Marcy, Ruben, and Joey. Ryan lifted his arms and cried out.

"Where's my mother!"

Marcy broke out in tears, ran over, and placed her arms around him as Jim replied and got straight to the point. "Son, your mother was killed in a car accident."

Ryan started hollering and screaming as Teddy, locked in the basement, stood at the top of the steps, barking without ceasing. Ruben, Kevin, and Joey began sobbing, looking helplessly at Ryan, unable to say anything that would comfort him.

CHAPTER 18

The Gift

Several people stood around the gravesite as the minister concluded the service with The Lord's Prayer. Ryan was standing next to his father with Sarah by his side, and around the circle was Jim's brother Frederick, his wife Pauline, Clara, Tiffany, Melvin, Ruben, Joey, Steven, and Thelma. The week had tested the resiliency and endurance of the immediate family. Now it was time for everyone to retreat to a neutral corner and start all over again. The group slowly walked away from the gravesite and exchanged words of support and encouragement. Ruben walked over to Jim and shook his hand.

"Jim, if there is anything you need me to do at any time, just call me."

"I will, Ruben, and thanks."

Clara reached out and grabbed Jim's and Ryan's hands and then hugged them around the neck. "I love both of you, and we must always stay in touch."

Tiffany, now fifteen, walked over and started sobbing as she hugged Ryan and her Uncle Jim.

Melvin patted Jim on the back and reached his arm around Ryan's back. "You know we're family, and we'll always be there for one another. Ryan, your father, will need you more than ever."

"I know, Uncle Melvin."

Jim replied, "Thanks, Melvin."

Frederick looked over at the Polanski and Jones families. "It was a pleasure meeting everyone. I wish it had been under better circumstances, and you two have a lovely daughter. She'll make my nephew a fine wife."

Steven and Thelma thanked him as Steven walked over and shook his hand.

Clara walked over to Thelma. "Thank you so much for coming."

"Honey, I was glad to be here to help support the family, and once Ryan and Sarah set a wedding date and get married, we will be a family." They both smiled.

Clara walked over and gave Frederick and Pauline a hug. "I appreciate you two coming, especially so far."

Frederick said, "I loved Brenda like a sister. She was a special lady."

Pauline replied, "We both did."

They all smiled, and Clara said, "Well, everyone, my family and I must leave for the airport. Our flight departs in two hours. Melvin has to be at work in the morning. Keep us in your prayers."

Everyone waved as they walked toward the car. Ryan wrapped his arms around Tiffany.

"I'll see you soon, little cousin, only you're not so little anymore."

Tiffany smiled. "That's right; I'll be sixteen next month. I'll be back for your wedding, and I want you to send me the first invitation."

"I will, Tiffany."

Tiffany and her parents got into the rental car and drove off. The Jones family said their goodbyes before departing, followed by Ruben and Joey. The family car driver opened the door and escorted Jim, Ryan, Frederick, and Pauline into the limo. He asked everyone to fasten their seatbelts and slowly drove out of the cemetery.

It was a beautiful spring afternoon, and Ryan and Sarah were to become newlyweds. It had been a long, strenuous journey to becoming an attorney, and at twenty-six years old, it was time to start a family and a new career. Sarah's father, Steven, had the honor of giving his daughter away. Ryan's Aunt Clara and his cousin, Tiffany, had flown in from Atlanta. Now eighteen, Tiffany had grown up to become a beautiful young lady and a flower girl at her cousin's wedding. In her second year of college, attending Harvard University, her goal was to obtain a medical degree at the University of Massachusetts Eye & Ear Infirmary at Harvard in Ophthalmology.

Family and friends filled the wedding chapel, waiting patiently for the bride's appearance. The officiating minister was the pastor of the church where the Joneses attended. Ruben sat next to his son Joey, and seated to his right was his wife, Priscilla. He married Priscilla three years ago, and they were expecting their first child, which made Ruben happy. Today was Joey's thirty-second birthday, and he'd been an automotive design engineer for four years.

Everyone stood, and the roar from the crowd echoed throughout the chapel as Sarah strolled down the aisleway in her beautiful wedding dress. It was a joyful moment for the Jones and Henning families and the beginning of a new generation. The wedding ended with the minister announcing the newlywed couple as Mr. and Mrs. Ryan and Sarah Henning.

Ryan and Sarah spent their honeymoon in Barbados, courtesy of Sarah's father, Steven. He also purchased a house in Grosse Pointe, a suburb of Detroit, below market value, sold it to Ryan at one-third of the cost, and made good on his promise by connecting Ryan with his business contacts. Ryan got an interview with the Taylor and Schluter Law Firm and joined the team as a junior attorney. For the next two years, Ryan concentrated on his law career, and Sarah taught part-time at a local elementary school. Jim retired and spent most of his time watching sports on TV. Since his wife died, he didn't have much interest in anything else, and his only companion was Teddy. Teddy developed arthritis in his legs, making it difficult for him to walk around. On Thanksgiving holidays, Sarah and Ryan spent the day with Jim while spending Christmas with her family.

It was a warm June afternoon, and Sarah was excited about the news she had received from her doctor. She was pregnant and envisioned the joy that would be on Ryan's face when he found out and stuck to her routine of having dinner ready when he got home. She thought telling him after dinner while he was in the family room relaxing would be a perfect time. Minutes later, Sarah heard Ryan driving into the garage. He shut the car door and walked into the house through the garage entrance, and Sarah ran over to him and wrapped her arms around his neck. It was her usual way of greeting Ryan when he came home from work.

"Hello, honey. How was your day at the office?"

"Hectic as usual but workable. Mark presented me with a new case. I think he's more confident in me, because he's doubled my workload this past month."

Sarah smiled. "Hmm. Just so Mark knows that additional workloads require additional pay."

Ryan smiled. "Believe me, sweetheart, I'm on it."

"Come on, Ryan, let me fix your plate."

After dinner, Ryan stood up and kissed Sarah on the cheek. "That was a good dinner, dear. I'm going into the family room to chill out."

Ryan headed for the family room as Sarah sat at the kitchen table and smiled. Ryan was lying in the recliner and had fallen asleep when Sarah gently sat on his lap and lay across his chest. Ryan woke up and wrapped his left arm around her waist. "Caught me napping, dear. I was more tired than I thought."

"Well, Ryan, honey, I'd suggest you get as much rest as you can now because in about nine months, rest is going to come at a premium."

Ryan slowly opened his eyes and looked at Sarah. "In about nine"—Ryan quickly stood up and held Sarah in his arms— "Sarah! We're going to have a baby!"

Ryan started running around, carrying Sarah throughout the house.

———————————

Sarah and Ryan stood at the front door of her parents' home and rang the doorbell. Thelma opened the door and gave a big smile.

"What a surprise, I didn't expect to see you two today."

"We were in the area, Mom, and decided to pay a visit."

"I'm in the family room. Let's go back."

They went into the family room and sat down. Ryan and Sarah sat next to each other and held hands.

"Mom, where's Dad?"

"He upstairs lying down because he wasn't feeling well. Let me go and see if he feels like coming down."

"No, Mom, don't bother."

"Sarah, he can tell me if he feels like coming down or not. He'd be madder than hell if you left and I told him you'd been here."

Thelma walked to the bottom of the steps and hollered out to Steven, "Steven, the kids are down here!"

A couple of minutes later, Steven came down wearing pajamas and a housecoat. "Hey, you two. What's going on?"

"Dad, are you okay? You don't look so well."

"I've felt worse. I'll survive."

Sarah decided to get straight to the point so her father could go back to bed. They planned to let Ryan give them the news, so she squeezed his hand firmly.

"Mom, Dad, Sarah's pregnant, and you're going to be grandparents!"

Thelma jumped up, and Steven started clapping.

Thelma replied, "So that's why you two came over here, handing me that bull that you were just in the area."

Steven nodded his head. "Thelma and I have waited for this moment. Congratulations, you two."

Sarah replied, "Okay, Dad, that's enough excitement for one day. Now you get back to bed."

Steven slowly walked away, looking over at Ryan. "Son, you can see your wife got her mother's disposition"—talking slowly—"bossy as hell!"

Everyone started laughing as Steven made his way upstairs.

CHAPTER 19

The Gift

The next morning Ryan and Sarah were on their way to visit Jim and tell him the news. Unlike the surprise visit they made to her parents' home, this Saturday-morning visit was part of their weekend routine. Ryan used his key to gain access, and as always, Teddy hobbled to the door to greet them. Ryan bent down and wrapped his arms around his neck.

"Hey, boy. how are you doing?"

Teddy's bark was much more profound, and his tail moved back and forth much slower as Jim's voice called out from the den.

"Come on back; I'm in the den."

Jim was sitting in his favorite chair, watching TV. Sarah reached down and kissed him on the cheek. "Hey, Dad."

"Hi, honey, and hello there, Son."

"Hello, Dad, what are you watching?"

"An old western. You know I watch a lot of them along with my baseball games."

"Yes, I do, Dad. You love your westerns."

"Sarah, Ryan tells me your dad's a big baseball fan?"

"Yes, Dad, he's a Detroit Tigers fanatic."

"Maybe he and I can go to a few games together next season."

"He'll love that."

Sarah and Ryan sat down on the couch and held hands and smiled.

"Why are you two sitting over there smiling like a couple of Cheshire Cats?"

This time Ryan squeezed Sarah's hand.

Sarah said, "Dad, you're going to be a grandfather, I'm pregnant!"

"A grandfather! What do you know about that? You finally brought me something besides dad, how you doing, what did you eat, and all that crap. Have you got any names picked out?"

Sarah said, "No, Dad, we just found out, so we have plenty of time to choose a name."

Jim got up and walked over to the bar. "Well, I think I'll have a little brandy. Care for one?"

Both declined and laughed when Jim drank down a shot. "Here's to our new addition and my first grandchild."

––––––––––––

It had been a couple of days since Steven and Thelma received the news about their daughter's pregnancy. Steven still wasn't feeling good, and Thelma was getting him dressed for a doctor's appointment. Steven excused himself to go to the bathroom and fell to the floor at the bathroom entrance. Thelma rushed over, helped him up, and noticed his face, severely twisted. She managed to get him to his feet, walked him over to the bed, and sat him down. She picked up the phone next to the bed and dialed 911.

Thelma stood there and watched the emergency crew wheel her husband through the double doors. A staff member led her to the emergency waiting area and instructed her to have a seat and wait for an update on her husband's condition. It was Monday morning at ten thirty-seven when she nervously took out her cell phone and auto dialed Sarah's number. Sarah immediately recognized her mother calling. "Hello, Mom."

"Yes, dear, it's me."

Sarah was unable to sense her mother's distress, preoccupied with household chores.

"What are you doing? Ryan isn't home, is he?"

Sarah immediately stopped what she was doing because her mother asked a question that had an obvious answer. "Mother what's wrong? Where are you?"

Thelma paused before speaking and spoke in a low tone of voice.

"Sarah, I'm at Providence Hospital. I believe your father had a stroke."

"Oh my God! I'm on my way!"

Twenty minutes later, Sarah rushed into the waiting room and saw her mother sitting with her head down. She walked over to her mother, and Thelma stood up. They embraced each other and began crying silently.

"Mother, what happened?"

"We were getting ready to go to his doctor's appointment. He said he was going to the bathroom and fell to the floor in the hallway. I helped him up, and we walked back into the bedroom. He sat down on the side of the bed, and I called 911."

They sat there for another five minutes before Ryan rushed in and hurried over to Sarah and Thelma. Sarah stood up and moved over one chair, and Ryan sat in the middle. He extended his arms around them, and they lay their heads on his shoulder. Thelma explained to Ryan what she told Sarah about what happened, and they sat quietly, waiting for a report on Steven's condition.

It was eleven thirty-five, and they had been sitting for thirty-three minutes when a man dressed in blue scrubs walked in and called for Thelma Jones. He was a tall man in his mid-forties with black hair bulging out beneath his blue cap. The three of them stood up, and he walked over and introduced himself. Thelma slowly raised her hand, acknowledging that she was the wife.

"I'm Thelma Jones, and this is my daughter Sarah and her husband, Ryan."

"I'm Dr. Hanson. Would you please follow me?"

They followed him out of the waiting area and down the hallway. They saw a young lady wearing scrubs standing at the doorway of an unoccupied room. Dr. Hanson led them into the room, and she shut the door behind them. He motioned toward the young lady with him, a short woman, in her mid-thirties, with a medium build and a dark brown complexion.

"This is Nurse Johnson, and she assisted me in the operating room. Would anyone care to be seated?"

The group declined and knew that it wouldn't be good news and waited for Dr. Hanson's next statement, making it official.

"Mrs. Jones, your husband suffered what is called a hemorrhagic stroke. A blood vessel ruptured in his brain, which restricted blood flow. He lost consciousness, and we were unable to revive him. I'm sorry for your loss. Does anyone have any questions?"

Everyone shook their heads and remained silent.

"Again, I'm sorry for your loss, and we're going to step away so the three of you can have time together. Take as much time as you like, and when you're ready, Mrs. Jones, Nurse Johnson will have some paperwork for you to sign."

Nurse Johnson followed Dr. Hanson out of the room, closing the door behind her. Thelma stood there, motionless before speaking.

"Well, you two, God knows best. I only wished that he could have seen his grandbaby."

Sarah reached out and held Ryan's and Thelma's hand and looked down at her stomach.

"Me too, Mom, but one thing's for sure, this baby will always be a part of my father."

Ryan turned and hugged Sarah. "Amen to that, honey."

The four of them stood around the gravesite, Thelma, Sarah, Ryan, and Ryan's father. Steven had no siblings, and his parents were deceased. On numerous occasions, he told Thelma that when he passed on, he wanted a short burial service. The four of them walked away from the gravesite, and Thelma turned her head to take one final look and grabbed Sarah by the arm.

"Your father always told me, Sarah, that he wanted a small burial service, nothing fancy, nothing elaborate. He said that he came into this world alone, and he'd leave it alone, so why bother with annoying crowds and insincere people?" Thelma paused and then continued speaking, "You know what, honey? He was right."

Jim embraced Thelma and Sarah and walked over to Ryan and hugged him.

"Son, that's exactly how I want my service to be when my time comes. Fred and his family can stay in England, and there'll be no need for Clara's family to travel from Georgia. There'll be nothing they can do, and I'll be in the hands of the Lord."

Ryan smiled. "Okay, Dad, but that won't be anytime soon."

Jim got into his car and drove off, and Ryan escorted Sarah and Thelma to his car and followed his father out of the cemetery.

CHAPTER 20

The Gift

Two weeks later, Thelma opened the door to her house and walked in with Sarah and Ryan, and they sat down in the family room. They had been to Steven's attorney's office to settle his estate. For the most part, everything was in order with the real estate properties and other assets secured. Still, substantial penalties due to late filings and improper documentation by Steven's attorney, Timothy Martin, had been levied. He asked Thelma to give him time to clear up the matter. Ryan wasn't pleased with his performance, and Thelma called him a crook.

"Son, don't you operate as that scoundrel did."

"Of course not, Mom, but for the most part, he had everything in order, so it didn't capsize the ship."

"I never was crazy about him, and I told Steven that. Timothy always wanted Steven to go fishing and play golf. He should have been focusing more on doing his job."

Sarah replied, "Well, Mother, things will work out. Come on, Ryan; we need to get our shopping done before it gets too late."

Sarah walked over and kissed Thelma on the cheek, and Ryan did the same.

It was March 15, 2008, and at precisely five forty-five a.m., a new edition arrived in the Henning household, a baby boy, Luke Christopher Henning. He weighed six pounds, eight ounces, and had Ryan's nose and his mother's eyes. They both agreed to name him Luke, a take from Ryan's father's middle name, Lucas, and gave him the same middle name as Sarah's father. Ryan, the proud father, stood and held his son while standing next to Sarah's hospital bed, grinning with pride. Ryan smiled while looking at his son.

"Hey, little guy. I'm your daddy."

Sarah said, "Well, Ryan, we have a son, and my mom and your dad will be chomping at the bit to see who will spoil him first." They both chuckled.

It was Luke's fifth birthday, and Sarah, Ryan, Jim, and Thelma sat at the dining room table. Luke sat in the middle, wearing his ice-cream cone birthday hat. At the center of the table, a birthday cake displaying the words Happy 5th Birthday Luke had five lighted birthday candles standing on top. Ryan picked up Luke and held him over the cake, and he blew out the candles.

They all applauded, and Luke reached out his hand to his father, swinging it in a cutting motion.

"Come on, Dad, it's time to cut the cake."

Luke stood up in the chair, and Ryan placed the knife in his hand and guided it to the cake. "Okay, Grandma, you get the first piece."

He cut a slice and placed it onto a plate. Luke picked it up and gave it to Thelma.

"Okay, Grandpa, you're next."

He cut the second piece and gave it to Jim, followed by slices to Sarah and Ryan.

"Everyone has a slice. Now I get the biggest piece," said Luke.

Everyone chuckled as Ryan guided his hand, and Luke cut a larger slice.

Luke said, "Okay, everyone, it's time to eat," and he sat down and started eating.

Thelma took a bite and walked into the family room, and sat down. It was apparent that she wasn't feeling well, and her health had diminished over the past three years. She'd sold her house and moved in with

Ryan and Sarah. They tried to convince her to do so after Steven died, but Thelma refused until her health declined, and they insisted.

Sarah walked in and sat down with her mother. "Mother, I can tell that you're not feeling well."

"Just the usual, a little tired."

"Come on, Mother; I'm going to take you upstairs so you can lie down."

She grabbed Thelma by the hand and took her upstairs.

———————

It was Friday afternoon and another long day for Ryan. He sat at his desk when his cellphone rang, it was his father.

"Hey, Dad, what's up?"

Jim was sitting in his usual spot in the den, on the recliner.

"Well, Son, I'm sitting here looking at Teddy. He can't even stand up and is in a lot of pain. It's time to take him to the vet tomorrow."

There was a slight pause. "Okay, Dad, I'll be there in the morning."

"Are you bringing Luke?"

"I don't know, Dad. What do you think?"

"Leave him at home. We'll just tell him that Teddy went to a better place."

"Okay, Dad, that is probably better."

The following morning Ryan arrived bright and early. Jim was dressed and had eaten breakfast, and stood watching Teddy lying on the floor in the den.

"Teddy has barely moved since I spoke with you yesterday and hasn't eaten a bite."

"Dad, open the door, and I'll carry him to the car."

As Ryan bent over to pick him up, Teddy started yelping.

"Okay, Teddy, it's all right."

Ryan thought back on the day when he first got Teddy and held him in his arms. That was the first day that he brought him to the house. Teddy was just a puppy, but today he was an old, sick dog, and Ryan carried him for a different reason and for the last time. Ryan put Teddy into the car's back seat, and Jim sat in the passenger's seat. Ryan got behind the wheel, and they headed off to the veterinarian.

———————————

Two weeks had gone by since they had Teddy euthanized, and it was just Jim now, all alone. He felt a sense of abandonment with his wife dying years ago, and his son married, supporting his family. The only companionships left were baseball games and western movies. The baseball games were seasonal, and he'd seen those old western movies a hundred times. He used to have a hobby of making things but lost interest in that right after his wife died.

Jim never saw much of Ruben anymore because he spent most of his time at his son's in-law's house. He also had a nine-year-old granddaughter that occupied most of his time. After reminiscing for a while, Jim sat back and closed his eyes. Shortly afterward, he heard the front door open and familiar footsteps running toward the den. Luke ran over and jumped into his lap.

"Hey, Grandpa, I surprised you, didn't I?"

Jim held him around the waist and kissed him on the cheek.

"You certainly did, Grandson."

Ryan walked over to the couch and sat his laptop on the table.

"Hey, Dad. How's it going?"

"Oh, not bad. I see you brought your laptop. You got work to do?"

"No, I want to show you an article. Give me a moment."

Ryan turned on his laptop and navigated to an article on the web that he had bookmarked. He walked over to his dad and handed Luke the computer.

"Luke, hold this up straight for your grandpa so he can read this article."

Jim looked at the screen and saw a picture of a man and a woman standing together wearing white lab coats and recognized that the woman was his niece, Tiffany. He bent over and took a closer look, and read the article.

"Peter Cornell, MD, PhD., the director of The Georgia Golden Ophthalmology Center, is pleased to announce the addition of a new staff member, Tiffany Stein, MD. Dr. Stein completed her medical degree, residency, and internship at Massachusetts Eye and Ear Infirmary at Harvard University. She was the top honor student in her class and will be part of our twelve-team medical staff at the center. Son, that is outstanding!"

Ryan took the laptop from Luke and walked back to the couch, and sat down.

"Dad, I spoke with Tiffany a little while ago, and she's waiting for a call back from me to talk with you. She'll be on speakerphone, so we'll be able to converse together."

"Good, call her, Son."

Ryan took out his cellphone and called Tiffany, and she answered. "Hey, Ryan."

Jim replied, "Hello, Dr. Stein, and congratulations."

"Uncle Jim, thank you. How have you been?"

"I'm doing fine, and I'm so proud of you and your cousin, Ryan."

"Yes, Uncle Jim. I read the article a few months ago that Ryan won the most significant criminal justice case in Michigan in the past ten years."

"Yeah, he's an excellent attorney, all right. I just wish he worked for another firm. That Mark Taylor isn't paying Ryan what he's worth."

"With his accomplishment, Uncle Jim, he'll be rewarded."

Ryan replied, "Tiffany, I've been telling Dad I'll get a substantial raise, or I'll be working for another law firm. I've made a few connections."

Luke said, "Hello, Cousin Tiffany."

"Is that my little cousin Luke?"

"Yes, it's me."

"Your father used to call me 'little cousin' when I was about your age."

"I know, he told me."

"How old are you now?"

"I'll be six years old in March."

"Wow, getting to be a big boy. Uncle Jim, you remember when my mother and I spent Christmas with Aunt Brenda, and there was a big snowstorm? I think I was about six, and you and Ryan went to England, visiting Uncle Fred."

"I remember, sweetheart."

Ryan replied, "I remember too."

Tiffany said, "I also remember being sick, and I had this dream about an angel speaking to me."

Jim looked over at Ryan.

Ryan said, "I also remember that Tiffany."

Tiffany continued, "I recall that dream so vividly, and after the angel spoke to me, he disappeared into a lamp."

Jim saw Ryan looking over at him and quickly changed the subject.

"How are your parents doing?"

"They're doing fine, Uncle Jim. I'm planning a surprise cruise next year for their thirtieth anniversary."

Jim replied, "Good. They'll enjoy that."

"Uncle Jim, do you still read your Bible?"

"All the time. I just don't go to church much anymore like I did when your aunt was living."

"Hey, Cousin Tiffany!"

"Yes, little cousin."

"I go to church on Sundays with my mom and dad and grandma. I like going to church. The preacher talks about how Jesus loves us, and we should love everyone too."

"That's right. Okay, Uncle Jim, Ryan, and little cousin, I've got to get going. I've got a meeting to attend."

The three of them said goodbye, and Ryan disconnected the call. Ryan thought about Tiffany's dream and wondered what his dad had done with the lamp Ruben gave to him and looked over at his father. He could tell by the expression on his father's face that he knew what Ryan was thinking, but Jim never said a word. Ryan motioned to Luke to get down off his granddad's lap because they had to leave.

"We've got to go, Dad."

"Okay, Son. Thanks for stopping by and sharing that article with me."

"Goodbye, Grandpa."

"Goodbye, Grandson, take care."

"I'll talk to you later, Dad."

They walked out the front door and got into the car, and Ryan drove off.

CHAPTER 21

The Gift

I t was Tuesday, and Sarah had made an appointment for her mother with Dr. Ross. Thelma's headaches had become more frequent, and Sarah wasn't going to wait any longer. Thelma had acted stubbornly about going and had canceled two previous appointments. Thelma was sitting on the examining table, and Sarah was seated in the chair by the door. Nurse Amy Wright, a tall, thin, blonde-haired woman in her mid-thirties, introduced herself and took Thelma's vital signs.

Thelma replied, "Nurse Amy, you sure are tall. How tall are you?"

"Mother, please, that's not a question you ask a person."

"It is if you want to know the answer."

"Excuse my mother, Nurse Amy."

"Oh, it's all right; I get that question all the time. I'm six feet, two inches tall, Ms. Jones, and Dr. Ross will be in shortly."

Nurse Amy walked out of the room and closed the door. Thelma reached up and grabbed her head, and frowned.

"See there, Mother. You got yourself all worked up. Are you okay?"

"I'd be okay if my head would stop hurting."

Dr. Herbert Ross walked into the office and stood in front of Thelma. He was in his mid-fifties, medium height, with grayish black hair.

"Hello, Ms. Jones, how do you feel?"

He turned toward Sarah and addressed her. "Hello, Ms. Henning."

Sarah replied, "Hello, Dr. Ross."

Thelma said, "I've been better, Dr. Ross."

Dr. Ross replied, "Ms. Jones, you've had two other appointments within the last two months, and they were both canceled."

"Well, Dr. Ross, I started feeling better, and I canceled them. My daughter told me this time I was going to make this appointment, or my son-in-law would tie me up and bring me here."

"You've got to start taking better care of yourself, Ms. Jones. Didn't you tell me the last time you were here that you had a grandson?"

"Yes, I did, Dr. Ross. He'll be six years old in March."

"Well, if you want to be here for his graduation, you better start keeping your appointments."

"Okay, Dr. Ross, I will."

"How long have you had these headaches?"

"It started a couple of months ago."

Dr. Ross held up his hand. "Look at my finger while keeping your head still and follow my finger with your eyes. Okay, good. Ms. Henning, take your mother up to the third floor. I have her scheduled to get scans taken, and I want to see her back here next Friday. I'll have Amy make an appointment."

Dr. Ross opened the door and escorted them to the elevators.

———————

Jim had just finished eating breakfast and felt a numbness in his right arm and sat down. The phone rang, and he answered it, and it was Ryan.

"Hello."

"Hello, Dad. Just checking up on you."

"I just finished eating breakfast and felt a little dizzy, so I sat down, and I have a little numbness in my right arm."

"Numbness, I'm on my way over."

Ryan made it to his dad's house in less than twenty minutes. He opened the door and hurried into the den. Jim was sitting there and smiled.

"You made the trip in record time, Son. I don't think it's that serious."

"Dad, how do you feel?"

"I'm feeling much better now."

"Maybe you need to go to the hospital?"

"No, no, Son. It's just one of those things that happen when you get older."

"Maybe you should come and stay with me a couple of days?"

"Son, I'll be okay, but if I have a problem, I'll call 911. Besides, your mother-in-law and I would be at each other five minutes after I got there."

Ryan smiled. "Yeah, she is hard to get along with sometimes. I'm going to leave, and I'll check on you later. You sure you don't want to go and get checked out?"

"No, Son, I'll be fine."

Ryan went over and hugged his father. "I love you, Dad."

"I love you too, Son."

Ryan left, and Jim turned on the TV and started watching an old western movie that he'd seen several times before.

Dr. Ross walked in as Sarah and Thelma sat patiently.

"Hello, Ms. Jones and Ms. Henning."

They both said hello.

"I got the results of the scans back, and there's a small mask on the left side of the brain. There's nothing to be worried about; we just need to take a sample. I scheduled to have a biopsy taken on Monday at one o'clock. Is that okay?"

Sarah replied, "That will be okay, Dr. Ross."

Dr. Ross led them out into the hallway and said he'd see them next week. At first, Thelma was quiet on the way home and then started talking.

"Now I know why I've been having all of those headaches."

"Mother, missing your appointments certainly didn't help things. It may have made matters worse. I'm sure that after they run a few tests, we will find out more."

Thelma, embarrassed about missing her appointments, sat back and remained silent.

———————

It was eight o'clock when Ryan walked through the door. Sarah had been sitting in the living room, waiting for him to come home. Luke and Thelma were upstairs in bed, asleep. Sarah stood up, ran over to Ryan, and kissed him. She kissed him a second time and then started crying.

"Hey, hey, hey, sweetheart, what's the matter?"

"They found a mask on mother's brain, and they want to take a biopsy."

Ryan wrapped his arms around her waist and hugged her.

"It's going to be all right. How did your mother take it?"

"She hasn't said much because I know she's worried. She should have gone to see Dr. Ross two months ago, instead of being so stubborn."

"It's going to be okay, honey."

"I hope you're right, dear. Come on in the kitchen, and I'll warm up your dinner."

———————

It was Wednesday morning, and this was the third time in the last two weeks that Thelma and Sarah had visited Dr. Ross's office. They sat patiently for his entrance, and he came in with a smile and greeted them.

"Well, ladies, I hope you've had a pleasant morning."

Thelma sat there quietly as Sarah replied. "We're doing okay. My mother seems to be feeling better."

"Is that so, Ms. Jones?"

"The headaches are not as bad. Just a little tired."

"Ms. Henning, take your mother up to the lab on the fourth floor for her blood work and come back to my office while she's having it done. I have a few pamphlets I want to give you."

"Okay, Dr. Ross."

Sarah and Thelma took the elevators up to the fourth floor as Dr. Ross stood in his office, waiting for her return. When Sarah came back to the office and saw the look on his face, she knew that the results weren't favorable.

"I can see by the expression on your face, Dr. Ross, that you don't have any good news to tell me."

Dr. Ross put his hand on her shoulder and looked her in the eye.

"No, I don't, Ms. Henning. The results came back positive. Your mother has a malignant brain tumor, and it's in stage four. I'm sorry."

Sarah started crying, and Dr. Ross reached over, took a box of tissue off the desk, and gave it to her.

"How long does she have, Dr. Ross?"

"A year, eighteen months maybe. Only God knows for sure. I'm going to give you a prescription; it will help minimize the pain. I want to see her back in two weeks."

The following eight months was a mental struggle for the Henning family. Thelma's health declined, and Ryan's father was taken to the emergency room on two occasions for shortness of breath. Ryan walked into the den carrying a replacement cylinder for his father's portable oxygen machine. Jim sat in his usual spot watching TV.

"Here's another tank, Dad. How's that one holding up?"

"Just fine, Ryan. Son, you don't have to come over here checking on me two and three times a day."

"You won't come and live with me, and you don't want anyone else staying with you."

"Son, don't worry about me. I'm all right. You can call me every day, but please, just come over every other day. You have a wife, a sick mother-in-law, and a kid to take care of at home."

"I'm not guaranteeing you anything right now, Dad, but we'll see how it goes."

Ryan and his father smiled at one another and embraced.

"I'll see you later, Dad."

"Okay, Son, and you take care."

Ryan's Monday morning started as usual. He ate breakfast with his wife and son, and Sarah prepared a breakfast tray for her mother and carried it upstairs. Ryan kissed Sarah goodbye, dropped Luke off at school, and headed off to work. He went along with his father's request to visit him every other day, and today was a visitation day. Ryan had a nine o'clock appointment in court and planned to go over to his father's house afterward. His court case lasted about two hours; pleased with the results, he smiled and headed over to his father's house. It had been a good morning up to this point. Ryan walked into his father's house and heard the TV coming from the den. He thought it was odd that his father didn't holler out his signature greeting: *Come on back; I'm in the den*, which always brought a smile to Ryan's face because where else would he be but sitting in his favorite chair? When Ryan walked into the room, his father's head didn't turn to greet him, and Jim continued looking straight ahead. Butterflies filled Ryan's stomach when he placed his hand on his father's shoulder and felt the stiffness in his body. It was the ending of a father and son's relationship, the family torch now placed in Ryan's hand.

Ryan sold the house, so everything had to be out before the new owner took possession. Two men were upstairs, moving boxes, tables, and chairs out of the attic. Ryan had donated most of his father's belongings, which were things he'd made or collected over the years. A man pointed to a wooden box located in the back against the wall.

"Would you like me to take this wooden box out, too, Mr. Henning?"

Ryan walked over to the box and slowly opened the lid, and there was the lamp. His eyes widened because he hadn't seen it in more than twenty-three years, and he shouted out, "The lamp!"

CHAPTER 1

The Discovery

Ryan shakes hands with a couple, each carrying a bag under their arms. They walk down the steps and exit to the left as two men exit the front door carrying a couch. They walk behind a large van with Salvation Army on its side and load it into the truck. As it drives away, Ryan closes the front door, picks up a small wooden box, and places it under his arm. He puts it into the back of a late-model Jeep and turns to take one final look at the house—which was once his home in this quaint little city of Melvindale, Michigan. It is the ending of a chapter in his life, but the memories of his youth growing up here will last a lifetime.

He gets into his vehicle and drives away, revealing an old, well-kept neighborhood, and passes an old school building scheduled for demolition, making room for a new office complex. A sign reading New Center Square is displayed on the fence surrounding the area as he continues driving down I-94 east and exits onto south M-10, John C. Lodge Freeway. He travels down Jefferson Avenue, which directs him through Downtown Detroit and the city's east side. Jefferson Avenue winds its way around, becoming Lake Shore Drive and the city of Grosse Pointe, Michigan.

The scenery is a beautiful coastal view of Lake Sinclair. He turns right onto Woodland Place Drive and pulls up into the driveway of a luxurious two-story brick home that he purchased from his father-in-law ten years ago. Ryan enters the living room and sees Sarah sitting on the couch, thumbing through a magazine.

"Hi, honey, did you get everything taken care of?"

"Yes, I did. I disposed of Dad's things and only kept a few keepsake items. The rest of the things I gave to neighbors and friends. After Mom died, Dad never cared much for having too many things around the house."

"What's that in the box?"

"It's a lamp my father acquired some years ago. He had it stored away in the attic."

"Hardly seems worth the effort to keep it since your father never used it."

"It's a special lamp, and it's unique looking, so I'll hang onto it. Besides, Luke needs a new lamp for his room."

———

The following morning, Ryan, Sarah, and their seven-year-old son, Luke, eat breakfast at the kitchen table as Ryan addresses Luke.

"Well, Son, how was school yesterday?"

"Okay, Dad. Ms. McCants said I was the best math student in her class."

"It doesn't surprise me, Son, your tutor, Ms. Ramsey, is the best tutor in Wayne County."

Sarah frowns while looking at Luke.

"Finish up your breakfast, dear; it's time for us to leave for school. I'm going to check in on Mother before I leave."

Ryan reaches over and grabs Sarah by the hand. "I checked up on your mother on my way down, honey, and she's sound asleep."

"Thank God. I'm so relieved that she can finally get a little rest. She had a rough time last night."

"I am too, honey. Dr. Ross said the only thing we can do for her now is to keep her comfortable."

"Mom, is Grandma gonna be all right? She's been sick a long time."

Sarah looks over at Ryan and then over to Luke.

"I hope so, sweetheart"—big sigh—"I hope so."

"Oh, by the way, Son, that lamp I promised you will be in your room when you come home from school today. It was my dad's, and it's a beautiful lamp. I only hope it works because he had it stored away." He smiles at Luke. "But if it doesn't, I'll go out and buy you a new one. Either way, you'll have a lamp in your room when you get home."

Luke looks at Ryan with a big smile. "Promise, Dad?"

"I promise."

Ryan picks up the newspaper and reads the front page. Sarah and Luke exit the front door as Sarah hollers out to Ryan.

"I'll be back shortly, dear."

"Okay, my love, I'll be here."

"See you later, Dad, and don't forget the lamp."

"Take care, champ, and I won't forget."

The front door shuts, and Sarah and Luke leave as Ryan continues reading the newspaper.

The doorbell rings, and Ryan looks at his watch. He opens the front door, and Ms. Donna Edward is standing there, smiling. Ms. Edward is the home care nurse of his mother-in-law. She's in her late forties and is a short, stocky-built woman, toting a black medical bag and wearing dark-rim prescription glasses.

"Hello, Ms. Edward, please come in."

They walk down the hallway into the living room and sit down on the sofa.

"How is Ms. Jones doing today, Mr. Henning?"

"Well, Ms. Edward, she had a rough night but was sound asleep a couple of hours ago."

"You know, Mr. Henning, she's in the final stages before her body is just going to shut down completely."

Ryan pauses. "I'm aware of that, Ms. Edward, but I feel so helpless, and my wife, Sarah, she's still trying to hang on, hoping that her mother is going to get better."

"That's a natural reaction from those who are closest to the person who is ill. They want to hold on to that feeling of hope that their loved one isn't going to leave them. That hope is what keeps them going, Mr. Henning, but unfortunately, that isn't enough to keep them from dying."

"The reality of living, Ms. Edward, knowing that one day we all must die."

"Yes, Mr. Henning, a fact of life. I need to go up and check on Ms. Jones, Mr. Henning."

"Certainly, Ms. Edward, she'll be in her room."

Ms. Edward is standing in front of Thelma's bedroom door and gently knocks.

"Come on in. It's either my daughter or you, Donna, because the counselor and my grandson never knock."

Ms. Edward slowly walks into the room and makes her way over to Thelma. Thelma has lost weight, looks frail, and sits up against the headboard.

"Hello, Ms. Jones, how do you feel? Are you in any pain?"

"I'm always in some kind of pain, Donna, but isn't everybody?"

"Ms. Jones, I'm only concerned about you at the moment."

"With the medications that I'm taking, the pain is manageable."

"That's good to hear. Let me take your vital signs, Ms. Jones. Take a deep breath for me. Good, now open your mouth and lift your tongue. Good, now the last thing is to take your blood pressure. Well, Ms. Jones, your vital signs are stable. You get your rest now, and I'll see you tomorrow."

Thelma smiles. "God willing, I'll see you tomorrow, and if not, I hope to see you someday on the other side."

Ms. Edward looks at Ms. Jones with a stern expression. "Like I said, get more rest, Ms. Jones, and I'll see you tomorrow."

The front door opens, and Sarah walks in and sees Ryan with his legs crossed and sitting on the couch.

"Hi, honey, I see Ms. Edward is here."

"Yes, dear, she went upstairs about fifteen minutes ago."

They hold hands while sitting on the couch together and have a look of concern on their faces. Ms. Edward walks into the living room to report on Thelma's condition.

"There is no change in Ms. Jones's condition Mr. and Mrs. Henning, so that means she hasn't gotten any worse."

Sarah looks down at the floor. "My mother has completely lost her appetite and refuses to eat. Two cups of tea a day is about all she cares about or wants."

"I know it's difficult for the two of you. Just hang in there and continue praying. I must be going to my next appointment, and I'll see you two tomorrow."

They exchange goodbyes, and Sarah leads Ms. Edward down the hallway to the front door.

"Goodbye, Ms. Edward, and I'll see you tomorrow."

"Take care, Mrs. Henning."

Sarah slowly shuts the door and walks down the hallway into the living room and addresses Ryan.

"Honey, I'm going to run to the store and pick up a few things. You need anything?"

"No, dear, I'm going to pull out this lamp and see if I can get it working for Luke."

"Don't spend too much time on that old lamp because there are more important things to do around the house. Remember, you promised me that during your next couple of days off you'd finish repairing the broken tile on the basement floor."

Ryan is smiling. "How can I forget? You've been reminding me every five minutes. I promise I'll get it done, but I also promised Luke I'd have a lamp in his room before he came home from school."

"Well, young man, you better get started. I'll leave you to your chores, and if I'm not back within the hour, please check in on mom."

Ryan smiles. "Sure thing, General, good as done."

Ryan walks over, takes the lamp out of the box, and places it onto the end table. Intrigued by its mesmerizing beauty, he takes out a light bulb from the drawer and plugs it into the light socket.

"Well, old buddy, Let's see if you work."

A big smile comes over Ryan's face.

"Wow, what a break, it works! I guess I'll polish you up, old fella, and grab a lampshade from the storage area upstairs. Luke will have his lamp, and that's chore number one completed."

CHAPTER 2

The Discovery

Ryan exits the room and heads upstairs to the attic to find a lampshade. He returns a short time later with one that's gold-and-black colored, places it on top of the lamp, and fastens it into place. Ryan hurries up to Luke's bedroom with the lamp and puts it onto Luke's dresser. He plugs it into the wall socket and stands back to take a final look.

"Well, I think that will do the job perfectly."

Ryan exits the room and closes the door behind him. He walks down the hallway toward his mother-in-law's bedroom door and slowly opens it. Thelma lies in bed and opens her eyes, and sees Ryan standing over her.

"Hello, Son. Well, one thing about you, I don't have to worry about you knocking and waking me up, unlike that wife of yours. Checking to see if I'm still breathing?" Thelma smiles. "I'm still very much alive, but if you came up here to ask me to have our last tango in Paris, I'd have to decline."

"Oh, Mom, you're ridiculous sometimes."

"Sarah always did say you didn't have much of a sense of humor. Well, this isn't a courtroom, Counselor, and I'm not on trial here, so loosen up."

"Okay, Mom. Are you hungry?"

Thelma smiles. "Where I'm going, I won't need any food, Son, but I'd like a cup of that cinnamon tea with plenty of lemons, and make sure it's sizzling hot, and for now, Counselor, court's adjourned."

Ryan grimaces, shakes his head and exits the bedroom as Sarah calls out from the kitchen downstairs. "Ryan, are you upstairs?"

"Yes, honey. I'm on my way down."

Ryan enters the kitchen and kisses Sarah, then leans back on the cabinet with his arms folded. "I can say one thing for your mother; she hasn't lost her feistiness."

Sarah chuckles. "The old counselor thing again?"

"Yep. Man oh man, that attorney who handled your father's estate sure did put a bad taste in your mother's mouth toward attorneys."

Sarah smiles while squinting her eyes. "Well, you know, honey, some of you attorneys are sly devils. That's why I keep a close eye out on you. My father was the only attorney she trusted."

Ryan looks at her with a sarcastic smile. "Don't rub it in, dear. I asked Mom if she was hungry, and she looked at me and said that where she's going, she won't need any food."

Sarah's facial expression turns to a look of concern. "Like you said, dear, we must prepare ourselves for the inevitable."

"She did say she wanted a sizzling-hot cup of tea with plenty of lemons."

"That seems to be all she wants these last couple of weeks. Let me get her tea ready and take it up to her, and I'll take a small breakfast plate up to see if I can get her to eat a little bite."

Ryan slowly shakes his head from side to side. "Good luck."

Sarah stands in front of Thelma's door with a breakfast tray and hollers out to her mother, "Knock, knock, Mother."

"Girl, come on in here. You don't need a formal invitation to enter a room in your own house."

Sarah walks in with the tray and places it onto the bed.

Thelma continues, "You should take a lesson from your husband. He never knocks. He said he doesn't want to wake me if I'm asleep, but he really comes up here to check on me to see if I'm still alive."

"Mother, please, don't be silly. He comes up here to make sure you're comfortable and to see if you might need anything, and it's always proper to knock when entering someone's bedroom, and it doesn't matter whose house you're in."

"Well, I suppose. What, more food?"

"Mother, you know you need to eat. You haven't been eating much lately."

Thelma turns her head and looks up toward the window. "Baby, where I'm getting ready to go, I won't need any food, just waking up in the morning and seeing the sunrise with the Lord."

"Mother, you're ridiculous."

"Ridiculous! That's the same thing your husband told me this morning. You know, the counselor!"

"Mother, Dr. Ross said that if you don't eat, he'll have to put a feeding tube in you."

"Hmm, that's what he thinks, but he better find out what I'm thinking first."

"Then you better start eating, Mother. I'm going downstairs to finish up the dishes, so is there anything else you need?"

"No, dear, I'm just going to lie here and rest."

Sarah places the tray onto the table next to Thelma's bed and exits the room as Thelma takes a deep breath, closes her eyes, and falls asleep.

Later that afternoon, Sarah picks up Luke from school, and he's awfully excited. He rushes through the front door and hurries toward the hallway steps leading up to his room.

"Luke, honey, slow down. Why are you in such a hurry?"

Luke is running and is halfway up the stairs and hollers out to his mom, "I want to see if dad kept his promise and has a lamp in my room."

Luke opens his bedroom door and runs up to the lamp that's on his dresser. "Wow, that's a cool-looking lamp."

Still excited about his lamp, Luke runs over to his grandmother's room, opens the door, and quickly walks up to her. Thelma sits on the side of the bed and gives Luke a big hug.

"Hi, Grandma."

"Hello, my dear. How is my grandson doing today?"

"Okay, Grandma. Dad just brought me the lamp he promised, and it sure looks great."

"Well, that's good, honey. You know your dad always keeps his promises."

Luke stares at Thelma with a look of concern. "Grandma, why don't you come downstairs anymore like you used to?"

Thelma speaks back softly to Luke with a dazed look. "Well, honey, your grandma isn't that strong anymore, and I'm a bit more tired"—Thelma focuses her attention on Luke—"but don't you worry about your grandma. She'll be okay."

"Promise?"

"I promise."

Sarah calls Luke to dinner. "Luke, honey, wash your hands and come down to dinner."

"Okay, Mom, I'm coming."

Luke gives Thelma a big hug.

"I love you, Grandma."

"I love you, too, sweetheart."

Luke leaves the room, and Thelma lies back on her pillow and closes her eyes. Luke enters the kitchen and sits at the table. Sarah places a plate of food in front of him as the front door opens, and Ryan walks into the kitchen. Luke looks up at his dad and smiles.

"Hey, Dad."

"Hello, there, Son. It looks like I'm just in time for dinner, sweetheart?"

Sarah smiles. "Yes, you are, Counselor. Did you find your new set of golf clubs?"

"Yes, I did, dear, but I had to special order them. Let me go upstairs and get cleaned up; then we can sit at the table, have prayer, and eat our dinner together. By the way, what are we having, because it sure smells good."

"Your favorite, smothered lamb chops, mashed potatoes and gravy, buttered broccoli, and fresh apple pie for dessert."

Luke quickly comments, "Yum, yum, except for the broccoli."

Ryan and Sarah chuckle.

"Dad, thanks for the lamp. It looks neat. I told Grandma that you promised me one, and she said your dad always keeps his promises."

"You're welcome, champ."

Ryan exits the room as Sarah speaks with Luke.

"I see you paid your grandmother her usual visit. How's she doing?"

"She told me that she was tired and that's why she doesn't come downstairs anymore. Mom, is grandma going to get well again?"

Sarah grabs Luke's hand with a gentle squeeze. "Well, Son, we can only pray and hope so, because it's all in God's hands now."

———————————

Ryan enters the kitchen and sits at the table, joining the other two. Ryan spreads out his arms, holding Sarah's hand with his left hand and Luke's hand with his right hand, and in unison, they bow their heads as Ryan leads the group in prayer.

"Dear Heavenly Father, we thank you for this food, which we are about to receive for the nourishment of our bodies, and we pray that you keep us safe and in your care. We also pray that you secure a special blessing for Mom, who needs your blessings and saving grace. Amen."

Sarah and Luke say, "Amen."

Thelma, from her bedside, hears the voice of Ryan blessing the food and his prayer to God for her well-being. She closes her eyes and speaks softly to herself. "Dear Lord, I know I don't have much time left. All I ask is that you take care of my family, protect them, and strengthen their faith, in Jesus's name I pray, amen."

The family finishes eating, and Sarah places a plate of food on a tray as Ryan and Luke stand next to their chair.

"Now that was an excellent dinner, my dear."

"Yeah, Mom, and you know the best part was the apple pie." Sarah and Ryan chuckle.

"While I take Mother her food, you go upstairs to your room, young man, and do your homework."

"Oh boy, I can try out my new lamp that used to be grandpa's."

"Well, Son, it may not be new, but it certainly was your grandfather's lamp. I'm going to the family room to do a little reading, and you get that homework done, champ."

Sarah replies, "And when you finish your homework, start running your bathwater, and I'll put a fresh pair of pajamas on your bed."

"Okay, Mom."

Luke exits the kitchen with Sarah following behind him with a food tray as Ryan walks toward the family room.

CHAPTER 3

The Discovery

L uke wakes up when Ryan comes into his bedroom.
"Did you finish your homework, champ?"

"I have just one more problem to do, Dad."

"I'll leave the lamp on so you can finish that last problem. You can turn the lamp out when you finish."

Ryan exits the room and heads down the hallway toward his bedroom. Sarah is sitting on the side of the bed and addresses Ryan. "Honey, I think Mom has given up. She only speaks about being with the Lord."

"Yes, I know, dear. There's nothing more we can do but continue to pray."

Ryan and Sarah continue their conversation about their plans for her mother's funeral arrangements and the closing out of her affairs after she dies. After a lengthy discussion, it's one thirty-five a.m. They decide to retire, and Ryan makes a final bed check on Luke and Thelma. Just before Ryan opens the door to check in on Luke, his lamp goes out. Ryan is thinking to himself, *Luke has turned his lamp off. Way to go, champ*. He checks in on Thelma and finds her sound asleep. Ryan quietly closes the door and walks back to his bedroom.

"Goodnight, Sarah, my dear. Sleep tight, and don't let the bedbugs bite."

Sarah smiles. "You're funny, sweetheart, because the only thing that's been biting on me lately is you."

That gets a slight chuckle from Ryan.

Sarah says, "Goodnight, dear."

At two a.m., Thelma awakes to a bright light illuminating at the foot of her bed, and she becomes frightened.

"What is this! What is this I see?" She rubs her eyes. "I must be dreaming!"

As Thelma continues looking, she sees a bright light of an angel at the foot of her bed with its wings stretched out and speaking to her.

"Do not be afraid. I'm an angel of the Lord, and because you have faith in the Lord Jesus Christ, you have been made whole."

Ryan wakes up and raises his head because he hears talking in Thelma's bedroom. He puts on his robe and house shoes and walks down the hallway to Thelma's bedroom door. Thelma looks on in amazement as a flashing light quickly covers her body and then extinguishes. She immediately falls asleep. Ryan opens the door about halfway and peeps his head into her room. Thelma is sleeping peacefully, and everything is quiet. He checks in on Luke, only to find that his lamp is on. He thinks to himself, *Luke must have gotten up to go to the bathroom and forgot to turn his lamp back off.* Ryan walks over, turns it off, and heads back down to his bedroom, shaking his head.

Sarah is setting the table for breakfast, and Ryan walks over and kisses her on the cheek.

"Good morning, honey, did you sleep okay last night?"

"Actually, I was sleeping fine until you got up to go to the bathroom."

"Well, Ms. Actually, I thought I heard voices coming from your mother's room."

"You know, dear, that Mother will occasionally talk in her sleep."

"I'm aware of that, but this was different. I'm almost sure I heard another voice as well, but when I went in to check on Mom, I found her sound asleep."

"Well, Counselor, it's time for you to go back to work, or you'll be trading your briefcase in for a room at the mental center down the street."

Sarah walks to the hallway and stands at the base of the stairs calling up to Luke.

"Luke, your breakfast is ready, time to come down."

"I'm coming down now, Mom."

Luke enters the kitchen and sits down at the table.

"Good morning, Son."

"Good morning, Dad. Oh, you too, Mom."

"Son, I see you turned your lamp back on last night. You must have gotten up to go to the bathroom and left it on."

"No, Dad, I fell asleep reading my book and forgot to turn it off. I didn't wake up until this morning."

"When I checked in on you before I went to bed, Son, your lamp was off, and when I checked on you again an hour or so later, it was back on."

"Honest, Dad, I never got up out of bed after I went to sleep."

Sarah looks at Ryan with a smirking smile. "Really, Ryan, hearing strange voices in Mother's room and a lamp turning on and off by itself?"

Ryan frowns. "Okay, dear, I get it. Ease up, will you? Finish up your breakfast, champ, because today is Saturday, and we've got to go and get our haircuts."

Everyone begins eating, when a loud thump rumbles from upstairs. Sarah hurries up the steps, calling out to her mother.

"Here I come, Mother!"

Sarah opens her mother's bedroom door and sees her spinning around as if dancing to an orchestrated ballet song and puts her hand over her mouth in disbelief.

"Mother, oh my God! What are you doing out of bed?"

"Quiet, Sarah, can't you see that I'm dancing with the spiritual angels of the Lord?"

Sarah rushes out of the room to the top of the steps and cries out loud to Ryan.

"Ryan, come up here! I don't know what's happening with Mother!"

Ryan runs up the stairs and rushes into Thelma's room. He looks in amazement as Thelma dances around the room.

"Sarah, is this real? Am I seeing what I'm seeing?"

"Hello, Son. Well, don't just stand there. Come over here and dance with your mother."

Sarah and Ryan rush over to Thelma, each grabbing her by the arm, leading her to the bed, and sitting her down. Sarah sits next to her on the bed as Ryan stands over Thelma.

Sarah says, "Mother, are you all right?"

"Of course, honey. Your mother has never felt this good in all her life. Well, at least not since my early thirties."

"Mother, are you in any pain?"

"Not at all, my dear Sarah. Why? Should I be?"

"Mother, you've been gravely ill." Her speech is unsteady. "You just haven't been feeling well these last few months."

Luke comes running into the bedroom and runs over into the arms of Thelma.

"Grandma, Grandma, are you're okay?"

Thelma puts her arms around Luke and kisses him on the cheek. "Little Luke, your grandma is just fine, and what is all of this fuss about me not feeling well?"

Ryan looks over at Sarah. "Sweetheart, I'm going downstairs to call Dr. Ross. You and Luke stay up here with your mother."

Ryan exits the room while Sarah sits next to her mother, and Luke stands between Thelma's legs facing her.

"Mother, what can you remember over the past few days?"

"Well, if you want to know the truth, the last thing I remember was lying down because I wasn't feeling well. I think I may have had a fever."

"Mother, do you have any idea of how long ago that was?"

"It couldn't have been more than a couple of days ago."

"Mother, it's been three months."

"Yeah, Grandma, you've been sick a long time."

"So that's what all the fuss has been about. I've been gravely ill over the last three months." Thelma begins speaking softly and looking as though she's in a trance. "I had a dream, and there was this warm and sensational bright light that seemed to touch me throughout my entire body."

Sarah looks at her mother intently as Thelma continues to speak.

"It gave me the greatest peace and comfort that I've ever known, and a voice spoke out to me."

"What did the voice say, Mother?"

"I can't remember, honey, but I was in a state of ultimate peace and comfort."

Ryan enters the room after contacting Dr. Ross's office.

"The nurse on call this weekend said to have your mother come into Dr. Ross's office at nine o'clock Monday morning."

The doorbell rings, and Ryan grabs Luke by the hand. "Come on, champ. It's ten o'clock, and that must be Ms. Edward to check up on your grandma."

Thelma stands straight up, pulling Sarah up with her, and reaches for her robe and house shoes.

"Hold on, Son; I'm going to do the honors of opening the door for Donna."

As Thelma hurries downstairs, Sarah looks at Ryan with a puzzled look.

"Ryan, what are we going to do?"

"I don't know, honey. I just don't know."

CHAPTER 4

The Discovery

Ryan, Sarah, and Luke hurry downstairs to the living room just as Thelma opens the door.

"Hello there, Donna. Guess who?"

Donna looks up at Thelma and begins to faint at the doorway entrance, and Ryan catches her by the arm as Thelma comments, "Well, it looks like the only person who needs a doctor around here is Donna."

Ryan helps Donna over to the couch and sits her down.

"Are you okay, Ms. Edward?"

Donna begins talking to Ryan while staring at Thelma. Thelma stands cheerfully within six feet of her, looking astonishingly well.

"I'm okay, Mr. Henning, but how is your mother-in-law?"

"Why ask the jockey when the horse is staring you right in the face? I'm doing fantastic!"

Sarah motions to Donna to follow her, and both women exit the living room as Ryan and Luke walk Thelma over to the couch. Sarah and Donna stand in the middle of the family room face-to-face with each other.

"What has happened, Mrs. Henning? Your mother looks and acts like a different person. I've seen patients diagnosed with terminally ill conditions appearing to get better before the final stages of death, but never anything like this."

"I truly don't have an answer, Ms. Edward. The only thing I can tell you is that the three of us were having breakfast this morning when we heard a loud noise coming from my mother's room. When I went to her room, she was joyfully dancing around and has been the way she is now, since."

"Unless this is just an extreme temporary condition that will soon turn back around, this is the most amazing thing I've ever seen."

"My mother talked about a dream she had where she saw a bright light that gave her peace, and heard a voice speak to her. She believes that's when she woke up and started feeling better."

"When is she scheduled to see her doctor again?"

"She's scheduled to see Dr. Ross at nine o'clock Monday morning."

"He'll more than likely order a new set of scans to see what's happening with the brain tumor. With the cancer spreading as it did, I don't see how she's standing on her feet, let alone dancing around. I'm going to check her vital signs before I leave."

The two women walk back into the living room. Ryan is sitting next to Thelma as Luke lies across her lap, sound asleep.

Sarah replies, "Luke, go upstairs and finish your nap, dear. Ms. Edward has to check on your grandmother."

Luke walks toward the stairway to go upstairs as Ryan walks out of the room and heads for the family room. Ms. Edward walks over to Thelma and places a blood pressure cup around her arm.

"One ten over sixty-five, not bad, Ms. Jones. Now breathe in and out for me. Now open your mouth so I can take your temperature. Ninety-eight point six. I must say, your readings are quite remarkable compared to yesterday. How do you feel, Ms. Jones?"

"I feel good enough to have my daughter make up a batch of those blueberry pancakes, along with some crispy bacon and a steaming cup of coffee. I'm starving!"

Sarah looks at Ms. Edward in disbelief.

"I'll be going now, so you can fix your mother's breakfast. Please let me know what the doctor says on Monday."

"I certainly will, Ms. Edward. I'll be in touch."

Donna bids Thelma goodbye as the two women walk to the front door, and Donna leaves.

Sarah immediately walks over to her mother. "Come on, Mother, you can sit and talk with me while I fix your breakfast."

The two women exit the living room and walk toward the kitchen. Ryan stands at the foot of the stairs and calls out to Luke. "Come on down, Son. It's time to go get our haircuts." Ryan looks over at Sarah. "We'll see you in a bit, dear."

"Okay, Ryan, drive safely."

Ryan and Luke leave out the front door. They get into the car, parked in the driveway, and fasten their seat belts.

"Dad, is Grandma, okay?"

"At this point, Son, it's just too early to tell. We'll know more on Monday after she sees Dr. Ross. We better get going, champ, or we're going to be late for our appointments."

Ryan drives out of the driveway and heads down the street to the barbershop. Sarah places a plate on the table and pours her mother a cup of coffee. Sarah sits down at the table and watches her mother eat.

"Mother, slow down. I've never seen you eat that fast before."

"Baby, your mother feels like she hasn't eaten in months."

Sarah stares at her mother with a look of concern while taking a deep breath. After eating breakfast, Thelma tells Sarah that she's tired and is going upstairs to rest. Sarah hugs her mother, and Thelma walks up the steps to her bedroom.

Sarah sits in a chair across from her mother, while Thelma is sitting on the examining table at Dr. Ross's office. Nurse Kelley Nelson, a young lady in her late twenties, is taking Thelma's vital signs.

"My name is Kelley, and I'm your nurse this morning. Your previous nurse, Amy, got married last month, and they moved to Florida."

Sarah replies, "I was wondering if she still worked here. Mom, you remember her, the nurse you joked about being so tall?"

"Yes, I remember her. She was especially friendly."

"Yes, she was friendly, Ms. Jones, and made the transition process quite easy for me when I replaced her. Your vital signs are stable, Ms. Jones, and everything looks good. Dr. Ross will be with you shortly, so you two ladies enjoy the rest of your day."

Sarah says, "You too."

Nurse Kelley leaves the room, and Thelma comments to Sarah, "Sarah, I always thought a nursing career would have been a better career choice for you instead of teaching. At least you'd be working now instead of being laid off."

"Mother, please, don't start on that again. With your illness, I wouldn't be working because I'd be home taking care of you, as I should be."

Dr. Ross walks in and greets them.

"Good morning, Ms. Henning, and good morning—" Dr. Ross hesitates. "My goodness, Ms. Jones, is that you?"

"Of course it's me, Dr. Ross. The last time I remember seeing you, you had a dreadful look on your face that maybe you'd seen me for the last time. Isn't that right?"

Dr. Ross grimaces. "Not at all, Ms. Jones. I was just concerned about your condition, but you appear to be doing quite well. How do you feel?"

"I feel like I could go ten rounds with Mike Tyson and beat 'em!"

Dr. Ross and Sarah glance over at one another.

"That's good to hear, Ms. Jones. Ms. Henning, take your mother up to the third floor to radiology. I have ordered a new set of scans. When they finish, you and your mother are free to leave, and I'll call you by the end of the day to discuss the results."

Dr. Ross escorts them over to the elevator, waves goodbye, and slowly walks away with a puzzled look on his face.

———

Sarah has driven to a local park, with a view of Lake Sinclair.

"Thank you, honey, for bringing me out here. Your father and I used to come out here and sit on Sundays after church, and that was long before you were born. Once you were born, your father focused more on his law career, and I spent more time with you at home."

"I guess that's why I fell in love with Ryan. He reminded me of dad. They had the same drive and ambition."

"Steven and I had some wonderful times together. Oh, how I miss him."

"Mom, it seemed that after dad died eight years ago, you didn't care about things like you used to. Things like sewing, cooking, and socializing with your friends never appealed to you anymore."

"Well, honey, you're right. I didn't care much anymore. You had your family and seemed to be happy, and me, well, I just felt that I was in the way."

"Nonsense, Mother. You had me, Ryan, and what about little Luke?"

"I must admit that when Luke was born, it did bring some joy into my life, but then I started not feeling well. It must have started about two years ago. I thought maybe it was just signs of depression from not having your father with me anymore. Then I began having these severe headaches, and I knew that I had to tell you about it. It wasn't fair to you, Ryan, or little Luke to continue hiding what was going on with me."

"Mother, I just wish you had told me sooner than—" Thelma interrupts.

"Than what? Do you think that telling you sooner would have prevented the stages of sickness that I'm experiencing now? Sarah, your mother may be a little naïve, but I'm neither crazy nor stupid enough to believe that I'm not terminally ill, and I have been for a long time. I also know that there is a tumor on my brain, so how much time did Dr. Ross tell you that I have left?"

Sarah starts to cry. "Oh, Mother! Mother!"

Thelma hugs Sarah. "Honey, it's okay. We all have a time that God has destined for us to leave this world. We must make this transition to be with him. Don't you worry; your mother is going to be all right."

"Mother, I just can't bear the thought of losing you. I'm hopeful that the scans are favorable and your health has improved."

"I know what you mean, honey. I've seen the surprised look on everyone's faces; you, Ryan, Donna, Dr. Ross, and even little Luke. Everyone seems surprised that I'm walking around as if nothing's wrong with me. I'm either in the final stages of death, or God has spared my life."

"Mom, let's just wait to see what Dr. Ross finds out from the scans. Then we'll know something for sure."

"Sounds like good advice to me. In the meantime, you sit here while I take a stroll down memory lane and go to the spot me and your father used to visit."

"Okay, Mom, be careful."

Thelma opens the door, gets out of the car, and walks across the grass toward the lake.

———

Dr. Herbert Ross and his associate, Dr. Benjamin Riley, examine Thelma's previous brain scans with the ones taken this morning. Upon reviewing the scans, they find no brain tumor present.

"Herbert, I don't even have words to explain what has happened. The scans show that Ms. Jones's brain is normal and shows no signs of a tumor."

"Ben, all I can say is that it's simply remarkable. If I didn't know better, I'd think that someone has taken out her old brain and transplanted a new one in its place."

"Herbert, that's exactly what has happened—it just wasn't done with a knife and scalpel."

"Well, Ben, they'll be glad to hear the good news, but I wish I could explain how this happened."

"Herbert, with good news like this, who cares how it happened?"

Dr. Ross sits halfway on the table with his arms folded and looks at Dr. Riley with a look of concern.

"I do, Ben, my boy." Dr. Ross takes a deep breath. "I do."

CHAPTER 5

The Discovery

S arah sits on the couch, reading a magazine when Ryan comes in from work.

"Hello, honey, it sure feels good to come home. I've been in court most of the day and have barely had time to sit down. How did things go with your mother at Dr. Ross's office?"

"Dr. Ross examined her and took scans. He told me that he'd call me this afternoon with the results and was quite amazed at how well she's getting around. He didn't say much of anything about her condition. I think he's reluctant to make any comments because he didn't want to give me the impression that things might be getting better until he examined the scans."

"I can understand his reluctance. It's highly unlikely that the tumor has disappeared, but we can still have hope. I'm not being too pessimistic, am I, dear?"

"No, sweetheart, you're just being practical. It's that attorney blood in you. Are you hungry?"

"No, honey, Mark and I had dinner at his favorite restaurant down the street while discussing the Hamilton case. I think I'll go into the family room and chill out on the recliner."

Ryan exits the room as Sarah continues thumbing through the magazine, when the phone rings.

"Hello."

"Hello, Ms. Henning!"

"Yes, is this Dr. Ross?"

"Yes, it is, Ms. Henning. Are you in a place where we can talk privately?"

"I'm alone in the living room. My son is upstairs doing his homework, my mother is taking a nap, and my husband just went into the family room, so this is perfect timing."

"Good. I have the results back from your mother's scans."

Sarah places the magazine on the couch and is extremely nervous. She tightly closes her eyes and braces herself for the information Dr. Ross is about to give her.

"Okay, Dr. Ross, what did you find out?"

Dr. Ross speaks slowly but deliberately. "Now I don't know how to explain this, but the scans came out negative. Your mother no longer has a brain tumor. She's completely normal and—" Sarah throws the phone on the couch "—Ryan! Ryan! Come here, quickly!"

Ryan comes running into the living room, which prompts Luke and Thelma to hurry down the stairs.

"Honey, what's all the excitement about?"

"Sarah, let us in on what's got you scaring the death out of everyone," says Thelma.

"Yeah, Mom, you scared me too."

"I was just on the phone with Dr. Ross, and he said that mother's brain tumor"—Sarah's almost too excited to speak—"was, was, gone! She's completely normal!"

Ryan yells out, "Oh, thank God! Hallelujah!"

"Grandma, you're gonna be all right! I knew God would fix it, and he did!"

"Little Luke, God can truly answer prayers if you believe in Him and His Word!"

Ryan shouts out, "Amen to that, Mother!"

The four of them are jumping up and down with excitement as Dr. Ross listens from his phone and hears joy and exuberance emanating from the Henning family.

Ryan is reviewing paperwork at his desk in his law office, preparing for an upcoming court appearance. Ralph Snyder, a short, stocky-built man in his mid-fifties, sits at his desk in a plush office setting in Stone Ridge, Virginia, and calls Ryan's cell phone from his office phone.

"Hello, this is Ryan."

"Hi, Ryan, it's Ralph Snyder of the Lawson and Snyder Law Firm in Stone Ridge, Virginia. How are you doing?"

"I'm doing fine, Mr. Snyder. How about yourself?"

"I'm doing fine, Ryan. I'm calling to inform you that your interview with us went quite well. You have an impeccable track record and are rated in the top five percent of criminal law attorneys in Michigan. My partner, Tom, said that he's never interviewed anyone with such confidence and poise. That indicates strong leadership capabilities."

"Thank you, Mr. Snyder. I've always been a take-charge person, especially when it comes to presenting the best argument possible when representing my clients."

"Good to hear, and that's why I'm calling you. Tom and I would like to offer you a position as a senior partner with our law firm, with full equity benefits. We feel that with you added to our team, we can rapidly solidify our firm as the number one law firm in Loudoun County."

"That sounds great, Mr. Snyder, and I appreciate the opportunity to work for your law firm. I'll talk things over with my wife this evening and get back with you tomorrow afternoon."

"Sounds good. I'll have Tammy email you with our proposed offer, which will include salary options and our benefits package for your review. I'll expect to hear from you tomorrow. Enjoy the rest of your day."

Ryan smiles. "You too, Mr. Snyder, and thanks."

Sarah is watching TV and hears the garage door opening. She walks over to the side door and greets Ryan as he enters the room.

"Where have you been, young man?" Sarah smiles as she wraps her arms around Ryan. "I'm going to have to reheat your dinner."

"Working late again, honey. When I called you earlier, I told you I had a meeting with Mark and Linda, going over the Jackson case. It just took longer than I expected."

"How's that case going?"

"It's a difficult case, but I should have it wrapped up in about forty-five days. Honey, come over here and sit down. I have some great news to tell you."

Ryan walks Sarah over to the couch, and they both sit down. Sarah looks at Ryan and smiles.

"Oh no, not another miraculous healing event. I don't think my heart can take another one."

"No, dear, my news isn't as spectacular as that, but it is good news. You remember the interview that I had with the Lawson and Snyder Law Firm in Stone Ridge, Virginia, a month and a half ago?"

"Of course I do. Other than worrying yourself to death about mother's illness, that's all you talked about. I guess it kind of got pushed to the back of our minds when mother's condition began to worsen."

"Ralph Snyder called me this afternoon and said he'd like to bring me on board as a senior partner. Ralph told me that he and Tom were extremely impressed with my track record and said I'd be the perfect fit for joining their team."

"That's good news, sweetheart, and with mother back to her old self, she's just fine to travel."

"Sarah, my love, do you know what this means? My salary would increase at least two to three times what it is now, and I'd also receive profit-sharing revenue. So are we ready to go?"

"Of course, dear. You've worked hard and have become an excellent attorney in Michigan. Ryan, you deserve this opportunity."

"Thanks, honey, we both do."

"Ryan, Mark won't be happy about you leaving and may make you a counteroffer."

"No doubt, but he'll never make me a senior partner with equity benefits. Besides, after eight years with the firm, it's time to move on. Mark has had plenty of opportunities to offer me a better package before now, but he hasn't. Fortunately, someone else did, so it will be my gain as well as the new law firm's."

"Ryan, let's wait and tell mother and Luke in the morning. Mother has been getting out more and has acquired a few new friends at the Senior Citizen Activity Center, but I know she'll be as happy as I am for you. She'll meet new friends in Virginia, and Luke will too."

The family is sitting at the kitchen table, eating breakfast, when Sarah tells Thelma and Luke about Ryan's new position.

"Well, Mother and Luke, I have some exciting news to tell you concerning Ryan's job."

Thelma replies, "I knew I had detected something different about you and Ryan this morning, so I was just sitting here waiting for one of you to confirm it."

"Ryan has been offered a position with the Lawson and Snyder Law Firm in Stone Ridge, Virginia, as a senior partner."

Thelma says, "Are you kidding me? Stone Ridge, Virginia, is in Loudoun County, which is the richest county in the country. Congratulations, Son. Does that mean we'll be packing up and leaving soon?"

"Yes, it does, Mother."

Ryan replies, "I'm going to tell Mr. Snyder that the second week of July would be a perfect time to make a move. Luke will be out of school for the summer, and I'll have all my cases closed out by then. That's two and a half months away, and it will give Mark a chance to add another attorney to his staff."

"Oh boy, Dad. I'll get a chance to meet new friends and go to a new school."

"Yes, you will, champ."

Ryan sits at his desk and calls the law firm of Lawson and Snyder. After a couple of rings, Diane, the receptionist, a thirty-two-year-old redhead, answers the phone.

"Law offices of Lawson and Snyder. How may I help you?"

"Good morning, Diane. This is Ryan Henning. I met you about a month and a half ago when I flew out there for an interview."

"Oh, yes, Mr. Henning, I remember. How are you?"

"Doing great, and how are things with you?"

"Things are going well, thank you. Mr. Snyder has been waiting for your call, and if you hold on, I'll connect you."

"Certainly."

Ryan hears a short buzz, and Mr. Snyder answers.

"Hello, Ryan. Tom and I were just discussing you, and we're excited about you joining our team. That is, of course, if you've decided to come on board."

"Yes, I have, and again, I'd like to thank you and Mr. Lawson for this excellent opportunity."

Mr. Snyder sits back in his plush chair with a big smile on his face.

"That's excellent, Ryan. Tom will be glad to hear the good news. When do you think you can start?"

Ryan flips through the pages of his desk calendar. "I'm looking at the second week in July. That will give me enough time to get things closed out here. I also must get with my realtor, Carlton, so he can put my house on the market. I think he can have a buyer for my house before then."

"Excellent, excellent. I'll have Tracy, our travel coordinator, contact you. She'll make arrangements for moving expenses, temporary housing, and travel expenses. I'll be in touch with you from time to time, and welcome aboard, Ryan."

"Thanks, Mr. Snyder."

"Call me Ralph, partner."

Ryan has a big grin on his face. "Sure thing, Ralph. I'm looking forward to working with you and Tom, along with all of the other staff members, and I'll be talking with you soon. Goodbye."

"Goodbye, Ryan."

Both parties hang up, and Ryan walks over to the table and picks up a bottle of water. He raises the container in the air and proposes a toast before taking a sip.

"To the success of the Lawson, Snyder, and Henning Law Firm."

CHAPTER 6

The Discovery

Ryan walks into a storefront resale shop. The sign at the top of the building reads Don's Treasure Chest. Ryan browses through the store filled with various items, including furniture, lamps, paintings, beautiful rugs, and more. As he's browsing, Cheryl Emery, a thirty-five-year-old woman, greets him.

"Hello, sir, anything in particular you're looking for?"

"Not at this time. I came here to speak with Don. Is he available?"

"Yes, of course, and whom should I say is asking for him?"

"Just tell him Ryan, his neighbor."

"Okay, I'll tell him you're here."

"Thank you."

Cheryl walks away and heads toward the back of the building as Ryan continues browsing. Don Mason, in his mid-fifties, tall with broad shoulders, walks up after a few minutes.

"Well, well, well, if it isn't Ryan, my neighbor. How's it going, neighbor?"

"Not bad, Don, actually quite well."

"Good to hear."

"How is that software program going that your company is working on? You know, the one that is supposed to revolutionize the twenty-first century?"

"Going great. I even got a promotion to principal engineer."

"Congratulations, Don, I must admit, you've come up with several unique software programs over the years."

"It took them long enough to promote me. It's only been twenty-three years. That's long enough to retire."

"Well, you know how it works, Don. It takes a lot of dedication and perseverance, and one day, it pays off."

"You're right about that, Ryan. I've worked hard all of my life, and most of the time, it has paid off."

Don picks up a small statue of a horse and turns it upside down, displaying the base. There's a half-inch-by-half-inch black-and-white label on the bottom.

"Take a look at that label on the bottom. Any idea what that is?"

"I don't know, is it some kind of a barcode?"

"It's called a QR code label. That stands for *quick response* because it instantly displays information about a product or service through the use of a smartphone. Take a picture of it with your phone."

Ryan takes a picture of the QR code label and then navigates to the image displayed on his phone.

"Now touch the image."

Ryan touches the image, and a picture of the statue appears with a write-up about the sculpture.

Ryan reads the information aloud: "Statue name: The Great Stallion, manufactured by the Craig Corporation in Erie, Pennsylvania, in 1973. The statue was inspired by a soldier in the Civil War who was rescued by his white stallion during a fierce battle."

"Now touch the link, and my website comes up."

Ryan touches the link, and Don's website is displayed.

"What do you think, my boy?"

"That's pretty good, Don, quite ingenious. Did you create this app?"

Don says with a sarcastic smile, "Naw, some guy in Japan. They finally made something I can use. None of my merchandise goes out of here without a QR code label. Anyone in the world can locate my business and view my inventory using my QR code label. Pretty neat, huh?"

"Yes, Don. It's quite a setup you have here."

"Well, Ryan, my boy, I know you didn't come here to talk about crawling up the ladder of success or to be given a crash course on QR code labels 101. I hope you're here to tell me that you're finally going to sell me the antique furniture you have, especially that antique bedroom set you've been storing away for years."

"Well, Don, that's exactly why I'm here."

Don's eyes widened. "Come on, Ryan, don't play with me like that. Are you serious?"

"Very serious. I've accepted a position with a law firm in Stone Ridge, Virginia."

"You don't say. Did you know that Stone Ridge, Virginia, is in Loudoun County, which is the wealthiest county in America? Man oh man, Ryan, you've made it to Hollywood."

"Slow down, Don, I haven't made my debut yet. Funny you should mention that Stone Ridge is located in the richest county in the country. That's the same thing my mother-in-law said."

"By the way, Ryan, your wife, Sarah, and her mother were here about three weeks ago browsing around."

"Oh really? No, she didn't tell me."

"The word had gotten around that your mother-in-law only had a short time to live."

Ryan gives Don an intense look as Don continues talking.

"I think they said she had a, let's see now was it a hmm—"

Ryan quickly interrupts. "It was a brain tumor, Don. I'm sure that Doris next door made it public notice."

Don looks at Ryan sheepishly as Ryan continues, "Doris is always running her big mouth." He looks sarcastically at Don. "You know what I mean, don't you, Don?"

Don looks tentative. "Yeah, sure, Ryan. So what happened to it? The tumor, I mean. I heard it just disappeared. Is that true?"

"Yes, Don, it's true. It just disappeared."

"When I saw her a few weeks ago with your wife, she didn't look like she'd been sick a day in her life."

"It was a miracle from God. You do believe in miracles, don't you, Don? You being a church-going man."

Don looks bewildered. "Sure, sure, Ryan, a miracle."

"Since we got that straight, let's get down to business. Here's a list of the things I want to sell. Can you come by this Saturday and look at what I have?"

"Sure, Ryan. I'll be glad to."

"I don't have time for garage sales or local auction vendors, and you're familiar with the furniture items and accessories I have. I know you'll offer me a fair price. Most of my stuff is valuable merchandise; you said so yourself."

"Sounds good to me, Ryan, and thanks for the opportunity. You do have nice merchandise."

"Good. Let's say Saturday morning around ten o'clock?"

"That works perfectly for me."

"I'll have most of the items in the garage before you arrive."

"Okay, Ryan, I'll see you then."

The two men shake hands, and Ryan exits the front door as Don's assistant, Cheryl, walks up to him.

"Cheryl, you remember the guy whose mother-in-law was supposed to have a massive brain tumor?"

"Oh yeah, you said no one knew what happened to it. It just disappeared."

"Well, the guy I was just talking to, it was his mother-in-law."

"Oh yes, the Hennings."

"If you ask me, I think it was just a bunch of horse shit to get attention."

"You don't believe him? It could have truly been a miracle."

"Miracle, they got you bamboozled too."

Cheryl is looking confused. "What do you mean, Don?"

"I had an aunt six years ago diagnosed with a brain tumor, and you know where she is now?"

Cheryl looks at Don but is no longer confused as he looks back at her with a quizzical expression on his face.

"Don't answer that. I can tell by the look on your face that you already know what I'm about to say."

Cheryl nods her head in agreement.

"That's right"—he pauses—"she's six feet under."

Sarah sits on the couch, reading a book when Ryan walks in.

"Well, honey, was your day off a productive one?"

"Yes, it was. I met with our banker, Tom Williams, and went to Mike's garage and got the car inspected. I also stopped by Don's shop to have him come over and take a look at the things we plan to sell."

"My mother and I went to his shop about three weeks ago."

"Yes, he told me."

"How's he doing? He had a slight cold when I saw him."

"He seemed to be okay. You know, Don, the good, the bad, and the ugliest."

"Now, Ryan, you know it's not nice to talk about people. You sound like Doris next door."

"Now, now, honey. If I told you a skunk was black with white stripes and stunk like hell, would I be talking about the animal or describing it?" Ryan smiles. "You get my point?"

Sarah looks at Ryan with a big smile. "Yes, dear, I certainly do."

Ryan is driving to work, and his phone rings. He activates his car's Bluetooth and answers the call.

"Hello."

"Hello, Mr. Henning, this is Carlton."

"Hey, Carlton, what's going on?"

"I think I hear the windshield wipers on. Are you driving?"

"Yes, I'm on my way to the office."

"Continue to stay focused on the road, because I have some good news for you."

"Hang on, Carlton. Maybe I should pull over because it's hard to hear with the wipers on and the rain pouring down." Ryan pulls over to the curb and gives a big sigh of relief. "Okay, Carlton, hit me with it."

"Mr. Henning, you have two offers on your house, and both are offering about thirty-five thousand dollars more than we expected."

"Carlton, you're a genius! The last six weeks have been unbelievable. My mother-in-law's miraculous recovery, a new job position, and now this."

"I must admit, Mr. Henning, you must be living right. Your house has only been on the market for three weeks. We can have this whole deal signed, sealed, and delivered before you leave in July."

"Wow, would that be a blessing!"

"I'll get things set up, and we should be able to meet early next week to go over things."

"Okay, Carlton, I'll wait to hear from you."

The two men hang up.

CHAPTER 7

The Discovery

Ryan is arranging things in his garage when he hears a knock on his garage door. When he opens it, Don is standing outside with a big smile.

"Good morning, neighbor."

"Good morning, Don. I had the garage door shut because I didn't want the neighbors to think I was having a garage sale."

"I understand. Good move."

Ryan leaves the garage door open as Don begins looking over the merchandise.

"Wow, this love seat is beautiful."

Don comes across an object wrapped up in newspaper, lying diagonally on a chair, and gently removes the paper.

"What do we have here, some kind of a lamp?"

Ryan looks in amazement. "What is this lamp doing here! Excuse me, Don, I'll be right back. In the meantime, you can look over the other items."

"Sure thing, Ryan."

Ryan hurries into the house and walks up to Sarah, washing the breakfast dishes.

"Sarah, where's Luke?"

"He should be in his room. I just sent him upstairs to put his clothes away. Is there a problem?"

"I'll let you know after I speak with Luke."

Ryan quickly hurries upstairs. Luke is sitting on the side of his bed and begins crying when he hears his father's footsteps. Ryan opens the door and walks over to Luke.

"Luke, what's going on with the lamp? Is that why you're crying?"

Luke answers his dad while still sobbing. "I knew you were going to be upset with me when you found out that I didn't want the lamp anymore, Dad."

"But I thought you liked the lamp, Son, because it was your grandfather's. Why did you change your mind?"

Luke is still sobbing. "I didn't want to Dad, but I'm afraid of it."

"Afraid of the lamp, but why, Son? And stop crying so I can clearly understand what you're saying."

"You remember the morning—the morning that me, you, and Mom were having breakfast? It was the morning Grandma got better."

"Yes, go on."

"You told me that I had gotten up in the middle of the night and turned the lamp back on, but I didn't, Dad."

"I could have been mistaken, Son. It could have had an electrical shortage in it. But that's no reason to be afraid of the lamp, Son."

Luke thinks back on the events that night and visualizes the things that he saw and heard take place.

"I heard voices coming from Grandma's room, too, just like you did, and it woke me up. A few minutes later, after the voices stopped, the bottom of the lamp started glowing, and it came back on." He starts sobbing more heavily. "Then I became afraid."

Ryan sits on the bed next to Luke and cradles him in his left arm.

"Okay, champ, It's okay. Why didn't you tell me this before?"

"I was afraid that you and Mom wouldn't believe me."

"I believe you, Son. Now put your clothes away, and we'll talk more about this later."

"You're not upset with me, are you, Dad? You said yourself that Grandpa never used the lamp."

"No, Son, of course not."

Ryan exits Luke's room and enters the garage through the side door, where he finds Sarah and Don talking.

"Did you find out from Luke why he didn't want the lamp anymore, dear?"

Ryan hesitates. "He just said he wanted a new lamp for his new room in Virginia."

"What about the fact that it was his grandfather's lamp?"

"He said that my father never used the lamp, so he's okay with letting it go."

"Okay, guys, I'll let you get on with your conversation," Sarah says.

She exits the garage, and Don carefully examines the lamp.

"Ryan, about this incredible-looking lamp. You said it belonged to your father?"

"Yes, he talked about it a couple of times, but I never saw him use it."

"Did he tell you where he got it from and why he didn't use it?"

"I remember when he first got it, and I have my suspicions of why he never used it."

"Sounds a little mysterious to me."

"You could say that."

"Ryan, tell me what you know about this lamp. All of it, please, I've got time."

"It was given to my dad as a birthday gift from a coworker named Ruben Polanski. They worked together at the Ford Motor plant in Dearborn. I remember when my dad brought it home. I was only thirteen at the time. My father tinkered around making things, like tables and chairs. It was kind of a hobby for him. Mr. Polanski knew that my father would appreciate the lamp because of its superb craftsmanship, but my dad found out that Mr. Polanski was given the lamp by his son, Joey. He became infuriated with Mr. Polanski, knowing that his son was on drugs. My dad insisted that it was probably stolen. Ben Williams worked with my father and Mr. Polanski, and Ben's wife, Eileen, was a social worker who volunteered her services at the homeless shelter. Joey frequently slept there, and she kept an eye out on him. She reported back to Ben about Joey, and Ben informed Mr. Polanski about his son's whereabouts. Joey said that a kid who stayed at the homeless shelter for a few days brought the lamp to the homeless shelter."

"Interesting, go on."

"Joey said the kid made the lamp himself and gave it to the old lady, who managed the shelter, as a gift for allowing him to stay there. She later took the lamp to the back of the building and discarded it into the dumpster. That old—"

Don quickly answers, "Bitch! Go ahead, Ryan, continue."

"Joey saw what she'd done with the lamp and fished it out of the dumpster. Joey took it to his father and told him what had happened and gave it to his father. Mr. Polanski never accepted anything from his son because he thought that it might be stolen merchandise, but the lamp was so extraordinary that he took it anyway. Mr. Polanski later spoke with Eileen, and she confirmed that Joey was telling the truth about how he obtained the lamp. That's when Mr. Polanski decided to give it to my father as a birthday gift. My father later apologized to Mr. Polanski for his outburst after he found out the truth and accepted the lamp. But there were mysterious rumors going around about the lamp and the origin of the boy."

"What do you mean, Ryan?"

"People in the shelter believed that the lamp was magical and that the boy was a genie. My father had gotten wind of this and wanted to get rid of the lamp, but instead of discarding it, he kept it stored away in the attic. This lamp had been stored up in the attic for twenty-three years until I discovered it a couple of weeks ago when I was disposing of my father's belongings."

"You obviously didn't believe those rumors, or you'd never have given it to your son to use."

"My grandparents were from Derbyshire, England, and practicing black magic and sorcery during that period was prohibited. My grandfather told my father that there lived a so-called witch in his town, who mysteriously disappeared. He believed that some of the town's people killed her, making them murderers, and because of the mystery surrounding the lamp, my father thought there might have been an evil spell put on it. That's nonsense. The lamp is just a masterful piece of work and nothing more."

"You have a point, Ryan. The lamp is magnificently made and would enhance the surrounding of any indoor setting. Not to mention the magnificent, engraved angel on the front."

"That's right, Don, and that's why I gave it to my son."

"An intriguing story. That explains why there's no manufacturer's label on it. Whatever happened to the kid? He was incredibly talented to make a lamp this exquisite. You have to wonder how he ended up in a homeless shelter."

"Your guess is as good as mine, Don. According to Joey, the boy disappeared and was never seen or heard from again."

"Hmm, is that so? Then tell me, Ryan, why does your son really want to get rid of the lamp?"

Ryan stares at Don and hesitates before answering.

"Well, Don, that's a discussion for another day."

Ryan goes into the house, brings out a few more things to add to his merchandise collection, and looks over at Don.

"Now it's time to get down to business, so what is your offer for this fine merchandise? Don't forget to include the antique bedroom set in the guest bedroom you always wanted, and the other things Sarah showed you that we're going to let go. As you know, Don, most of this stuff has a great deal of value, and you wouldn't have any trouble selling it."

"Don't be so quick to count my chickens before they hatch, my boy. As you know, Ryan, nothing is quite that easy, and you still haven't told me what price you're looking to get."

"I did a little checking around, and the bedroom set is from the Villa Valencia line, and that Italian chair is a Lucca love seat. Together they are worth around fifteen thousand dollars. I figure you can sell what I have and make a substantial profit. I'm asking thirty thousand dollars for everything, including the antique bedroom set, so with that said, how much will you offer me?"

Don looks at Ryan with a big devilish grin.

"Since we've been neighbors a long time, I'll offer you twenty-five thousand dollars, and I'll have everything out of here by Monday morning."

"I'll take twenty-seven thousand dollars, and I want everything out of here no later than tomorrow."

Don gives Ryan a stern, serious look.

"Ryan, my boy, you drive a hard bargain. I guess that's what makes you such a good attorney. You've got a deal. I'll have my crew come over here later this afternoon and start moving this stuff out. I'll have the cashier's check ready for you first thing Monday morning."

Ryan and Don shake hands, and Don walks down the driveway, headed across the street to his house, whistling as he leaves.

CHAPTER 8

The Discovery

Ryan grabs the last of the family's luggage and shuts the door, and joins the rest of the family. They're standing on the walkway in front of the house. A group of neighbors walks up to say goodbye to the Henning family, with hugs and handshakes extended from everyone. The group includes Don Mason, Sylvia Mason, Doris Fleming, Oliver Rollins, and Tommy Rollins— Oliver's eight-year-old son. Don is the first to greet the family.

"Well, Ryan, ole boy, hate to see you go. You've been a good friend and neighbor."

Sylvia comments, "That's for sure. Don and I will miss you two. Sarah, you keep in touch with me."

Doris hugs Sarah. "I'll keep you informed about what's going on just in case you get homesick."

Ryan smiles. "I'm sure you will, Doris."

The group chuckles, and Oliver replies, "I've got to find me a new golfing buddy, Ryan."

"That won't be hard to do, Oliver. There're plenty of avid golfers around here."

Thelma addresses the group. "I don't know many of you that well, but I want to thank you for keeping me in your prayers."

Don and Sylvia look over at one another as the airport limo pulls up. Tommy is standing next to his father, Oliver, and addresses Luke.

"Hey, Luke, maybe we can stay in touch on Facebook."

"Maybe so. What do you think, Mom?"

"I don't know, Son; we'll have to see about that."

Everyone says goodbye as the Hennings get into the airport limo. As the limo drives away, Luke looks out the back window and waves toward the house.

"Goodbye, old house. You take care of yourself and be nice to the new people who will be moving in."

Don and Cheryl are surveying the inventory at Don's Treasure Chest when Don motions to Cheryl to come over to where he's standing and has the lamp that he bought from Ryan in his hand.

"Cheryl, my dear, have you ever seen a lamp this elegant before? It's made from a wood called Bocote, a wood native to Mexico, Central America, and the West Indies. Just look at the beautiful wood grain pattern, absolutely stunning."

"No, Don, I can't say I have. Wow, there are no nicks or discoloration anywhere, and the edges are perfectly beveled, and the engraved image of the angel on the front is breathtaking."

"That's why I hired you, Cheryl. You have an eye for detail and beauty. I spent the last two days putting QR code labels on the items I bought from Ryan. Get with Robert and Larry this evening and have them put those items on the showroom floor. I want to be ready for the Grosse Pointe Festival that starts tomorrow."

Cheryl nods her head, and the two walk off in different directions.

It's just after ten in the morning, and Don is standing outside his shop with his door open. People are leisurely walking back and forth along the sidewalk, browsing through the various shops. An attractive young woman in her early twenties, with light brown hair, walks into Don's shop. He follows her as she inspects his inventory.

"Hello, young lady, just browsing?"

"That depends on what you have that interests me."

Don smiles cheerfully. "Well, let's see if I can perk up your interest. Don Mason, the proprietor of this establishment, and whom may I have the pleasure of addressing?"

"Melanie Jenkins of Jenkins Interior and Designs."

"Interior designer, how nice. Are you from this area?"

"No, I'm just passing through. I live in Ashburn, Virginia."

"Really, a neighbor of mine just moved to Stone Ridge, Virginia. So what brings you to Grosse Pointe, Ms. Jenkins?"

"I'm on my way to Fishers, Indiana, and I heard about the weekend festival here. My mother owns The Gold Diamond Health Care Facility, which has recently opened in Fishers. She's contracted my company for the interior decorating and hired her brother, my uncle Jason, as the facility administrator. I'm looking for a lamp for my uncle's office and to maybe pick up a few unique items for myself. I had no idea how splendid and magnificent the city of Grosse Pointe is, Mr. Mason."

"That's what the rich do, Ms. Jenkins, they keep the money in the family, and that's how they remain rich. And thank you for noticing how splendid our city is, Ms. Jenkins. You not only have an eye for discerning inner beauty but also external beauty as well."

"You have a fine collection, Mr. Mason. How did you acquire a discerning eye for such elegance?"

"My mother was an art collector and taught me how to be a collector of fine things. I'm a software engineer by profession, and this is kind of a hobby for me."

"I find that fascinating, Mr. Mason. Only a few men know the value of what items are truly worth or even care to know; they just like what they see and buy it. That is, of course, if they can afford it."

Melanie walks over to a lamp sitting on a glass table and picks it up to examine it closer.

"What an unusual-looking lamp. It isn't an antique, but the quality is incredible. I particularly like the engraved image of an angel on the front side. I don't see a manufacturer's label, Mr. Mason, and what is this label on the base of the lamp?"

"Let me hold the lamp. Ms. Jenkins."

Don turns the lamp upside down, with the base of the lamp facing Melanie.

"Kindly take out your cell phone and take a picture of the label. That's called a QR code label, Ms. Jenkins."

Melanie takes a picture of the QR code label, and an image of the label is displayed. Don instructs her to touch the image, and when she does, a picture of the lamp appears with a description of it, which she reads aloud.

"A gift from an angel. This lamp was made by a young boy who stayed in a homeless shelter in Detroit, Michigan, in the early nineteen nineties. Rumors circulated that the young boy was an angel, and he gave this lamp to the shelter for helping him. He was never seen again, and his whereabouts are unknown to this day."

"A touching story, don't you agree, Ms. Jenkins?"

"It makes for a good conversation piece at best, Mr. Mason; I'll say that much. The craftsmanship of the lamp is unlike anything I've ever seen before, and it is made of top-quality wood. I believe the wood composition is Bocote. Is that correct, Mr. Mason?"

"You're correct. You know your merchandise, Ms. Jenkins. Bocote is the best grade of wood on the planet."

"It's my job to know what I'm selling my clients, Mr. Mason. Does the lamp work?"

Don bends over and turns the switch, and the light comes on.

"How much are you asking for the lamp?"

"I haven't set a price, Ms. Jenkins. I figured I'd negotiate a price with whoever was interested in buying it."

Melanie takes out a small notebook, writes on it, and hands it to Don. He looks at what she's written and burst out with a loud reply.

"Twenty-five hundred dollars! Are you serious? Maybe you know something about the lamp that I don't know, Ms. Jenkins?"

"Mr. Mason, the lamp is in immaculate condition and uniquely made of quality wood. I've never seen a lamp this exquisite before, and I've purchased fifty or more. With that said, it has no manufacturer's label on it, nor does it reference who made it. In that case, it could be extremely valuable or worth nothing at all, depending on who's buying it."

"Then how did you decide on this price, Ms. Jenkins?"

"I offered you more than a fair price for the lamp because if my uncle doesn't like it, which he will, I can put it into my inventory to be used to decorate a client's home at a later date. I certainly can't place a lamp into a home that was purchased from a resale shop costing fifty dollars. I can, however, justify doing so with it costing twenty-five hundred dollars. My clients are wealthy, and they trust me, Mr. Mason. They rely on my expertise when it comes to decorating their homes."

"Not only are you attractive, Ms. Jenkins, but exceptionally wise as well."

"That's how I keep my clients happy and my bank account full. Here's my credit card along with my business card. I've got to be leaving so I can make it to Fishers by four this afternoon."

"I'll have Cheryl take care of you, Ms. Jenkins, and you'll be on your way in no time. Thank you for your business. By the way, that must be some uncle of yours. What did you say his name was, Ms. Jenkins?"

"Jason Perkins, Mr. Mason."

"I'm going to remember that name for future reference, Ms. Jenkins."

"Please do, Mr. Mason, and maybe I'll drop by again one day."

"I'll look forward to seeing you again, Ms. Jenkins, and have a safe trip."

"Thank you, Mr. Mason."

Cheryl gives her the lamp, secured in a rectangular cardboard box, along with a receipt and her credit card. Melanie exits the shop as Don's eyes follow her until she disappears out of sight.

CHAPTER 9

The Discovery

Melanie enters The Gold Diamond Health Care Facility and greets Nancy, the nursing administrator. Nancy walks over to Melanie, carrying the lamp in one hand and a decorative glass candle container in the other hand. Nancy's in her late thirties, medium built with dark brown hair.

"Good morning, Nancy, how are things going?"

"I can't complain. Things are okay. What's this you have?"

"I heard about a festival in Grosse Pointe, Michigan, on my way here. I visited this elegant little resale shop and found this lamp. Ever been to Grosse Pointe, Michigan, Nancy? It's such a beautiful place."

"No, Melanie, I haven't, but what an adorable-looking lamp, so well made, and the lampshade complements the beauty of the lamp. I've never seen such a remarkable-looking lamp before. Who made it?"

"I don't think anyone really knows. Something about a boy, who was an angel living in Detroit, back in the nineteen nineties. There's always a story behind the unique items you'll find in one of those shops, mainly to increase the value of their merchandise." She smiles at Nancy. "I truly understand. Being an interior decorator, I've created some stories of my own. Is my uncle in his office?"

"Yes, he is, Melanie. I just left his office."

"Well, Nancy, you take care."

"You, too, Melanie."

Melanie walks toward the hallway leading to Jason's office as Nancy walks over to the vending machines.

Jason Perkins, a forty-five-year-old, tall, medium-built man, is The Gold Diamond Health Care Facility administrator. He's clean-shaven with medium-length dark brown hair, tapered around the sides and back, wearing a dark brown tailored wool suit with a cream-colored shirt, light beige tie, and brown dress shoes. He's sitting at his desk when he hears a knock on his office door.

"Uncle Jason, it's Melanie."

"Come in, come in, my dear."

Melanie walks in and places the lamp and candle on Jason's desk, to the left of a family picture of him, his wife Margaret, and his seven-year-old daughter, Celeste. She plugs the lamp into the electrical socket and turns the switch, and lights the candle.

"Well, Uncle Jason, what do you think? A cinnamon-scented candle, which is your favorite, and a beautiful-looking lamp to compliment your mahogany desk."

Jason picks up the lamp to inspect it closer and turns it off.

"Yes, Melanie, your uncle does love the smell of cinnamon, and the lamp is especially nice."

"I thought you'd like it."

"What an intriguing-looking angel on the front."

Melanie smiles at seeing the approval on Jason's face.

"Let me guess, you picked it up from an exclusive little shop that only you could find."

"You're correct. Don's Treasure Chest in Grosse Pointe, Michigan. A gorgeous little city."

"I must also compliment you on the decor you chose for the facility. I must admit that no one can say that you got the interior decorating contract because your mother is the owner of the facility, but because you're simply the best."

"How nice of you to say that, Uncle Jason, and I met the deadline with a couple of weeks to spare."

"Perfection and promptness are two of your finest attributes, my dear, but your uncle has work to do. I must prepare for this afternoon's meeting."

"Yes, Mother was telling me about the meeting when I picked her up from the airport this morning. She said the entire corporation will be there. Well, Uncle Jason, I'll leave you to prepare for your meeting, and I'll speak with you later."

"Goodbye, my dear."

Melanie walks out of the office, closing the door behind her.

Jason puts both hands behind his head and leans back in his chair, breathing in the sweet cinnamon aroma emitted from the candle while staring at the angel on the lamp. He quickly sits up when his office phone beeps twice and answers it.

"Hi, Jennifer, what's up?"

"Mrs. Perkins is on line one."

"Fine, send her through."

Jennifer transfers the call to Jason, and he greets his wife, Margaret. She's an attractive, tall, thin woman in her early forties, with blue eyes and blonde hair.

"Hello, sweetheart, how's my favorite wife doing this morning?"

Margaret smiles. "Your favorite and only wife, dear. I'm just calling to see how your morning is going. You left out early this morning, and Celeste and I missed you during breakfast."

"My morning went fine, sweetheart. Melanie is back in town and just left my office. She dropped off a beautiful desk lamp and candle arrangement. I had to leave this morning because of the meeting I had to prepare for this afternoon. I thought I mentioned it to you before we went to bed last night?"

"No, Jason, I don't remember you telling me. What, another staff meeting?"

"No, no, dear, much more than that. This is a high-profile meeting, and all the corporate officers have flown in from Virginia. The board of directors will be in attendance, along with my sister Gloria and her Magnum Five Investment Group."

"Wow, I see what you mean." Margaret smiles. "You're sure that the Air Force One isn't flying in the president and his staff? That seems to be the only members that will be missing."

"Brilliant analogy, my dear, and not too far from the truth. Let me say a quick word to Celeste, and then I must get back to work."

Celeste is Jason's seven-year-old daughter. She has curly, light blonde hair and blue eyes.

"Hello, Daddy."

"Hello, pumpkin, and how is Daddy's little princes doing this morning?"

"I'm okay, Daddy. Mom and I are going to pick up some things today for my birthday party next weekend."

"Excellent, sweetheart. I know your party will be especially nice, and I'm looking forward to it. Well, dear, Daddy must get back to work. I'll see you and your mother this evening. I love you, pumpkin."

"Love you too, Daddy. Goodbye."

"Goodbye, pumpkin."

They hang up, and Jason sits back in his chair with his hands behind his back and stares at the angel on the lamp.

———————————

A group of five walks into Mandy's five-star restaurant as the maître d', in his mid-fifties, walks up and addresses Anthony Golden. Anthony is in his mid-forties and is the CEO of the Jennimen Corporation, the parent company of The Gold Diamond Health Care Facility. Accompanying him is Clifford Thomas, the litigation officer, and Michael Spears, the operations officer, both in their mid-fifties. The other two in the group are Roger Clemons, the chief financial officer, and Mark Simmons, vice president of marketing, both in their late thirties.

"Good afternoon, sir, a party of five?"

"We're here for the Jennimen Corporation meeting."

"Please follow me, sir." He turns toward one of the waiters. "Ronald, watch the floor while I escort these gentlemen to The Blue Diamond Executive Conference Room."

He leads the group to the rear of the restaurant to a set of elevators. They enter the elevator and arrive at the second level. The maître d' walks them down the corridor, stops in front of a double door entranceway, and escorts them into the executive conference room. Gloria Jenkins, in her late forties, with a figure of a twenty-five-year-old model, is the majority stockholder of The Jennimen Corporation. She's talking with Nancy and Jason and eating from the various hors d'oeuvre trays prepared by the kitchen staff. Gloria addresses the group's arrival with a big smile.

"Well, here comes the rest of our merry men. How's it going, everyone?"

The group, in unison, acknowledges Gloria with a warm greeting as Michael replies, "Splendid, splendid, Gloria, and how have things been with you?"

"Oh, I can't complain. Things are going pretty well." She directs her attention to Anthony. "And how are things going with you, Anthony?"

"I'm doing fine, Gloria."

Everyone prepares a plate and takes a seat at the table where table tents of their names are displayed.

CHAPTER 10

The Discovery

Chairwoman, Barbara Alexander, an attractive, middle-aged woman with long black hair, asks everyone to be seated and opens the meeting.

"Good afternoon, everyone. The board is pleased to announce that this is the first time that all our board members, corporate officers, and investors are in attendance together. We're here today to discuss the progress of our first Gold Diamond Health Care Facility in Fishers, which is a subsidiary company of The Jennimen Corporation. I want to start by introducing our board members and our investment group, after which I'll have Mr. Anthony Golden introduce himself and his corporate staff members. I'm Barbara Alexander, the chairwoman of the board. To my immediate right is Larry Henderson, our vice-chairman. To my immediate left is Beverly Jordan, our secretary. And to her left is Margie Welsh, our treasurer. We have The Magnum Five Investment Group, and from left to right are Ms. Gloria Jenkins, Ms. Maryland Rowlands, Mr. Michael Spencer, Ms. Joyce Cummings, and Mr. Jonathan Pep. Mr. Golden, you may introduce your staff members at this time."

"Thank you, Chairwoman Alexander. I'm Anthony Golden, chief executive officer of the Jennimen Corporation, and to my right and down the line is Michael Spears, chief operations officer; Roger Clemons, chief financial officer; and Clifford Thomas, chief litigation officer. To my left is Mark Simmons, vice president of marketing, Jason Perkins, facility administrator of The Gold Diamond Health Care Facility, and his nursing administrator, Nancy Sheldon."

Chairwoman Alexander replies, "Thank you, Mr. Golden. We had our first open house tour last weekend, and it was a big success. I understand that there were over six hundred people in attendance. Is that correct, Mr. Perkins?"

"Yes, Chairwoman Alexander, that is correct."

Chairwoman Alexander replies, "We'll start with you, Mr. Golden. Please give us an update on how things are going after our first two weeks of operation."

"Certainly, Chairwoman Alexander. As everyone knows, our goal is to provide platinum service to our residents. They're paying premium prices and expect premium service. Mr. Spears and I have ensured the comfort as well as the safety of our residents at the facility. We accomplished this by employing a knowledgeable and competent staff, starting from upper management to our nursing staff and down to our kitchen and housekeeping staff members. I'll let Mr. Spears elaborate more about our operations."

"Good afternoon, everyone. I must say at this point that if I were to judge our overall performance over these first two weeks, with ten being the highest mark, I'd give us an eleven."

Everyone chuckles, followed by an enthusiastic applause. Michael continues, "This is largely due to the excellent guidance of our facility administrator, Mr. Jason Perkins, and his staff. I've been traveling to different parts of the country, looking for new locations to build other facilities for the past two weeks. Jason and I have been in daily contact, discussing pertinent business matters concerning the operation of The Gold Diamond Health Care Facility. Jason, why don't you fill us in on some of the other details?"

"Certainly, Michael. The Gold Diamond Health Care Facility accommodates seventy-five residents. We have six levels, not including the basement. Level one houses our administrative offices, which include our physical and occupational therapy centers, conference room, indoor swimming pool, and cafeteria. Levels two to six comprise our seventy-five luxury residential suites, in which there are fifteen suites on each level, and our current residents are living in the second-level suites. It will be two to three weeks before we bring more residents into the facility. We want to use our current residents as our test group, to correct and modify our current procedures and policies if needed."

Chairwoman Alexander nods her head. "Thank you, Mr. Perkins. It sounds like a well-planned program. Would anyone else like to speak?"

Jonathan Pep is in his mid-thirties and the youngest member of The Magnum Five Investment Group. He motions to Chairwoman Alexander.

"Mr. Pep, you have the floor."

"Mr. Spears, you said that you've been traveling the country to find new facility locations. How's that going?"

"It's going quite well, Mr. Pep. I'm currently looking at two locations on the West Coast and three more in the eastern half of the country. We want to have at least two more facility locations secured by the end of the year."

Chairwoman Alexander looks around the room. "Anyone else?"

Anthony raises his hand.

"Mr. Golden, you have the floor."

"I'd like to say that we're pleased to have acquired Mr. Clifford Thomas, our litigation officer. Attorney Thomas has over twenty-five years of experience at the Malone Medical Center as their litigation officer. He has an impeccable track record, and we're glad to have him on board with us."

There's enthusiastic applause from everyone as Clifford motions to Chairwoman Alexander.

"Mr. Thomas."

"I'd like to thank Anthony and the entire organization for the warm welcome and support they've given me. As you're all aware, our residents are extremely wealthy. They pay forty-five thousand dollars a month to live in our private health care facility, and like most wealthy people, they're demanding, self-centered, and most of the time, hard to please. My job is to circumvent any legal confrontation with our residents as much as possible. They'll never sue us to fatten their pockets because they're already wealthy, but they will, however, sue us over prin-

ciples. So if we continue to cater to their needs by providing professional, courteous, and platinum service, we will have them all eating out
of the palm of our hands."

The group applauds, and Chairwoman Alexander asks for any more
comments before adjourning the meeting. She closes out the session by
wishing everyone well and praising them for their excellent work. As the
group disperses, Jason walks over to his sister Gloria.

"Well, my dear sister, you didn't have much to say."

"That's because everything seems to be quite in order, and you're doing a superb job. Keep it up."

"Thank you, Gloria. Will you be staying long enough to have dinner
with the family this evening?"

"Oh, I apologize, Jason. Melanie and I have a flight back to Virginia
at seven o'clock this evening." Gloria walks up to Jason and hugs him.
"Give this card to Celeste and tell her that her Aunt Gloria will call her
on her birthday next week."

"I'll make sure she gets it. Did Melanie tell you about the beautiful
desk lamp she gave to me?"

"Yes, she did, Jason. She showed it to me when she picked me up
from the airport this morning. It's a beautiful lamp. I wonder what the
designer had in mind when he made it? It's such an intriguing-looking
lamp. It takes my daughter, Melanie, to find a lamp that unusual."

"I agree, Gloria."

"Come on, Jason. The three of us can walk down together."

Gloria, Jason, and Nancy exit the room together, following behind
the other group members.

Jason then addresses Nancy. "That was an excellent report you gave,
Nancy. Continue to keep up the good work with our nursing staff."

"I will, Jason; you can count on that."

―――――――――――

Jason is sitting at his desk when his cell phone rings.

"Oh, hello, dear. I know it's quite late. I'll be home, say, in about forty-five minutes. Love you."

Jason puts his cell phone in his jacket pocket. He leans over his desk, blows out the candle, and turns on his desk lamp. Jason gets up from his desk, walks over to the light switch by the office door entrance, and turns the overhead lights out before leaving the office. He drives out of the parking lot and passes by his office window, and sees the light from his lamp illuminating through the light drape-covered window. As he turns right, heading down Meridian Avenue, the light in his office goes out.

———

Head nurse Beverly Sims, in her early thirties, and her assistant, Marie Santiago, in her late twenties, are working the night shift. They're both wearing black loose-fitting pants, black leather low-heeled shoes, and white blouses displaying name tags, which is the company's dress code. They're sitting at their desks in the nursing office, Suite 200, on the second level of The Gold Diamond Health Care Facility. Suites 201–215 are private living accommodations reserved for their residents. Beverly stands up and addresses Marie.

"Marie, I'm going down to the kitchen to get a couple of apples. Do you want anything?"

"Yes, Beverly. Would you bring me a bottle of water?"

"Sure, Marie, I'll be back in about ten minutes."

Beverly exits the office, and Marie continues to sit at her desk. Marie hears voices and walks down the corridor to suite 215 to investigate. She opens the door, walks into Mr. Johnson's suite, and sees a light shining from beneath his bedroom door. Marie slowly opens the bedroom door, but not before the light extinguishes. She finds Mr. Johnson sound asleep, so she walks back to her desk and sits down as Beverly walks in and hands her a bottle of water.

"Thanks, Beverly. I thought I heard voices coming from Mr. Johnson's suite."

"Well, you know, Marie, Mr. Johnson does have a history of talking to himself."

"I also saw a light shining beneath his bedroom door when I went to check on him."

"Are you sure the light you saw wasn't a reflection from his bedside lamp?"

"I don't think so, but I could be mistaken. Besides that, everything appears to be in order."

"Good. We have about four hours before Brenda and Patricia arrive. Let's get started on our paperwork."

CHAPTER 11

The Discovery

Beverly and Marie are standing and talking when the day shift nurses arrive; Brenda Holloway, in her mid-thirties, and Patricia Neal, in her late twenties.

Patricia says, "How did it go, ladies?"

Marie comments, "Not bad, Patricia, just the usual complaints: 'I'm cold,' 'I'm hot,' 'Where's my food?' I could go on and on, but that was earlier this evening. It has been quiet for the last four hours. A little bit too quiet if you ask me."

Beverly replies, "Ladies, Marie is just a workaholic. I found the peace to be a real joy."

"Just listen. No residents complaining, no nothing. I find that a little peculiar, and what about Mr. Johnson in 215, crying out for his pain medication at five-thirty every morning? Not to mention, Ms. Brown in 212, knocking against the wall every fifteen minutes, thinking she's locked out of her house again."

Beverly replies, "Calm down, Marie. Like I said, ladies, Marie is a workaholic. I think she's feeling neglected because no one is calling out for her assistance."

The three of them chuckle as Brenda speaks. "I just hope they keep it up; I certainly won't have a problem with quietness."

"I know that's right, Brenda. Well, girls, we'll see you tomorrow," says Beverly.

Beverly and Marie leave while Brenda and Patricia sit at their desks. During the first three hours of their shift, they both talk about how unusually quiet it has been since their arrival, and they wonder why none of the residents have awakened yet.

Patricia replies, "Brenda, I'm going to check in on the residents before the cleanup crew gets here."

"Okay, Patricia, I'll create a new login sheet while you're gone."

After about five minutes, Patricia hurries back to the nursing office as Brenda bends down in front of the file cabinet, taking out a folder. Patricia is frantically speaking.

"Brenda! Brenda!"

"What's wrong, Patricia?"

"Everyone is still asleep, and that's highly unusual!"

"Calm down, Patricia. I'll go with you to check on them. You'll see that everything is—" Suddenly, they both pause as loud talking is heard from each suite.

Brenda and Patricia hurry to suite 201, closest to the office, and open the door, only to find Diane Jefferson, a woman in her early nineties, gracefully dancing around.

Brenda says, "Oh my God! Ms. Jefferson, what are you doing?"

Brenda and Patricia hear laughing and talking in the corridor and rush out of Ms. Jefferson's suite. They're astonished to find that the residents are exuberantly walking down the aisle toward them. Betty Carmel, in her late eighties, waves graciously at Brenda.

Brenda says, "Ms. Carmel, is that you?"

"Of course it's me. Who did you think it was, and what's wrong with you two, standing up there looking like you've just seen a ghost?"

"Oh my God, this can't be happening! Brenda, you need to call Ms. Sheldon, now!"

Brenda rushes into the office with three nursing assistants, who have just arrived, running behind her. She frantically begins dialing from the phone on her desk, and she hears Nancy's voice. "This is Nancy."

"Ms. Sheldon, this is Brenda on the second floor. Please come up here as quickly as you can!"

"What's going on, Brenda? Is there a problem?"

"Yes! No! I don't know, Ms. Sheldon. Just please get up here as soon as you can!"

————————————

Patricia, Brenda, and the three assistants look in amazement when Nancy dashes through the double doors that lead into the hallway. She joins the other five, all looking in disbelief. Nancy can immediately see that a strange occurrence has taken place because Ms. Carmel is no longer paralyzed and walks around waving at everyone.

Nancy replies, "Patricia and Brenda, I know the two of you can't explain what's going on here, and neither can I, so I'm just going to call Jason, and maybe he can figure out what in the hell is going on here! In the meantime, the five of you take the residents and sit them together in one suite, and I'll be right back!"

Nancy hurries down the corridor to the nursing office and sits down at Brenda's desk. She picks up the phone and dials Jason's cell phone number, and he answers. Jason's in his car driving through downtown Indianapolis.

"Hello."

"Jason, this is Nancy. Are you on your way to the facility?"

"No, Nancy, I'm going to have breakfast with Bruce, an old colleague of mine. He's in Indianapolis on a business trip, and his flight is scheduled to leave out for Florida this evening."

Nancy speaks emphatically. "Jason, you need to get here to the second floor as soon as possible!"

"You're kidding, right?"

Speaking in a loud, piercing voice, Nancy says, "Jason, I have never been more serious in all of my life!"

Jason hangs up the phone and calls Bruce, but now he's exceeding the speed limit.

"Bruce, this is Jason. I've got to get back to the facility. There seems to be a problem that needs my immediate attention. I'll try to catch up with you later this afternoon."

"Sure, Jason. I'll talk with you later."

Jason hangs up the phone and continues speeding through traffic. After a twenty-minute drive, he races into the parking lot, gets out of his car, and rushes toward the facility entrance. Jason hurries through the double doors and passes the elevators to the stairwell, oblivious to the greetings by his employees. He runs up the stairs leading to the second floor, enters the corridor, and hollers out Nancy's name.

"Nancy! Nancy!"

Nancy leans her head out of suite 208 and motions to Jason to come in. Jason walks into the suite and is surprised to see all fifteen residents sitting in a semi-circle of chairs, gracefully smiling. Nancy stares at Jason with a look of perplexity and addresses him. "Jason, have you met our residents?"

Ms. Carmel, paralyzed from the waist down before this miraculous event, speaks out. "Hello there, Mr. Perkins, remember me? I was the first resident you visited a couple of weeks ago."

Ms. Carmel stands up and prances around the room. The other residents begin laughing and applauding, including Mr. Peter Johnson, Ms. Tracy Brown, and Mr. Marty Roth, all in their late eighties, and five men and six women, all in their early nineties. Jason says with an astonished look, "I don't know what to say. How is this possible?"

Ms. Carmel replies, "Something magical happened to us last night, Mr. Perkins, all of us." Looking as though she's hypnotized, she continues speaking, "All we can remember is a bright light encircling our bodies, giving us a warm feeling of peace, joy, and comfort. A feeling of real love. Not the bologna that people sing or write about, but real, genuine love."

Mr. Peter Johnson begins speaking. "There was also a voice that spoke to us, a voice like one we've never heard before."

Jason replies, "That's quite a story, Mr. hmm," trying to remember his name.

"It's Johnson, Peter Johnson, Mr. Perkins."

Jason pretends to clear his throat to get Nancy's attention. "Nancy, come with me. Brenda, you stay here with the other girls until we return."

Jason turns toward the residents and addresses them. "Would you please excuse us for a moment?"

Ms. Carmel replies, "Don't make it too long because I think we're all getting pretty hungry."

The group agrees with Ms. Carmel as Jason and Nancy walk down the corridor to the nursing office. Jason takes a seat at the end of a desk, with only his left foot touching the floor as he speaks. "What in the heck is going on here, Nancy?"

"What are we going to do, Jason? We've taken the vital signs of each resident, and they all seem to be in perfect health."

"Yes, Nancy, it certainly is incredible. We've got to get Dr. Cooper up here and have him thoroughly examine the residents. In the meantime, we've got to prepare ourselves for the family members who will be visiting today. There's going to be a lot of questions asked, and we don't have any answers."

"Jason, when the word gets out, there're be plenty of people from the media floating around here."

"Hmm, you're right. Tell you what, keep everyone contained into one or two suites and make the phones inoperable. Let them order from the menu, and keep them as comfortable and quiet as possible until Dr. Cooper gets here."

"How do you want me to address family members visiting today?"

"Get with Brenda and Patricia and ask them who usually visits on Wednesdays. I want you to personally call those families and inform them that we have a new program in place for the residents and that we will be implementing the program throughout today and tomorrow. Tell them that we will look forward to seeing them on Friday, and they'll be able to evaluate the results of the new program. For now, inform the residents that their family members will be visiting them on Friday to share in the good news about their health and not to try to contact them before then. Tell them we want it to be a surprise. It will give me about forty-eight hours to get with Gloria and the group, so we can come up with a plan."

"How long do we keep the residents contained in one suite?"

"Let's see, it's nine forty-seven now. I want you to call in additional nursing staff and assign one nursing assistant per resident. At that time, they can return to their suites. I don't want them together at any time, and the residents, along with the nursing assistants, must not leave their suites for any reason. We need to keep things stable and calm. Inform the staff that they're not to discuss this with anyone, and I do mean with no one."

"Anything else, Jason?"

"I want two head nurses per shift with an hour overlap. I'll let you work that out. I've got to break the news to my sister, Gloria. Meet me in my office after you have everything in place."

CHAPTER 12

The Discovery

J ason exits the nursing office, takes the elevator down to the first floor, and enters his office. He sits down at his desk, takes out his cell phone from his jacket pocket, and calls Gloria. Gloria is standing in front of the mirror, taking a final look at her appearance. Her phone rings and she walks over to her phone on the bed, recognizes Jason's number, and answers.

"Hey, Jason, make it quick. I'm already running late for my exercise class."

"I'll make it rather quick, my dear. I hope you're sitting down, my dear sister, because you and the crew need to get here, pronto."

Gloria sits on the side of the bed and continues talking. "Jason, what are you talking about?"

"Gloria, you may find this hard to believe, but when the residents woke up this morning, they were all in perfect health."

Gloria is chuckling. "You do mean they were happy to be in the best facility that money could buy?"

Jason leans over and places his elbows on his desk, and speaks emphatically into the phone. "No, Gloria, my dear. I mean, the terminally ill residents are no longer ill. The residents with dementia have minds as sharp as a razor, and Mr. Calvin, our only blind patient, is no longer blind."

Gloria stands straight up from her bed. "What!" She says frantically. "Jason, I'll call you as soon as I know when our flight is due to arrive!"

Jason sits in a white company minivan parked at the American Airlines arrival terminal. Gloria, Anthony, Michael, and Clifford exit the airport terminal and walk over to where Jason's parked. Jason gets out and greets everyone, and puts their baggage into the back of the vehicle. There's a moment of silence before Anthony speaks.

"So, Jason, what's all this talk about the residents miraculously being healed?"

"Well, I can tell you all this much: the lame walk, the blind can see, and the dying have been swept away from the clutches of death. Tuesday night, they were sick and helpless, and Wednesday morning, shazam! They woke up in perfect health. You go figure it out."

Michael comments, "What did Dr. Cooper find out?"

"He concluded that everyone was in perfect condition, and even a resident's acne cleared up. Now how's that for sensationalism?"

Gloria says, "Jason, what do you think happened?"

"Gloria, I'm like everyone else. I haven't any answers. I do, however, have everyone confined to their suites, with a nurse assistant constantly with them. I managed to delay family members from visiting until Friday. I also informed all staff members not to say anything to anyone until we've had time to sort things out."

Anthony comments, "Excellent, Jason."

Everyone sits back, with looks of concern on their faces as Jason drives down the highway to the facility.

———————

They arrive at the facility, and Nancy meets the group when they enter the second-level corridor. They walk into the nursing office as Beverly and Marie arrive after checking with the nursing assistants, and Nancy introduces them to the group.

"Everyone, this is Beverly and Marie, our night shift nurses. Ladies, you know Mr. Perkins, of course."

Nancy motions toward the group.

"This is Ms. Gloria Jenkins, Mr. Anthony Golden, Mr. Michael Spears, and Mr. Clifford Thomas. They're from our corporate office in Ashburn, Virginia."

Beverly and Marie extend a warm greeting to everyone.

Nancy continues, "Beverly is our head nurse on the evening shift, and both of them had just been relieved by our morning shift nurses a couple of hours before everything went crazy around here this morning."

Gloria comments, "Did you ladies notice anything unusual or out of the ordinary before this event occurred?"

Marie addresses Gloria. "Well, Ms. Jenkins, I remember it was unusually quiet, and around two o'clock this morning I heard voices coming from suite 215. When I went to investigate, the talking stopped, but I saw a light shining beneath Mr. Johnson's bedroom door. When I opened it, the light had gone out, and Mr. Johnson was fast asleep. Beverly said I probably saw the light reflecting from his bedside lamp. It may have been, but I know for sure, I heard voices."

Michael gives a big sigh. "Well, ladies and gentlemen, where do we go from here?"

Anthony stretches his arms over his head and comments. "I'm not sure, but it's going to be a long day tomorrow, and we need to get our rest."

Jason replies, "I suggest we all retire to suites on the third level and get an early start in the morning. We can meet in the conference room downstairs, say"—he looks at his watch—"about nine o'clock. That will give us about eight hours of sleep."

"I've had enough excitement for one day. That sounds good to me, Jason. I'll see everyone in the morning," says Gloria.

Jason addresses Nancy, "I want you at the meeting in the morning, Nancy, have Frank in maintenance bring up everyone's luggage."

The group walks down the corridor and exits through the double doors, taking the elevator to the third floor. Each one chooses a suite and bids goodnight to one another.

———————

Members of the group sit at the conference table, eating from the breakfast setup when Nancy and Jason arrive.

Jason says, "Good morning, everyone, and how's the food?"

Clifford replies, "Jason, this is by far the best omelet I have ever tasted."

"That's because we have two world-class chefs on staff, and their entrees can compete with chefs' in restaurants anywhere in the world."

Nancy walks over to the table and prepares herself a plate. Jason grabs a cup and saucer and pours a cup of coffee. They both walk over to the conference table and join the others.

Gloria comments, "Well, has anyone come up with any answers or solutions?"

Everyone shakes their heads, indicating they have no answers.

Nancy replies, "I've checked everyone's medications, and nothing has changed, and no medication is the same for any of them."

Anthony addresses Clifford. "Clifford, will we be faced with any legal allegations because of what has happened?"

"No, we haven't done anything wrong; on the contrary, most will be elated with the news."

"What do you mean most, Clifford?"

"There are some family members who will become the beneficiaries of their estates."

"I'm beginning to get the picture, Clifford," says Anthony.

Clifford continues, "They're waiting until that loved one, or should I say, that unloved one, passes on, and when they find out that they're no longer ill, it will greatly hinder their plans, and they'll blame us. That's because some are only concerned about their relatives' money—" he pauses slightly "—not about their relatives."

Gloria speaks out. "So what do we do?"

Clifford replies, "Gloria, someway, somehow, the residents are no longer ill. Whether it's divine intervention or something else that caused this to take place, I cannot say. I can say this, however, that the transformation of their health is truly miraculous, and we must somehow find a miracle of our own—" he pauses "—if we are to survive."

Jason addresses a group of nineteen family members: two male-and-female couples, five mother-and-daughter couples, and five single women. Their ages range from mid-thirties to mid-fifties.

"Hello, everyone, my name is Jason Perkins, and I'm the facility administrator." He directs his attention toward Nancy. "This is Nancy Sheldon, our nursing administrator. Before we escort you to the second level, I want you to know that what you're about to witness is astonishing and a mystery to us all. In other words, as of this morning, your loved ones are in perfect health."

Nancy comments, "We have medical staff members who are trying to come up with answers, but at this moment, we have none."

The group begins looking at each other, confused by their comments. Margaret Jefferson, Ms. Diane Jefferson's daughter in her late forties, speaks out, "What do you mean, Mr. Perkins, perfect health?"

"Without taking any more questions, Ms. Sheldon and I will escort you to the second level; please follow us."

They walk down the hallway to the elevators: facility employees, pretending to be working, glance at the group. Jason escorts half of them on the elevator to his right, and Nancy accompanies the other half on the one to her left, and they arrive at the second level. They escort them down the hallway and through the double doors, entering the second-level corridor, and Brenda greets the group.

"Is everything in place, Brenda?"

"Yes, Ms. Sheldon."

"Good, have the nursing assistants escort everyone to their family member's suite."

Brenda leads the group down the corridor, and the visitors unite with their relatives. Loud outbursts of joy and sobbing fill the rooms as everyone begins slowly walking out into the hallway. Mr. Marty Roth is vehemently spoken to by his nephew Dan Roth as his wife, Emma, stands watching. Cynthia Carmel, Ms. Betty Carmel's daughter, talks with her mother and is sobbing with joy.

"Oh, Mother, I can't believe it! Oh, Praise God! Praise God!"

Residents and family members walk hand in hand as Jason and Nancy continue watching in disbelief. Melinda Johnson, Mr. Peter Johnson's forty-five-year-old granddaughter, addresses Jason with tears running down her face.

"We don't know what's going on here, Mr. Perkins, but God bless you. It's truly a miracle."

"I appreciate the gratitude, but miracles are not within my power, madam. You have to thank someone higher up than me for that."

Everyone is thanking Jason and Nancy as Dan Roth, and his wife makes their way through the crowd and addresses Jason. "What kind of games are you playing here?"

"Games, what do you mean, sir?"

"You know exactly what I mean. I'm Dan Roth, Marty Roth's nephew, and this is my wife, Emma."

Jason politely nods at his wife.

Dan Roth continues, "Is my uncle tied up in some elaborate medical scheme, using him and the others as guinea pigs for some new experimental drug?"

"I assure you, Mr. Roth, that isn't the case."

"Well, if they are, I'll find out."

He walks away, looking back at Jason. "You'll be hearing from my attorney."

Jason looks over at Nancy. "Nancy, it's apparent that Mr. Marty Roth is one of the unloved ones that Clifford spoke about in the meeting, and it's quite evident that his nephew is his beneficiary."

Jason turns and addresses the group, "May I have your attention, please. In case you're wondering when the residents can be released, our doctors must complete a final examination, and the release documents must be prepared. It may take two to three days. In the meantime, spend as much time as you like with your relatives."

Nancy gives final instructions to Brenda and Patricia. Jason and Nancy exit through the double doors and head to the conference room.

CHAPTER 13

The Discovery

The group is seated at the conference room table when Jason and Nancy arrive. They sit at the table, and Anthony addresses Jason. "How did things go, Jason?"

"Better than we expected, but Mr. Roth's nephew and his wife weren't too happy about it. A beneficiary of his uncle's estate was quite evident. He said we've been using his uncle and the rest of the residents as guinea pigs for a new experimental drug, and we'll be hearing from his attorney."

Everyone begins laughing as Clifford comments, "If that's the best he can do, he's wasting his time. After the word gets out to the public, we'll be flooded with media vultures trying to be the first to get the story. How do you want to handle it, Anthony?"

"I'll handle the media myself. I want Jason and Nancy's involvement to be as little as possible. I have no firsthand knowledge of what took place, so I can limit the comments to a few questions."

Jason comments, "Clifford, I told the families that it would take two to three days before anyone could leave the facility pending the completion of a final medical examination and the preparation of the release documents."

"That's correct. We should have things wrapped up in a couple of days."

Jason continues, "In a week and a half, the second group of residents will arrive. How are we going to handle that?"

Michael replies, "I suggest we continue with our program as scheduled. Clifford has already stated that we haven't done anything illegal, so there's no reason to delay the program. Besides, when the word gets out about this, the next group of residents and their families will insist that we honor our contract agreement with them."

Gloria comments, "One thing we do know for sure: whatever caused this to happen came after the residents had been here for a couple of weeks, and it happened to them all at once."

Clifford nods his head. "How true, Gloria, and it happened so spontaneously that whatever caused it could very well happen again, putting us in an extremely difficult situation."

Anthony comments, "Well, enough of the sci-fi theory. You're beginning to sound like Rod Serling of *The Twilight Zone*, and we're no closer to solving the mystery than we were when we first sat down. I say that we stay on course, as Michael suggested. Does everyone agree?"

Everyone nods in agreement. "Very well. Let's continue with business as usual as much as possible. Gloria, Michael, and I will be heading back to Virginia in a couple of days. Clifford, I need you to stay here with Jason to handle any legal matters that may occur. We'll get things calmed down before we leave and will return the night before the next group is due to arrive. If there aren't any more questions, we need to prepare ourselves for how we will be handling things over the next couple of days. It could be a real madhouse around here."

Anthony looks at everyone, and they all remain silent, so he dismisses the group, and they exit the conference room.

Jason and Clifford are picking up Gloria, Michael, and Anthony from the airport. Clifford remains upfront with Jason as the other three sit in the back of the vehicle.

Everyone remains silent for a moment until Anthony comments, "Well, gentlemen, how are things looking? Are we all set for tomorrow?"

Jason says, "Everything is in place. We have the second floor all prepared for the fifteen new arrivals."

Clifford comments, "We've been receiving pressure from the public as well as city officials to occupy the other four floors, and we've made it quite clear to everyone that until we get a better handle on this situation, we're going to proceed with caution."

Jason replies, "I have suites on the third level prepared for us, and the kitchen staff will be available to provide us with food and beverages. We've scheduled the new residents to arrive between nine o'clock in the morning and noon. We've also added extra security for the next few days, to control the media and meddling public. I'll greet everyone upon their arrival tomorrow. Nancy and her staff will escort them to their suites. There will be two blind residents, four with cancer, five with dementia, and four with brain tumors."

"If this miraculous event continues with this group, we have a real problem on our hands," says Clifford.

Gloria comments, "How bad can it get, Clifford?"

"Gloria, if it happens again, every wealthy person in the country will be lobbying for a suite at the facility. It will undoubtedly put us between a rock and a hard place. Not to mention the fact that only the wealthy can afford to live here."

Gloria gives a big sigh before speaking. "Completely shutting out the poor."

Anthony comments, "Well there's no sense in losing any more sleep over it. At this point, we'll just have to wait and see what happens."

Jason drives off and heads to the facility as everyone sits back quietly in their seats.

They arrive at the facility and proceed to the third floor, where Jason has made sleeping arrangements for the group.

"Michael, you're in suite 304, Anthony 306, and Clifford, you'll remain in suite 310. Gloria, you have the option of coming home with me tonight or taking suite 308."

"Jason, I'm going to stay here with the rest of the group. Tell Margaret and Celeste we'll have lunch together later this week."

"Fine, Gloria. Everyone get some sleep because we'll have a long day tomorrow. I'll have Frank bring up your luggage."

The group retires to their suites, and Jason escorts Gloria to her room. They enter the suite, and Jason sits down on the love seat as Gloria sits on the couch adjacent to where he's seated. Gloria starts sobbing. "Oh, Jason, what are we going to do?"

"It's going to be all right, Gloria."

"Richard told me that there would be tough challenges that I'd face with running the company, and he groomed me the entire year before his death. He wanted me involved in the Jennimen Corporation and said it was the future for Melanie and me. As the cancer got worse, he pushed me harder until he felt I was ready to manage the company. These last two years haven't been easy, Jason, and you've been a tremendous help."

"That's because Richard taught me well, and you're my sister; I'll do anything for you, Gloria. You never told me how Richard came about naming the company the Jennimen Corporation."

"It was Richard's middle name. Richard's father, Randall Edward Jenkins, was extremely close to his mother, Jennifer, Richard's grandmother. Jennifer was an astute businesswoman in marketing, advertising, and finance and taught her son how to excel in the business sector. Richard's father chose to pursue hospital administration as his goal because he saw a lack of quality in professional health care facilities. When his father married and Richard was born, his father gave him the middle name of Jennimen, named after his grandmother, Jennifer. He added the word *men* because he wanted him to grow up to become a great leader of men. My husband followed in his father's footsteps by forming the Jennimen Corporation, dedicating himself to building upscale, quality health care facilities just as his father did."

"Quite interesting. Richard was a brilliant and dedicated individual, Gloria, as well as a dear friend and brother-in-law. He was masterful in building and managing hospitals, and I was fortunate enough to work up under him. Richard gave me my first top-level position, and for that, I'm truly grateful. It was his dream to build a network of upscale health care facilities, and through your efforts and all of us involved, his dream has come true."

"And believe me, Jason, I'm grateful as well, but this current situation that we're dealing with has me extremely nervous."

"Yes, Gloria, it has us all scratching our heads, but everything has a cause and effect, my dear sister, and believe me, we'll get to the bottom of this. Now get some rest. I'll be heading home and will return before the new residents arrive in the morning."

"Thank you, Jason, and I'll see you in the morning."

Jason walks over, gives Gloria a light kiss on her forehead, and exits the suite.

Jason drives up into his driveway, featuring a beautiful three-story home with a horseshoe driveway. Jason enters his home and quietly walks up the steps and into his daughter's bedroom. He leans over the bed as she's sleeping and kisses her on the cheek. He exits the room, walks down the hallway to his bedroom, and finds his wife, Margaret, sitting up against the headboard reading a book.

"How did it go, dear? Did everyone make it in okay?"

Jason sits on the side of the bed and takes off his shoes as he turns toward Margaret with a look of concern.

"Yes, dear, everyone arrived safely, but Gloria is having an anxiety attack from worrying so much. I'm going to have to keep a close eye on her."

CHAPTER 14

The Discovery

J ason and Brenda are standing in the lobby when the first two residents arrive. Both are in wheelchairs accompanied by a family member, and Jason gives them a warm welcome.

"Good morning, I'm Jason Perkins, the facility administrator, and this is Brenda Holloway from our nursing staff. Welcome to The Gold Diamond Health Care Facility."

A woman in her mid-fifties, escorting an older woman in a wheelchair, graciously replies, "My name is Priscilla Atkins, and this is my mother, Jody Fitzsimmons. I think she's assigned to suite 212 on the second floor."

Brenda replies, "Yes, that is correct, Ms. Atkins."

Brenda turns toward the middle-aged man pushing the second wheelchair. "And you are, sir?"

"My name is Gregory Lance, and this is my father, Herbert Lance."

"Oh, yes, Mr. Lance. Your father will be in suite 203. Please follow me, and I'll take you up to the second floor."

Brenda escorts the group down the hallway leading to the elevators as Jason stands there waving them goodbye. Jason motions to James Turner, his security guard, in his mid-thirties, to come over. He's about six feet five inches tall, with a light brown complexion and broad shoulders.

"Remember, James, you make sure that the two television trucks camped across the street remain off our property, and none of the media personnel are allowed inside the facility without my permission."

"Yes, sir, Mr. Perkins."

Jason turns and heads to his office and sees the elevator doors closing with the new arrivals about to be shuttled up to the second floor.

———————

Jason sits at his desk and leans back in his chair when his phone rings. "This is Jason."

"Jason, this is Nancy. We got the residents checked in and placed into their suites. Brenda and I will check in the remaining residents once they arrive. Rosalyn and Ann will be coming on at two, and I'll give them instructions on how we want things handled this afternoon."

"Good. As soon as you get everyone settled in, I want you to go home and get some rest. I want you back here at nine o'clock this evening before Rosalyn and Ann leave at ten. I'll be here as well and will be checking with you and the girls throughout the evening."

"Okay, Jason, but if anything happens beforehand, be sure to call me."

"Nancy, you sound like you expect something to happen."

"Jason, to be perfectly honest with you, I don't know what to expect. I guess we'll just have to wait and see. I'll see you this evening."

"Sounds good."

———————

Jason stands in front of Gloria's suite and lightly knocks on the door. Gloria opens it, and Jason walks into the suite and accompanies Gloria over to the couch. He sits down on the love seat across from her.

"Hello, my dear. I figured we'd walk down to the conference room together."

"Okay, Jason, give me a minute. I just spoke with Celeste. She's such a little darling."

"Yes, she is, and she's quite fond of her Aunt Gloria. She'll grow up to be quite a special young lady."

Gloria smiles. "She should be. She acquired her intelligence from us and her good looks from her mother."

The two give a little chuckle together, exit the suite, and head toward the conference room.

Anthony, Michael, and Clifford sit at the conference table when Jason and Gloria walk in, and Anthony addresses them. "Come on in, you two. Take a seat and brace yourselves, everyone, because we don't know if this miraculous event will happen again, but if it does, pow!"

Gloria begins sobbing. "Oh my God, what are we going to do?"

Anthony quickly says, "Oh, I'm sorry, Gloria. I didn't mean anything by that."

Jason responds, "My sister Gloria is taking this extremely hard, so I'd appreciate it if everyone takes that into consideration."

Everyone nods in agreement as Clifford speaks. "As I've stated earlier, we haven't violated any laws. Just be sure that we don't make any claims to anything that happens, or for that matter, doesn't happen. Our employees aren't to speak to anyone, especially the media. Our strategy, expectations, and anything else concerning this matter are strictly confidential."

Jason replies, "I've alerted the nursing staff to report anything out of the ordinary, such as resident behavior, or any strange noises or voices that they may hear. I'll be floating around the facility throughout the night to monitor activities on the second level with Nancy and her staff. The rest of you can retire to your suites on the third floor, and I'll keep everyone posted if anything happens."

Anthony replies, "We're the center of everyone's attention this evening, The mayor, the media, family and friends, and everyone else in between. So with that said, I'm going to my suite to have a brandy before I retire. Anyone care to join me?"

Everyone agrees except Jason, who heads down the hallway to his office as the others follow Anthony to his suite.

Jason lies across his couch asleep when Nancy knocks on his office door. Jason sits up when he hears the knocking and tells the visitor to come in.

"Oh, it's you, Nancy." He looks at his watch. "What time is it?"

"It's about eight thirty."

Jason gets up and walks over to his desk, and sits down. "Have a seat, Nancy; you're early."

"I slept for about four hours. I figured I'd come in early to see how you were holding up."

"As well as can be expected. Trying to adjust to the new normal, which is anything but normal. Hold on, Nancy."

Jason picks up the phone, dials a three-digit number, and begins speaking. "Hi, Sam, have Lisa bring me a pot of coffee with a couple of cups. Thanks."

He hangs the phone up and continues speaking with Nancy. "Have you been upstairs yet?"

"No, I wanted to check in on you first. I'm going to head up there after I leave here."

There's a knock on the door, and Jason tells Lisa to come in. She's in her mid-twenties, with black hair and a medium build. Lisa walks in carrying a tray with a pot of coffee and two cups on saucers. "Oh, hello, Ms. Sheldon."

"Hello, Lisa, how have things been?"

Jason motions to Lisa to put the tray over on the table next to the couch.

"Oh, fine, Ms. Sheldon. Mr. Perkins, will there be anything else?"

"No, Lisa, that will be all, thank you."

Lisa walks toward the door, bidding Nancy goodbye. Jason walks over to the table and pours a cup of coffee. "Care for a cup of coffee, Nancy?"

"No, Jason, I had two cups right before I got here, and that was one too many. Well, I guess I'll get upstairs and check on things, and I'll touch base with you in a bit."

"Okay, sounds good."

Jason walks over to his chair and sits down. He puts the saucer on his desk and reaches across his desk, and turns on his lamp. He takes a sip of coffee and motions to Nancy.

"Nancy, would you turn the light switch off by the door on your way out?"

"Sure, Jason."

Nancy turns the overhead lights off and exits the room, closing the door behind her. Jason places his coffee cup on the saucer and leans across his desk, admiring the image of the angel on his lamp.

———————

Nancy, Beverly, and Marie are sitting at their desks when Jason walks in.

"Hello, ladies, any new developments?"

Beverly says, "No, Mr. Perkins, everything is quiet at the moment."

Marie comments, "If you ask me, I'd say it's a little too quiet. Kind of like it was the night before—" She pauses.

Jason replies, "Like what, Marie? Like it was the night that the previous residents woke up with no health issues?"

"Mr. Perkins, I'm having hot flashes. May I go grab a bottle of water?"

Jason smiles. "Certainly, Marie. I think we can hold things down until you get back."

They glance over at one another and smile.

"Well, ladies, if there's nothing else to report, I'm going to head back down to the office."

"Okay, Jason, we'll be here," Nancy says.

Jason leaves and heads back down to his office. He sits down at his desk, picks up the family picture, and gently kisses it. Jason leans back in his chair, closes his eyes, and falls asleep.

An hour later, he is awakened and startled by a light that covers his face. He notices that it's coming from the base of the lamp. He continues looking until it stops glowing, and the light goes out. Jason opens his top drawer and pulls out a flashlight. He points the beam of light at the lamp and discovers that the image of the angel is no longer present. Jason stands up and rushes toward the door, using the flashlight to illuminate his pathway.

Nancy, Beverly, and Marie are standing in the middle of the office when Jason comes rushing in.

"Nancy! Beverly! Marie! Go and check on the residents now!"

The three women rush down the corridor in different directions, entering each suite, as Jason follows behind Nancy. They hear voices coming from suite 211, and the four of them converge toward that location. Nancy opens the door to the suite, and they all rush in. The voices stop, but a light illuminates beneath the bedroom door. Beverly quickly opens the door, but not before the light extinguishes.

Marie shouts out, "This is just like before, Mr. Perkins! Just like before!"

More voices continue echoing throughout the corridor, and the group runs out and finds it coming from suite 209. They enter the suite, and the same events occur as in suite 211. More voices are heard in other suites until everything becomes calm and quiet. The group stands in the middle of the hallway, bewildered and speechless.

Nancy says, "Jason, you knew something was going to happen. That's why you came running up here. How did you know? What did you see?"

"It's just a feeling I had, Nancy. Call it a premonition. I don't know how else to explain it."

Beverly comments, "Does this mean that the residents are going to wake up this morning with no health issues?"

Jason replies, "I don't know what this means. I've got to get back to my office. Nancy, you and the girls stay here."

CHAPTER 15

The Discovery

J ason rushes down the hallway through the double doors and takes the stairwell down to his office. When he opens the door, he finds that the lamp is back on and calmly walks over to the lamp and sees that the image of the angel is back. Jason sits down in his chair, reaches into his lower left desk drawer, and takes out a bottle of brandy and a shot glass. He pours him a shot and slowly drinks the brandy down. He picks up the phone and dials a three-digit number, and Beverly answers the phone.

"Beverly, put Nancy on the phone."

"Hey, Jason, what do we do now?"

"I want Beverly and Marie to stay here when Brenda and Patricia arrive at six. I want you to call Gloria and the others at eight and tell them to meet me in the conference room at nine fifteen, sharp."

"Do you think that this miracle is about to happen again?"

"Well, Nancy, what do you think? Strange voices heard and lights shining beneath everyone's bedroom door. It sounds like a recipe for another miracle to happen if you ask me. You girls stay in position and call me when the residents wake up. If it happens like before, they'll wake up at the same time, which I believe is around daybreak. I'll be waiting for your call."

Jason hangs up the phone and looks intently at the lamp. He walks over to his couch, lies down, and closes his eyes.

Frank Sinatra's song *The Way You Look Tonight* echoes throughout the corridor. Nancy and Marie slowly open the door to suite 206, where the music is playing. Ninety-two-year-old Jeffrey Lanier is ballroom dancing with eighty-two-year-old Arlene Collins from suite 205.

"Come on in, kids. Arlene and I could dance to old blue eyes' songs all night long."

Marie collapses to the floor as Brenda and Patricia help her to her feet. Nancy rushes down the corridor to the office to call Jason. Jason, lying on his couch, opens his eyes and sits up. He looks at his watch and takes a deep breath as his office phone rings.

"Yes, Nancy!"

"You're right, Jason! It has happened again!"

Jason hurries up to the second floor, using the stairwell, as the day-shift maintenance man, Tom Griffin, in his late thirties, follows behind him. Jason and Tom enter through the double doors into the hallway and find Nancy standing in the office doorway as the music is still echoing throughout the corridor. Anthony hears the commotion down on the second level and alerts the group that they should go and investigate.

Anthony and the others arrive at the second level and exit the elevator as Tom, in maintenance, hurries toward the stairwell's exit door. The group proceeds down the hallway through the double doors and into the corridor. They look in amazement at seeing the residents laughing and celebrating. The residents are all waving their hands and giving praises to God.

———

Tom hurries through the kitchen area and opens the back door. He props it slightly open using a small wooden block, takes out his cell phone, and calls Keith Snider. Keith is the channel 12 news reporter working from his mobile news truck parked across the street from the facility.

"Keith Snider here."

Tom has hidden behind a trash dumpster, speaking softly on his cell phone.

"Mr. Snider, this is Tom. It happened again! Everyone is no longer sick!"

"Okay, good work, kid. You did a good job. Enjoy the hundred dollars, and I won't tell anyone who told me."

"Please don't, Mr. Snider, because if they find out, I'll lose my job."

"You have my word, kid."

Keith tells two of his cameramen to set up for a live newscast and tells another man sitting inside the truck to call the station and inform them that he has a breaking news story. The news report will be coming from The Gold Diamond Health Care Facility in Fishers.

Anthony and the group continue to look in amazement as Jason walks over and addresses them.

"I don't know if any of you have ever been to a circus before, but what you're observing is truly The Greatest Show on Earth."

Jason motions to Nancy to get her attention, and she walks over to him.

"Nancy, get the list of people who are authorized to see the residents and make sure the guard at the gate has the listing. These are the only people who are allowed to enter the facility at this time. Anyone else claiming to have business here must check with me first."

Jason turns and addresses the group. "Shall we proceed to the conference room? There's not much more we can do here."

The group follows Jason to the elevators, and they head down to the main floor. Keith Snider and his camera crew have set up, and Keith is preparing to go live remotely with the news story. Paul Adams is broadcasting live at the channel 12 news desk in downtown Indianapolis.

"This is Paul Adams at Action 12 News with a breaking news story. Keith Snider is reporting live from The Gold Diamond Health Care Facility in Fishers, where he states that the second group of patients woke up this morning in perfect health, just like the first group. Keith, what can you tell us about what's going on there, and is this true?"

Keith is reporting live from the mobile unit, and the TV screen switches to a screenshot of him.

"Paul, we've just been informed from a reliable source working inside of the facility that, indeed, the patients who checked into the facility yesterday woke up this morning in perfect health. As unbelievable as this might seem, we're talking about terminally ill patients, people with dementia and massive brain tumors. According to our sources, they show no sign of illnesses this morning."

"Keith, have you or your crew members witnessed any of the patients?"

"We haven't confirmed this information yet, Paul, but plan to do so before the end of the day. Another interesting note is that the first group was here for two weeks before this event occurred, but in this case, it literally happened overnight. This is Keith Snider from Action 12 News, reporting live from The Gold Diamond Health Care Facility in Fishers."

"Thank you, Keith. Stay tuned to Action 12 News for further updates on the miracle healing at The Gold Diamond Health Care Facility in Fishers."

The group is sitting around the conference table when Jason's cell phone rings, and he answers. "What! Okay, honey, thanks."

Jason addresses the group. "It's already reached the media. Channel 12 News has just aired a live broadcast informing the public of what has happened here."

Anthony responds, "Channel 12 News, that's their trucks parked across the street. An employee of ours must have informed them."

Gloria says, "Hey, guys, didn't we see the maintenance man run toward the stairwell when we came down from the third floor this morning?"

Clifford replies, "Yes, you're right, Gloria. What's his name?"

Jason says, "Tom, Tom Griffin. I'll speak to him later. Right now, we've got to come up with some answers."

There's a knock on the conference room door, and Jason responds, "Come in."

Carol Novy, the human resource manager in her mid-thirties, medium height, with black hair, addresses Jason, "Excuse me, Mr. Perkins, but we're getting flooded with telephone calls."

"Have Jennifer put the phone into automated message mode and leave it there until I tell you otherwise."

"Yes, sir, Mr. Perkins."

Carol leaves, shutting the door behind her.

Anthony replies, "Well, everyone, the next week or two will tell us what we're really made of. What do you think, Jason?"

Jason stares up at the ceiling. He's reliving the recent phenomenon in his mind, and everyone is surprised to see the blank look on his face.

Anthony continues, "Jason, are you okay?"

Jason regains his focus. "Yes, yes, of course, maybe just a little tired."

Anthony is annoyed. "Aren't we all! Everyone might as well be prepared to spend the next few hours here. We're going to have to make this our temporary headquarters for the time being, and I'll address the media at the appropriate time. Clifford, I want you to go back and review our resident contracts. We must make sure we haven't missed anything, and, Mike, you can work with me on some strategies that I have in mind. Jason, you continue working with Nancy and her nursing staff, keeping the residents comfortable."

Gloria says, "Is there anything you want me to do, Anthony?"

"Yes, there is, Gloria. I want you to go upstairs and relax, and we'll handle everything."

Anthony looks intently at everyone seated around the table.

"People, this is a delicate situation that we're in, and we must remain calm, alert, and focused on the responsibilities that lie ahead of us."

CHAPTER 16

The Discovery

J ason sits at his desk talking on his cell phone with his wife, Margaret.

"Hi, honey. I won't be home tonight, but you already guessed that. How's Celeste?"

Margaret is sitting on the couch in the living room, speaking with Jason on the house phone. "Oh, she's fine. She's been asking when her daddy is coming home."

"I'll be staying another night. That's the reason I'm calling you. I want you and Celeste to have lunch with me here at the cafeteria tomorrow."

"That will be fine, dear. At what time?"

"I'd say around eleven thirty."

"Now you know Celeste is going to want to bring Missy with her."

"I know, dear. Missy can stay in the office while we're having lunch. By the way, did Melanie make it in this afternoon?"

"Yes, she did. She's in the study, preparing for a meeting with the owner of the new Hawaiian Steak House Restaurant. The owner was extremely impressed with the decorative layout she's done at the facility and scheduled a meeting with her at six."

"That's Melanie. All work and no play will certainly keep her on the list of unmarried women. Tell Melanie that I want her to join us tomorrow for lunch. I look forward to the four of us being together. I could really use the support."

"I know, sweetheart. It's been a rough time for all of you. I'll talk with you later this evening. Goodbye, dear, and try not to worry so much. It will all work out."

They hang up, and Jason sits back in his chair, with his hands behind his head, staring at the lamp and speaking softly to himself. "I'm sure it will, my dear Margaret." He pauses. "I'm sure it will."

Later that afternoon, the group is seated around the conference table, and Anthony comments, "My interview with the press went well. I gave them just enough information to chew on for a while. Nancy, what's the status of the residents?"

"For the most part, the girls have kept them quiet and comfortable. They're all excited to be going home."

Jason comments, "We've had no problems with family members accusing us of involving the residents in some experimental scheme. However, six families opted out of their contract after the first group made a full recovery. They weren't going to take a chance of having them made—" he pauses "—whole, disrupting their plans. We had no problem replacing them because plenty of wealthy families cared enough for their loved ones and are truly grateful for this miraculous event. The question now is, where do we go from here?"

Michael replies, "Because of this, we've received phone calls from all over the world. There's even a prince in Saudi Arabia who's willing to pay a million dollars a day to have his mother stay here. The media calls this The Healing Center. Many of ministers insist that we make provisions for the poor, saying that Jesus never charged anyone for healing them. So where do we go from here, Clifford? As our legal advisor, what do you think?"

"We will continue our normal operation, since we haven't violated any laws. As you all are aware, we're being pressured from all fronts. The media wants a story, the wealthy want us to build more facilities, the public calls us a fake, and religious leaders want saving grace for the poor. People, the ball is in our court, we have two seconds left in the game, and we're down by two points. Any three-point shooters in the house?"

Michael comments, "I suggest we occupy all five floors and keep our pricing structure in place for the moment. We haven't a clue as to what is causing this and don't know if it will continue. We must, however, proceed with caution as we move forward. Any changes to our current operation may present legal challenges that we want to stay away from."

Gloria opens the door and takes a seat next to Nancy, as Anthony says, "Hello, Gloria. I hope you're feeling better."

"Much better, Anthony, thank you."

Anthony continues, "I agree with Michael. We must proceed with caution. One reporter asked me how is it that these so-called miracles are showing up only where the rich are living. I told him that I don't know how they came about, so I can't answer that question. This incident has created quite a bit of concern amongst the public. People are beginning to believe that God favors only the wealthy, leaving the others out there to fend for themselves. With that said, I agree with Michael. We should fill up all of the suites, and if it happens again, we must consider providing accommodations for everyone."

Jason comments, "Carol says that we've received over five hundred requests for suites, just today alone. How do we plan to select the next group of seventy-five residents?"

Michael says, "I suggest we have a lottery drawing. Secure a post office box that people can mail in their request and have a public lottery drawing."

Anthony replies, "Is that legal, Clifford?"

"I don't see a problem, but I'll check. It sounds like a logical solution since there will be those who will claim that bribery was involved in choosing the residents that are selected. It would certainly eliminate that problem."

Anthony continues, "Clifford, you and Jason work on that. Michael and I need to get back to Virginia to meet with the board. They've been pleased with how we've handled things up to this point. We also need to get with Mark and Roger to see how this chain of events could affect our next marketing campaign and our current budget structure. I'm going to announce to the press as soon as possible about our intentions. It will keep them off our backs and, hopefully, put everyone else at ease. Is there anyone else who'd like to speak?"

Anthony pauses for questions, and everyone remains silent. "Good. I'll see everyone back here in the morning."

———————————

Rosalyn Williams, a twenty-two-year-old, tall, brown-skinned woman, and Ann Bonner, a twenty-five-year-old, medium-built redhead working the afternoon shift, are sitting in the nursing office. Jason walks in and takes a seat in front of Rosalyn's desk.

"Hello, ladies, how are things going?"

Rosalyn says, "Everything is fine, Mr. Perkins. It's amazing how completely different the residents are now from yesterday when we left. Mr. Perkins, this must be the work of God, but I don't understand why so many people are angry. It should be a time of joy and celebration."

"I'm not a very religious man, but didn't Jesus heal people when he was on earth, yet they killed him?"

They both nod their heads in agreement.

Jason continues, "The world can be an extremely cruel place, Rosalyn. There are those who are happy and joyful over what has happened here, yet there are others who don't share that same sentiment. For everything that is good and great, there's a flip side that is equally bad and evil. You see, ladies, everyone would be okay if they could control the events that have taken place here, but no one can, not even us, and it's happening in our own backyard. I'll talk with you two later."

The girls bid Jason goodbye as he gets up from the chair and exits the office.

———————————

The following morning, the group is seated around the conference room table, as Jason comments. "I'd like to begin by saying that Tom Griffin is no longer with the company. As we expected, he's the informant who tipped off the news crew the morning this happened. The four of you were correct. When you saw him heading for the stairwell that morning, he was on his way to alert the reporter. He had to confirm his story first. That's why he came running upstairs behind me. His replacement is Keith Byrd."

Anthony replies, "Good. I'm going to make this short. We've formulated a strategy that will bridge the gap between where we are now and where we need to be, and it seems to be working, so everyone stay on course. Any questions?"

Clifford replies, "Yes, just one last thing. I've found no issues in having a lottery drawing. We can move forward with that plan."

"Great. Get that set up and keep us posted. We need to have this completed as soon as possible," says Anthony.

The group exits the conference room.

CHAPTER 17

The Discovery

Jason sits at his desk and calls his wife, Margaret.

"Hello, sweetheart, have you left the house yet?"

Margaret is backing the car out of the driveway. Now eight years old, Celeste holds her white Pershing cat, Missy, and is seated in the back. Margaret is speaking to Jason from the car's Bluetooth. "I'm pulling out of the driveway now, honey."

"Does Celeste have Missy with her?"

"What a silly question, dear. Of course she does, and Melanie said she'd meet us there."

"Excellent, I'll see you when you get here."

"Okay, dear."

There's a knock on his office door. "Come in."

Nancy walks in with a folder in her hand. As Nancy approaches Jason, he stares intently at the lamp as if he were in a hypnotic state of mind. Nancy watches him for a moment and calls out his name.

"Jason, Jason." Nancy speaks louder. "Jason!"

Jason snaps out of it and answers Nancy. "Yes, yes, Nancy. How are you?"

"You were staring at that lamp as if you were in some sort of trance."

Jason leans across his desk and lights his candle in the glass container.

"Like the rest of us, Nancy, I'm probably just a little tired." He waves his hand over the candle, directing the smoke in his direction.

Nancy stares at Jason. "I suppose Jason."

"Don't you just love the smell of cinnamon, Nancy? It has such a pleasant aroma."

Nancy ignores commenting about the cinnamon smell and focuses her attention on him.

"Jason, I remember the morning that Melanie brought this lamp to your office. It was the day before the first group of residents had a miraculous recovery, and they had already been here for two weeks. But this time, it happened to the second group the next morning after they arrived. At about two a.m. that morning, you stormed into the office, telling us to check on the residents immediately. It was like you knew something was about to happen. What did you see, Jason, that made you think so? Does this lamp have anything to do with this?"

Jason is irritated while looking directly at Nancy. "Of course not, what an absurd thing to say. It was just a feeling that came over me, a premonition, and nothing more. Be careful, Nancy. Making assumptions is an extremely dangerous thing to do. I think you have been working too much. We'll see about giving you a few days off after things have settled down a bit."

Nancy looks disturbed. "Here's the report you wanted. Is there anything else, Jason?"

"Yes, meet me in the cafeteria at eleven thirty. I'm having lunch with the family, and I'd like for you to join us."

Nancy, standing during the entire conversation, gives Jason a blank look and slowly turns around. She exits the room, closing the door behind her.

———————

Jason leans back in his chair when he hears Margaret and Melanie call out his name and immediately tells them to come in. They walk in and stand on the opposite side of his desk. Celeste runs with Missy in her arms and jumps onto his lap.

"Greetings, everyone," Jason says.

Margaret and Melanie greet Jason, and Celeste grabs him by the face and comments, "Daddy, when are you coming home? Missy and I miss you."

Jason gently rubs his hand across Missy's back and kisses Celeste on the cheek.

"I miss you, too, sweetheart. Daddy will be home soon, I promise."

Jason directs his attention to Melanie. "How's my favorite niece doing?"

Melanie smiles. "Well, since I'm your favorite and only niece, I take great pleasure knowing that I'm at the top of your list."

"Margaret, my dear, you're looking lovely as always."

"Thank you, sir. That's because I have a husband who takes excellent care of me."

Jason smiles. "Lucky you." He looks at Celeste. "Okay, sweetheart, why don't the three of you walk down to the cafeteria, and I'll be along in a moment."

"Daddy, what about Missy?"

"I'll take Missy. She'll stay in the office until we finish our lunch. Melanie, there's a table already set up for us. Minnie knows you're coming; she'll direct you to the table."

The three of them proceed toward the door as Celeste looks back and waves.

"Goodbye, Daddy. Goodbye, Missy."

They exit the office, and Jason immediately opens his desk drawer and takes out a large, black plastic trash bag. He puts his brandy and a group of folders into the bag and picks up the family picture from his desk. He hurries over to the glass coffee table and places the photo onto the table. Jason walks toward a small storage closet, opens the door, and sets the trash bag onto the floor. He walks over to the thermostat on the wall and slams the palm of his hand against the outer casing, causing it to crack, and picks up his phone and dials maintenance. Keith, a thirty-five-year-old, short, stockily built man with brown hair, sits in the maintenance office.

"Hello, Keith, this is Jason."

"Hello, Mr. Perkins, what can I do for you, sir?"

"There's a crack on the outer casing of my thermostat; please replace it right away. I'm getting ready to walk down to the cafeteria and have lunch with my family, so have the casing replaced before I get back."

"Sure thing, Mr. Perkins. I'll get right on it."

Jason hangs up the phone and looks for Missy. She's sitting in a guest chair in front of his desk. Jason takes pieces of paper from his top drawer and places them on his desk. He takes the candle container and lays it on its side, causing the flames from the candle to ignite the paper on his desk, and rushes out of his office—being careful not to lock the door.

Nancy, Jason, and his family are seated at the table in the cafeteria and hear a voice screaming out, "Fire!" Jason rushes up and heads toward his office, where the commotion is coming from, followed by the others. When Jason arrives, he sees Keith with a fire extinguisher, and he has the fire under control. When the others arrive, Missy runs out of the office and jumps into Celeste's arms.

"What happened here, Keith?"

"I'm not sure, Mr. Perkins, when I came into your office to fix your thermostat, your desk was on fire."

Jason looks behind him. "Everyone stay back." Jason saunters over to his desk. "I see what happened here. My daughter's cat must have jumped up onto my desk and knocked the candle over."

Celeste holds Missy by the head and looks her in the eye. "You naughty girl. Look what you did to Daddy's desk."

Melanie replies, "It appears the desk and this beautiful lamp I got you, Uncle Jason, have been destroyed. What happened to your family picture, Uncle Jason?"

Jason points over toward the coffee table.

"It's over there on the table. I took a nap earlier and wanted to look at the photo as I rested." Jason turns toward Nancy. "Nancy, check upstairs and make sure the residents are okay."

Nancy methodically stares at Jason as he stares back at her. Nancy slowly turns and exits the office. Jason sees Carol standing out in the hallway and motions to her.

"Oh, Carol, there you are. Call the insurance company and tell them I need someone out here today. There's no need to report the fire since no one was injured. We don't need any more attention from the public or the media than we already have."

"Okay, Mr. Perkins."

Melanie says, "Uncle Jason, I have all the receipts, so there won't be any problems replacing things."

"This time, Melanie, don't go out of your way to provide me with such an exquisite lamp. A conventional one from a local retailer will do just fine."

Jason looks toward the employees standing in the hallway.

"Everyone get back to work; the excitement is over. Well, family, no real harm is done. I think it's okay to continue with our lunch. I'll let Keith take Missy down to the maintenance office with him."

The family walks down the hallway back to the cafeteria. Jason walks over to his desk, lays the lamp across his desk, and unplugs it. He exits his office, closing the door behind him.

Brenda and Patricia are standing in the office talking as Nancy walks in.

"I just came up to check on things. Jason had a small fire in his office, but Keith from maintenance discovered it in time and was able to put it out."

Brenda replies, "Everything is fine up here. What started the fire?"

"Jason left his daughter's cat in the office. We were having lunch in the cafeteria, and he claims the cat jumped onto his desk and knocked the candle over."

"What a lucky coincidence that Keith came up to Mr. Perkins's office when he did," says Patricia.

Nancy replies, "Yeah, these coincidences are popping up quite frequently lately."

Brenda and Patricia take a quick look at each other as Nancy leaves the office.

CHAPTER 18

The Discovery

J ason, Melanie, and Carol are standing in Jason's office. Marty Johnson, the insurance agent, is just leaving to file a report.

Marty says, "Well, Mr. Perkins, you're lucky. This fire could have been a lot worse. The lamp and the desk will certainly need replacement, and there's smoke damage to a few other things."

Melanie says, "I have receipts for everything, Mr. Johnson. It was my company that furnished the facility."

"Good, here's my card. You can go online and fill out the necessary claim forms and fax them over to my office when you're finished. I'll be sending over a claims adjuster to assess the damages."

Jason replies, "Thank you, Mr. Johnson, and enjoy the rest of your day."

Mr. Johnson and Carol exit the office, and Melanie addresses Jason.

"Uncle Jason, Carol, and I will get started filling out those claim forms."

"Excellent. I'm going to stay here for a minute and go through a few things. I'll see you later."

"Okay, Uncle Jason."

Melanie leaves the room, and Jason walks over to the lamp lying on its side. He gently rubs his hand across the soot-covered lamp, and the soot comes off. It appears to have no burnt effects or singed marks. He quickly takes out a handkerchief from his pocket and begins rubbing furiously over the lamp, only to discover that it has been unharmed by the fire while the lampshade is in ashes.

Jason takes a light bulb out from the storage cabinet and replaces the broken bulb. He picks up the end of the electrical plug, inserts it into the socket, and turns the lamp switch, and the lamp comes on. Jason frantically runs over to the storage closet, grabs the black plastic bag, and dumps everything onto the floor. He hurries over to his desk and puts the lamp into the trash bag. Jason cradles the bag under his arm and leaves the office.

The group sits at the conference table, and Anthony addresses Jason.

"Jason, I understand you had a fire in your office?"

"Yes, a small one, but we immediately got it under control, and there were no reports filed other than with the insurance company."

Jason looks over and sees Nancy staring at him.

"Good. The last thing we need is to have the facility burn down with the residents still here after they've miraculously been given a clean bill of health. What was the cause of the fire?"

"My family and I were having lunch in the cafeteria, and my daughter's cat knocked over the candle that was on my desk."

Jason glances over at Nancy, and she stares at him a second time.

"You must be more careful, Jason, and I'd suggest that in the future, you leave your daughter's cat at home."

Looking directly at Nancy, Jason says, "I totally agree, and my apologies to everyone for my negligence."

Anthony says, "The residents will be leaving tomorrow. I suggest we tighten up any loose ends that need our attention over the next couple of days; then everyone take a few days off. There won't be much of a staff needed since there won't be any residents in the facility. Mike, Clifford, and I will be leaving on Sunday for Virginia, and we'll be having meetings all next week. So that gives us the rest of the week and most of the weekend to finish things up here. Any questions?"

Anthony looks around the room at everyone, and they all remain quiet.

"Good, so let's keep things going, and we will meet back here in the morning."

The group disperses.

Jason is sitting in the conference room alone and dials Bruce's phone number on his cell phone. Bruce recognizes Jason's number and answers his mobile phone.

"Hello, Jason."

"How's it going, buddy?"

"Jason, good to hear from you. How's it going? You must be kidding. It seems that all the action is over your way. What in the hell is going on?"

"It all started the day you and I were on the phone and I got an urgent call."

"Yes, I remember."

"I'm taking a few days off next week, and I'd like to come down for a few days, alone. I'll fill you in when I get there."

"Hey, you're always welcome. Ilene and I will be glad to have the company. When do you think you'll get here?"

"I'll leave here next Monday and should arrive on Wednesday afternoon."

"Great. Touch base with me before you leave, and I expect to see you next week."

"Thanks, Bruce, and give my love to Ilene."

Jason and Bruce hang up.

Jason and Margaret are lying in bed as Jason addresses Margaret. "Honey, I called Bruce this evening and told him I was coming down for a couple of days next week. The residents will be leaving tomorrow, and I could use a couple of days of downtime. Besides, it will be a couple of weeks before my office is finished."

"That sounds like a good idea. Will you be flying down?"

"No, I've decided to drive down and take in the scenery along the way."

"Are you sure you're up to it? That's a pretty long drive."

"Margaret, after what I've been through these last few weeks, I could drive to Florida standing on my head, blindfolded."

Margaret smiles. "I'll make sure you're not blindfolded and sitting straight up in your seat. You've got to get back here in one piece."

They both chuckle, and Jason turns toward Margaret, kisses her on the cheek, and says goodnight. He turns the lamp off next to the bed, and they both retire for the evening.

———

Jason loads up the van as Michael, Clifford, and Anthony get in and take a seat. Jason takes his place in the driver's seat, and they head off to the airport. After a few moments of silence, Anthony comments, "With the residents gone, we can focus on some personal things and exhale for a minute. Clifford, it's been close to eight weeks since you've been home. I know you'll be glad to see Michelle and the kids."

"Yes, I will. The kids have been calling me every day for the past week. The funny thing is they've been calling for firsthand information about what has happened here. I had to finally tell them that I wasn't at liberty to discuss any details about what has occurred. Only then did they start asking me when I was coming home."

The four of them laugh, and Anthony addresses Jason. "Jason, you'll be going to Florida for a few days next week. A few days in Florida should do you good."

Michael replies, "What part, Jason?"

"Bradenton. It's about fifty miles south of Tampa. It's a lovely place, and I'm going to visit an old friend of mine."

Anthony replies, "Gloria called me about three o'clock this afternoon, saying she arrived safely in Ashburn. She took an early morning flight out to attend a social event she had tickets for this evening."

Jason responds, "Good for her. My sister has had a rough time dealing with this situation."

"Yes, I know. I told Gloria to spend the next two weeks doing absolutely nothing but relaxing and enjoying herself, a suggestion I recommend for all of us. When we reconvene in a couple of weeks, it will be a long and strenuous journey."

The group remains silent as Jason merges onto the freeway, heading to the airport.

———

Jason walks up the steps from his basement, carrying a black nylon bag. He goes into the garage, opens the trunk of his Silver Mercedes CLA Coupe, reaches for the lamp, and places it into the bag. Jason heads over to the garage corner and puts four bricks inside. He zips it closed, puts it back into the trunk, and walks back inside the house.

The following morning, Jason puts the last of his luggage in the trunk of his car and shuts it. Celeste and Margaret stand in the driveway, and Jason turns to Celeste, picks her up, and kisses her on the cheek.

"Well, pumpkin, you take care of your mother while I'm gone."

"I will, Daddy. When are you coming back home?"

"Daddy will be back home next weekend."

He puts Celeste down and embraces Margaret. "Okay, dear, I'll call you from the hotel I'll be staying in on the way."

"Okay, sweetheart, drive safely, and give our love to Bruce and Ilene."

Jason gets into his car and pulls out of the driveway as Celeste and Margaret wave goodbye.

———

Anthony, Michael, and Clifford are sitting at the table in the conference room at the home office of the Jennimen Corporation. It's a beautiful, historic red-brick, four-story building located in downtown Ashburn, Virginia. They're joined by Robert Kraft, president of market research, in his late thirties; Mark Simmons; and Roger Clemons as Anthony addresses the group.

"Gentlemen, as you know, it's been a long and difficult journey over the last few weeks for the three of us. We've managed to get a handle on things, at least for now. Mark, I want you to hold off on our marketing program until we see what's going to happen with the next group of residents, and, Roger, we need to make adjustments to our third-quarter revenue projections. These two incidents at the facility in Fishers have created interest throughout the nation and internationally as well."

Mark replies, "This is still quite unbelievable to me, and I'm sure it is to everyone else. Have you determined what our next strategy will be, Anthony?"

"Yes, I have, Mark. I'll go over the plans that we've put in place with the three of you when we reconvene. Clifford will be spending time with his family, and I'll be off to California for a few days of golf. Jason is leaving this morning for Florida, and I advise everyone to just relax this next couple of weeks."

"It sounds like we have everything in place," says Roger.

Anthony asks Michael and Clifford if they have anything to add before closing out the meeting, and they have no additional comments.

"Well, since there are no more questions or comments— "he looks at his cell phone "—today is Monday, the eleventh, and we'll meet here week after next, on the twenty-fifth."

Everyone nods their heads in agreement, and Anthony dismisses the group.

CHAPTER 19

The Discovery

J ason turns left onto 143rd Street and then turns right onto 9th Terrace East, drives about a hundred yards, and pulls up into a red-glazed marbled-tiled, circular driveway. The house is a beautiful ranch-style home. He blows his horn once, and Bruce Spillman and his wife, Ilene, come out to greet him as he gets out of the car. In his late forties, Bruce is of medium height and build, with light brown thinning hair. Ilene, in her early forties, is tall and slim with black hair.

Bruce says, "Hey, buddy, you made it."

Bruce greets Jason with a brief handshake and a hug, and Ilene embraces him.

"How about that? Here I am once again in the Sunshine State with two of my favorite people."

Ilene says, "Good seeing you again, Jason. How's Margaret and Celeste doing?"

"Just great. They both send their love to you and Bruce."

Bruce replies, "Well let's go inside. We've got a lot of catching up to do."

Ilene has prepared a meal, and they sit down on the back patio deck. Ilene gives Jason a plate of food and pours him a glass of wine.

"You two are always the perfect hosts. Thanks, Ilene."

Bruce says, "Well, Jason, I could tell you to save the suspense for later, but Ilene and I want to know what in the hell is going on up there in Fishers?"

"I'm sure you probably know just as much as I do with all of the media coverage. The residents checked into The Gold Diamond Health

Care Facility with all types of illnesses, and one morning when they awoke, shazam! No more sickness, and as incredible as it might seem, it happened not once but twice."

Ilene replies, "Jason, no one has a clue as to how this might have happened? People don't just heal overnight, do they?"

"Ilene, at The Gold Diamond Health Care Facility, they do, or should I say, they did."

Bruce replies, "Jason, I believe in miracles, but not in the manner you just described."

"Most of the people say it's a fake publicity stunt to fill up our facilities—" Jason pauses for a moment as Ilene pours him another glass of wine "—others say that it's a miraculous healing from God, while the rest just don't know what to believe."

"And what's your theory, Jason, since you have firsthand knowledge of what took place?" says Bruce.

"I believe that it was simply a force of nature, an energy force that happens once in a millennium, that was present in the facility at the time the residents were there. If my theory is correct, the energy force will soon dissipate, and everything will return to normal."

Bruce is chuckling. "That's quite an analogy, Jason. How did you come up with that theory?"

"Elementary, my dear Watson, elementary. It's like an atmospheric storm, whereby the warm and cold air come together and produce an enormous storm. The storm not only produces rain, high winds, and thunder, but also the greatest force of nature in the form of lightning. Just as quickly as it appears, it dissipates as if it never happened."

Bruce has a big smile on his face. "I can say one thing about your hypothesis, Sherlock, it sure sounds good."

The three of them laugh as Ilene clears away the table and exits the patio.

"I'll let you two talk over old times together while I go and do the dishes."

Ilene opens the patio door and walks into the kitchen.

"How's Peter doing in law school, Bruce?"

"He's in his last year of school at Yale, and he plans to spend a couple of weeks with me and Ilene before him and his fiancée, Jane, take a vacation to Italy."

"Splendid, he's going to make a fine attorney. By the way, how's the boat rental business? Have you added to your inventory?"

"Going well. I just picked up two new twenty-one-foot Star Decks."

"Is Victor still managing the operation?"

"Oh, yes. Victor's been with me for six years now, and I couldn't run the business without him."

"Great. I'd like to go out in the morning and smell that fresh coastal ocean. I bought myself a new rod and reel and want to try it out for a few hours."

"Not a problem. I'll have Victor set up a new Star Deck, and Ilene will pack you a nice lunch. What time do you think you want to head out?"

"I figure I'll get out there around seven o'clock tomorrow morning."

Bruce picks up his mobile phone and calls Victor Pena, who stands in a boat, cleaning it out. Victor, a tall, lean Mexican man in his late thirties, answers his mobile phone.

"Hello, Bruce."

"Victor, how did things go this morning?"

"Things went fine. Fourteen of our twenty boats went out this morning, and I'm cleaning out the last boat that came in about an hour ago."

"Good. You remember my friend Jason Perkins from Indiana?"

"Yes, sir, I sure do. How is Mr. Perkins?"

"He's doing fine. He just arrived here this afternoon to get away for a few days. I want you to prepare a new Star Deck for him. He wants to go out about seven in the morning and do a little fishing alone."

"I'll have everything set up for him when he arrives in the morning."

"Excellent. I'll talk with you later this evening."

Bruce and Victor hang up.

"Okay, Jason, you're all set. Do you remember how to get there?"

"I believe so. I take Tamiami Trail to US 41 and then a right onto 14th Street."

"Hey, pretty good memory. It seems like you got things all mapped out. Let's go and grab your bags out of the car and take them to the guest room."

They walk off the deck and head toward the front of the house to the driveway.

Jason walks out of the parking lot and around to the boat docking area. Sounds and sights of seagulls are flying above. Jason wears tan cargo shorts with a short-sleeved, cream-colored shirt and brown leather sandals with an Australian outback hat tied under his chin. He carries a container of food prepared by Ilene, a tackle box, and the black nylon bag containing the lamp. He walks down the pier, and a tall, thin man walks up and greets him.

"Mr. Perkins, how are you?"

"I'm doing fine, Victor, and how are you doing?"

Jason sets his things on the pier and shakes Victor's hand.

"I'm doing fine, Mr. Perkins. You came to spend a few days with us?"

"Yes, yes, indeed. Do you have things ready for me?"

"Yes, sir. I have one of our new Star Deck boats prepared for you. It seats six people in luxurious black, butter-soft leather seats and is fully equipped. How does that sound for a great day of fishing?"

Jason has a big smile. "I see why Bruce considers you an invaluable employee. You certainly know how to wow your customers." They both laugh.

"You have all the fishing equipment you need, Mr. Perkins, with artificial lures and live bait. How long do you think you'll be gone?"

"Probably most of the afternoon. I should be back around, hmm . . . around four."

"Sounds good. Let me help you with your stuff."

Just as Victor reaches down to grab the black nylon bag, Jason immediately stops him.

Jason smiles. "I'll get those things, Victor. Why don't you go down to the office and grab me a cup of coffee?"

"Sure thing, Mr. Perkins."

"I've got a new rod and reel in the bag, and I don't want you to jinx me by taking off the lucky spell I placed on it." The two of them chuckle.

"I understand, Mr. Perkins. You see that boat over there?"

Jason turns and looks over at the boat.

"I always make sure I clean it last because I usually get a lot of rentals the following day"—Victor is smiling—"at least most of the time." They both laugh.

"I'll be right back, Mr. Perkins."

Victor runs down to the office as Jason loads his things into the boat. Victor returns with the coffee in a big, black porcelain mug and hands it to Jason from the pier. Victor removes the rope tied around the dock, carefully tossing it into the boat as Jason drives away.

Jason waves, looking back at Victor. "I'm going about five miles out. See you when I get back."

Victor waves. "Okay, Mr. Perkins. Enjoy yourself and have a safe trip."

Jason turns his attention to steering the boat and puts it into high gear, and speeds away.

———————

Bruce stands at the kitchen counter, pouring himself a cup of coffee, as Ilene sits at the table eating her breakfast.

"Come on, honey, sit down and eat your breakfast before it gets cold."

Bruce sits down and takes a sip of coffee. "I see Jason got his early start."

"I offered to fix him breakfast before he left, but he said he wasn't hungry, so I put a little extra in his food container."

"You know, Ilene; we touched on it briefly before we went to bed last night, how calm he seems to be about The Gold Diamond Health Care Facility incident. He even came up with his own take of what he thought was the reasoning for the occurrence. Jason seemed awful certain that it was just a spontaneous event that took place and now it's all over."

"It was strange. Do you think he knows more about what's going on than he led us to believe?"

"I'm not sure, honey—" he pauses, "—but if he does, he better be careful of how he handles it."

CHAPTER 20

The Discovery

Jason stops the boat and looks around. He's about five miles out with no sign of land in sight. Jason drops the anchor, sits down, and looks up at the sunny sky. He reaches into his left pants pocket, takes out a glass flask container of brandy, and takes a large sip. Then he reaches over on the floor of the boat, picks up the black nylon bag, and takes a deep breath. Jason slowly places the bag into the water and watches it submerge deep into the ocean until it disappears out of his sight.

He takes out a CD, puts it into the CD player, and turns it on. Louie Armstrong's voice cries out as he sings, *"What a Wonderful World,"* and the music echoes throughout the warm ocean air. He lays his seat back and stretches his legs out across the seat opposite from him. Jason grabs the front of his hat and brings it down over his eyes, and falls into a deep sleep.

Victor finishes talking with a customer when he sees Jason heading for the dock. Jason cuts the motor off, and Victor reaches over, grabs the rope, and ties it to the pier. Jason picks up his gear and steps out of the boat as Victor notices he's without his nylon bag.

"Mr. Perkins, what happened to your black bag with your new rod and reel in it?"

"I laid it up on the side of the boat and accidentally knocked it into the water"—he speaks explicitly—"how careless of me!"

"It doesn't appear you used any of the other fishing gear I gave you."

"After that, I didn't feel much like fishing, so I decided to take in the ocean breeze and enjoy the day on this beautiful boat. Well, Victor, so much for my lucky spell. Besides, it was a very relaxing and peaceful outing, and I can buy another rod and reel, but there's no price for happiness and peace of mind."

Jason reaches into his pants pocket and pulls out a hundred-dollar bill, and gives it to Victor.

"Thank you, Mr. Perkins!"

"You're quite welcome, Victor."

Victor picks up Jason's food container and tackle box and follows Jason to his car. Jason has Victor put them into the trunk, and the two of them bid each other farewell. Jason gets into his car and drives off.

———————

Jason, Bruce, and Ilene are having dinner at the dining room table.

"Ilene, this roasted duck is simply superb."

"Thanks, Jason, it's Bruce's favorite."

Jason smiles. "Ilene, your husband always did have a taste for the finer things of life."

Bruce replies, "Jason, Victor tells me you accidentally knocked your new rod and reel off the side of the boat this morning."

"He's absolutely correct, Bruce. I wasn't paying attention, and when I turned around to reach for the bag, my left arm knocked it off the side of the boat, and it went flying into the water."

"I'm sure we can find a replacement. What were the make and model?"

"I'm not sure. Margaret gave it to me as a gift a couple of months ago. It's not important. I'll find out when I get back. I'd rather take in a few rounds of golf that you promised me. Is that still on, Bruce?"

"We'll go out on the course in the morning. How's that?"

"Sounds good. I think I'll take a shower and go to my room and do a little reading. I'll see you two in the morning. Goodnight."

Jason exits the dining room as Bruce and Ilene continue talking.

Bruce says, "Jason didn't seem fazed at all about losing his new gear. You'd think that if Jason brought it to Florida, he'd show a little more concern about losing it. Jason also told me that he purchased it for himself. Now he says that Margaret bought it for him a couple of months ago as a gift. What's that all about?"

"I agree, honey, Jason is acting a bit peculiar about things."

"Another thing."

"What's that, dear?"

"Victor told me that Jason tipped him a hundred-dollar bill."

"A hundred-dollar bill! Even I know that's not Jason based on what you told me his nickname was in college. What was it?"

"The Campus Scrooge." They both laugh.

Ilene says, "Come on, honey. Let's go out on the patio and get a little fresh air. The air in here just got a little too thick. I'll clean the table off later."

They shake their heads and walk out onto the patio.

Jason, Bruce, and Ilene are standing in the driveway as the house phone rings. Ilene goes to answer it and looks back at Jason.

"Don't leave yet Jason. Let me take this call first."

Ilene walks into the house and over to the coffee table, and answers the phone.

"Hello."

"Hello, Ilene, this is Margaret, just checking on you and the fellas."

"Hi, Margaret, Jason's out in the driveway talking with Bruce. He's getting ready to head back to Indiana."

"That's good. I know Jason enjoyed himself. I want to thank you and Bruce for letting him stay there for a few days. I hope he didn't drive you crazy with all the anxiety he's had lately over what has happened at the facility."

"On the contrary, he's been as cool as a cucumber. Even when he went out fishing alone and lost the new rod and reel you bought him, he didn't let it bother him."

"The new rod and reel I bought him? Ilene, what in the devil are you talking about?"

"Jason brought with him a black nylon bag, and when he met Victor at the dock the morning he went fishing, he told him that it contained a new rod and reel. When Jason returned later that afternoon without the bag, he told Victor that it had accidentally fallen overboard by mistake."

"I'm still a little confused, Ilene. What does that have to do with me?"

"That evening when the three of us were having dinner together, Bruce volunteered to replace the rod and reel. Bruce asked Jason for the make and model, and Jason said that he didn't know because he received it as a gift from you a couple of months ago."

"Are you sure he said me, and maybe not Melanie, his niece, instead?"

"No, he said you. I was sitting right there."

"I think the stress of the situation is really getting to him, even though he's not showing it."

"He's right out front. Do you want me to get him for you?"

"No, just tell him to call me on his cell phone when he gets a chance, and I want to thank you and Bruce again for being such dear friends."

"Anytime, Margaret, you know that. Take care, and I'll talk with you later."

The two hang up the phone, and Ilene walks back out into the driveway where Bruce and Jason are standing.

Ilene smiles. "Jason, that was your better half. Margaret says to give her a call on your cell phone when you get a chance."

Jason says, "Well, you two, I really must be heading back, and thanks for everything."

A hug is extended from Bruce and Ilene as Jason gets into his car. They wave goodbye, and Jason drives off. As the two of them walk into the house, Ilene turns to Bruce with a frown on her face. "Talk about the icing on the cake."

"What are you talking about, Ilene?"

"Margaret was calling to check up on how things were going. She said with all the anxiety Jason has been having; lately, he must be driving us both up the wall, in so many words. I told her that Jason has been relatively calm, even after losing the new rod and reel she bought him. Her reply was, 'What rod and reel? I never bought Jason a rod and reel.'"

Bruce is looking surprised. "Then, if she didn't buy him a rod and reel, there probably wasn't one in the bag."

"Then what was, Bruce?"

"I don't know, honey, but I can tell you this much: the accidental incident of knocking the bag into the water was no accident."

They shake their heads and walk back into the house.

Jason drives along the highway with a view of palm trees and ocean-front property and sings, "It's a Wonderful World."

CHAPTER 21

The Discovery

FOUR WEEKS LATER

Anthony, Michael, Clifford, Gloria, Jason, and Joan Harper, the new nursing administrator, are seated at The Gold Diamond Health Care Facility's conference table. Joan is in her mid-thirties, about five feet, four inches tall, with blonde hair.

Anthony comments, "All seventy-five residents have checked in, and everything is in place. There're reporters from all over the globe and a street full of public onlookers waiting to see what happens when the clock strikes twelve. Jason, is your nursing staff prepared?"

"Yes, all staff members are in place and on high alert. I'd like to take a moment to say that Joan has done a splendid job since taking over as our new nursing administrator these past couple of weeks."

Anthony replies, "Yes, Joan, I've only heard great things about you. Keep up the good work."

"Thank you, sir, I certainly will."

Anthony continues, "Okay, let's all get back to work, and we'll see how this thing goes. Keep your fingers crossed."

Anthony dismisses the group.

Melanie stands on the opposite side of Jason's desk and addresses Jason.

"Well, Uncle Jason, tonight's a big night."

"Every night's a big night, Melanie."

"Yes, of course, Uncle Jason."

Melanie gently places a new lamp on Jason's desk, plugs it in, and turns it on.

"Except for this replacement lamp, Uncle Jason, your office looks as if it was never in a fire. I purchased this lamp from Roxy's Lamp Shop down the street, and although it may not be as special as the other one, it will do just fine."

"Yes, Melanie, sometimes simple works just as fine, at least in this case."

"I guess I'll head out to the house, Uncle Jason. That is if I can get through the sea of reporters and bystanders camped across the street."

"Be careful, dear, and I'll see you later. Wait a minute, Melanie; I'll call and have James escort you to your car and out of the parking lot."

As Melanie leaves, Jason picks up his office phone and arranges for James to meet her in the lobby. Jason decides to head up to the sixth-floor nursing office. He turns his desk lamp off and takes the elevator up to the nursing office on the sixth floor, looking for Joan. Upon arrival, he addresses Darlene Anderson. She's the second shift nurse, medium built, with a dark brown complexion, and sits at her desk.

"Hello, Darlene, where is Joan? I told her to come up here and check on things and to wait for me until I arrived."

"Oh, hi, Mr. Perkins. She'll be right back. She had to go down to her office to get her notebook and put away the nursing report log. Would you like for me to call down to her office?"

"No, that won't be necessary. Just tell her to call me in my office when she returns."

Jason returns to his office and sees his desk lamp is on, and he panics. Jason runs to Joan's office and finds her sitting at her desk.

"Joan, what are you doing in your office?"

"Jason, but you told me less than half an hour ago to take the nursing report logs off your desk and put them back into the filing cabinet."

"Then you've been in my office?"

There's a slight smile on Joan's face. "How else could I have gotten the reports?"

"I left my lamp off; did you turn it on?"

"I had to turn your lamp on to locate the file key. It was hidden beneath the papers on your desk. Are you okay, Jason? You act as if you sense that something is about to happen."

Jason calms down and stares Joan directly in the eye.

"No, Joan, I was only trying to find out how my lamp got turned back on, and don't make any more assumptions. That's the reason your predecessor, Nancy, is no longer with the company. Do I make myself clear?"

Joan is feeling intimidated while looking Jason in the eye.

"Yes, sir, Mr. Perkins, perfectly clear."

Jason walks out of Joan's office and closes the door. He proceeds to his office and sits down at his desk, staring intently at his new lamp. Jason opens his bottom left drawer and takes out a bottle of brandy along with a shot glass. He pours a drink into the glass and quickly drinks it down and sits back in his chair with his hands cradled behind his head, and softly sings, "It's A Wonderful World."

Anthony stands at the podium of The Blue Diamond Executive Conference Room at Mandy's five-star restaurant. In attendance are the Jennimen Corporation's board of directors, the corporate officers, and the Magnum Five Investment Group.

"I'd like to thank everyone here for the excellent job and support that you've given us during our crisis. It has been two months now, and everything has returned to normal, with no incidents. We have three new facilities planned to be operational over the next eighteen months, and occupancy for those facilities is secured. With that said, I'd like to propose a toast to the future success of the Jennimen Corporation, and may The Gold Diamond Health Care Facilities grow in more significant numbers across the country."

Everyone stands and raises their glasses and shouts out, "To the Success of The Gold Diamond Health Care Facilities!" And they all applaud.

CHAPTER 22

The Discovery

FOUR YEARS LATER

A group of four geological oceanographers approaches Spill-man's Boat Rentals in two of the chartered boats. Ralu Nyondo is brown-skinned, of medium build and height, with a slight South African accent. Danny Starks is a tall, slender-looking man; Robert Riley is short and medium-built, and Tim Moss is medium height and muscularly built. Among the group are Arnold Taylor, the company owner, and project manager, Shannon Hill. When they approach the boat dock, Victor is waiting to greet them. They toss him the ropes, Victor ties the boats to the pier, and the men step out onto the dock.

"Welcome back, guys, did you get the rock samples you needed?"

Danny replies, "Yes, Victor, we got some good samples and one more thing. Look at what Ralu found. A bag with a lamp inside."

Victor looks down at the bag as Ralu takes the lamp out.

"Hey, I recognize that bag. It's the one Mr. Perkins lost about four years ago."

Ralu says, "Mr. Perkins? Who is he?"

"Mr. Perkins is an old friend of my boss. He went fishing on one of our boats about four years ago. He said the bag accidentally fell off the boat, and it contained a rod and reel he just purchased."

Ralu replies, "The only thing that was in this bag was this lamp, and it was weighed down with four bricks."

Victor scratches his head in disbelief. "I know it's been a while since I saw that bag, but I could swear that this is the same one."

THE SACRED LAMP — 239

Arnold says, "Someone wanted to get rid of it because they put bricks inside, making sure it sunk to the bottom. But why would anyone want to get rid of a lamp so bad that they'd bury it on the ocean floor?"

Robert replies, "Good question, unless it was involved in some foul play."

Ralu begins wiping the lamp off with a towel and carefully examines it.

Ralu replies, "This is amazing! The lamp isn't even wet, and it looks new. Take a look at the angel engraved on the front of it. Have you ever seen such a lamp like this before?"

Robert replies, "No, I haven't. What a beautiful-looking lamp. Are there any identifying labels, such as a manufacturer's label?"

Ralu says, "No, but there's a label on the base of the lamp. It's a QR code label. The same type we put on our rock samples to identify them. I may sound a little crazy, but I'm interested in getting it back to the hotel to see if it works."

"Come on, guys, let's head back," says Arnold.

The group walks to the parking lot, gets into a blue cargo van displaying the name Taylor Research Group on its side, and waves goodbye to Victor.

————————————

Ralu and Danny share a room at the Quality Inn Hotel in Bradenton. Danny sits at a table examining his rock samples, and Ralu is sitting across from him at another table, studying the lamp.

"Well, Danny, let's see if this baby works."

Ralu removes a bulb from the desk, puts it into the lamp, and turns the switch.

"Fantastic, Danny! The lamp works!"

"How about that, Ralu? That must be a special lamp. What are you going to do with it?"

"My dad has been attending a conference in Tampa and is going to visit me in the morning. I'll give it to him. He's an antique collector."

"Didn't you say that your dad was a hospital administrator somewhere in Africa?"

"You're correct. The hospital is Kamuzu Central Hospital in Lilongwe, Malawi. The country borders Mozambique and Zambia and is our native country. My father attended medical school at Harvard University in a special student exchange program some years ago. With his education and experience, my father could have worked at any hospital in the world, but he chose Kamuzu Hospital, located in an extremely poverty-stricken area. He said that the people there needed his help."

"How is it, then, that you became an oceanographer?"

"I always loved the ocean, and I wanted to know everything about it. I've seen enough sickness and dying in my life, growing up in my country. All I wanted to do was to get as far away from that place as I could. In my senior year in high school, I got accepted at the University of Washington in Seattle in their oceanography program, and the rest is history."

"That was my passion, too, and I went to Hawaii Pacific University and have never regretted a moment of it."

"So here we are, Danny, pursuing our dreams."

Ralu stretches both of his arms out behind his head and yawns.

"Well, Danny, my father will be here in the morning, so let's get some sleep."

"I'm with you, Ralu. It has been a long day for both of us."

Danny walks over to his bed and lies down. Ralu turns the lamp off that he found, walks over, gets into his bed, and the two men drift off to sleep.

CHAPTER 23

The Discovery

Early the next morning, Ralu's father arrives at the hotel. He drives up in a rented late-model Jeep and parks in the parking lot. As he gets out of the jeep, Ralu walks up to meet him. Ralu's father, Dr. Kendall Nyondo, is in his late fifties, with a medium build and height and a dark complexion. He has short, black, wool-like hair and a strong South African accent. The two men embrace each other.

"Hey, Dad, good to see you."

"Hello, my son, good to see you as well. How are things going?"

"Good, Dad. Our company has a contract with a private geological firm to collect rock samples along the coast of Florida, and this is the area Arnold has chosen to begin our research. Come on in, Dad. Everyone is up and waiting to meet you."

The crew is in the lobby, preparing to leave, when Ralu walks up to the group and introduces his father. Everyone greets Dr. Nyondo with handshakes, and Arnold addresses him, "Dr. Nyondo, I must say, Ralu has been a great addition to our staff over the past six months."

"An oceanographer was always his first passion."

"Well, he made the right choice. It's been a pleasure meeting you, Dr. Nyondo. Ralu, why don't you take the rest of the day off and visit with your father?"

"Thanks, Arnold. I'll continue documenting the rest of the rock samples."

The group bids goodbye to Ralu and his father and exits the lobby.

"Hey, Dad, let's go to my room. I have something to show you."

The two men exit the lobby and walk down the corridor. Ralu opens the door to his room and directs his father to sit down on the chair at the table.

"Close your eyes, Dad." Ralu places the lamp on the table in front of his father. "Okay, Dad, open your eyes."

Dr. Nyondo opens his eyes and is fascinated when he sees the lamp. "Wow! What a beautiful-looking lamp, and the engraved image of the angel on it is magnificent! Son, where did you get such a lamp?"

"I found it on the bottom of the ocean floor yesterday when we were out searching for rock samples."

"Son, it must have been thrown overboard off of a boat or ship by mistake. I don't believe it was on the ocean floor as a result of an old shipwreck because the lamp doesn't appear to be that old. I wonder how it got there?"

"Dad, you may find this hard to believe, but the lamp was in a nylon bag weighed down with four bricks. It appeared someone was trying to get rid of it, and oddly enough, it doesn't appear to be affected by the water because it still works."

Dr. Nyondo looks puzzled. "Interesting. It doesn't make any sense, at least not to us, but I'm sure it does to someone else."

"The manager of the boat rental said a friend of his boss had lost a bag that looked like this one about four years ago."

"Did he say anything else?"

"The man claimed he had a new rod and reel in the bag, and it accidentally fell overboard."

"Did he tell you the name of the man who lost the bag?"

"He just said his name was Mr. Perkins."

"I wonder what Mr. Perkins had in mind?"

"Dad, look at the base of the lamp; it has a QR code label on the bottom. We use QR code labels to identify our rock samples. We can store information such as the date and time we collected samples and the location of the discovery. I waited until you got here before doing any further research on the lamp."

Ralu grabs his phone and tells his father to hold the lamp with the base facing him so he can take a picture of the QR code label. Ralu takes a snapshot, and an image is displayed. He touches the image, and a picture of the lamp appears with its description, which he reads aloud.

"A gift from an angel. This lamp was made by a young boy who stayed in a homeless shelter in Detroit, Michigan, in the early nineteen nineties. Rumors circulated that the young boy was an angel, and he gave this lamp to the shelter for helping him. He was never seen again, and his whereabouts are unknown to this day."

"What an amazing story, Ralu. Is there any more information?"

"There's a web address."

Ralu clicks on the link, and the website for Don's Treasure Chest appears. Ralu reads the company's name and the city location of the business out to his father. "Don's Treasure Chest in Grosse Pointe, Michigan. Dad, write this phone number down."

Dr. Nyondo takes an ink pen out of his shirt pocket, picks up the stationary lying on the table, and writes down the phone number given to him by Ralu.

"Well, Dad, since I gave the lamp to you, I'll give you the honor of calling Don's Treasure Chest to find out more information about the lamp. You can use my laptop on the table to do any additional research."

"Son, it will be my pleasure. I can't wait to get some background information on the lamp."

"Dad, I have some things to check on. I'll see you in a bit."

Ralu opens the door and exits into the hallway.

––––––––––––––

Dr. Nyondo takes his cell phone out of his sport jacket and dials Don's Treasure Chest. After two rings, Cheryl, Don's assistant, answers the phone.

"Don's Treasure Chest."

"Yes, my name is Dr. Kendall Nyondo, and I have a lamp containing your QR code label. It may have been purchased at your store a while ago."

"Well, if it has our QR code label on it, it's probably an item that we sold to someone."

"Yes, of course. I'm calling to inquire about its origin because it has no manufacturer's label."

"Well, Dr. umm"—Cheryl is trying to remember his last name—"Dr. Nay."

"It's Dr. Nyondo."

"I'm sorry, Dr. Nyondo, if it doesn't have a manufacturers label on it, there's probably not much we can tell you."

"It does, however, make mention on your website that the lamp has a connection to a boy who stayed in a homeless shelter, and it has the image of an angel engraved on it."

"Just a minute, Dr. Nyondo, I'll be right back."

Cheryl returns after about two minutes.

"Hello, Dr. Nyondo, I do remember that lamp, and it did have an image of an angel."

"Yes! Yes! That is correct!"

"You'll have to speak with Mr. Mason, the owner. He'll be able to provide you with more information. Hold on, and I'll connect you."

A slight pause, and Don answers the phone. "This is Don. What can I do for you, Doc?"

"Yes, Mr. Mason, I was inquiring about a lamp that was purchased in your shop."

"The lamp with the angel on the front?"

"Yes, Mr. Mason, that is the one."

"Hmm, how did you get your hands on that lamp?"

"It's a long story, Mr. Mason, and why do you still have it featured on your website since it's no longer part of your inventory?"

"It's a unique item and eye-catching to everyone who visits my website. You know how remarkable it is since you have it in your possession, Doc. I continued featuring it because it shows people the type of quality merchandise I specialize in selling to my customers. By the way, Doc, a young lady paid me twenty-five-hundred dollars for that lamp."

"She obviously has a special talent for recognizing beauty and value, and you're absolutely right, Mr. Mason, it's quite a remarkable-looking lamp."

Don pauses for a moment and rubs his forehead. "If I remember correctly, she bought it for her uncle's office and left here traveling to Fishers, Indiana, to some home health care facility her mother owned. That's where all that miracle bull was supposed to have taken place."

"Miracle, I don't understand."

"Come on, where you been, Doc? About four years ago, a group of people in a home health care facility in Fishers, Indiana, was supposed to be miraculously healed. It was all over the news."

"Oh yes, I did read an article about it, but I was out of the country, and I heard it ended up just being a hoax."

"Now you're talking, Doc. A hoax is all it was."

"I'm trying to get some background information about the lamp and thought you'd be able to help me since it was sold in your shop."

"Well, Doc, I bought the lamp from an ex-neighbor of mine name Ryan Henning about four years ago. Ryan was a lawyer and moved to Virginia to work for a law firm. I don't know the name of the firm, but you can look his name up on Google."

"Any idea what part of Virginia he may have moved to?"

"I believe it was Stone Ridge, Virginia. By the way, he had a mother-in-law that had brain cancer, and one morning she woke up and boom! It was gone. What a crock of bull."

"Did her doctor ever confirm that she had brain cancer, because brain tumors don't just disappear without being surgically removed."

"All I can tell you, Doc, is that according to Ryan, she had a tumor, and it disappeared. Excuse my language, Doc, because there's bullshit, and there's bullshit, but this is the whole stockyard wrapped up into one." Don is chuckling.

"The description about the lamp stated the boy was an angel. Where did that come from?"

"Well, Doc"— Don chuckles sheepishly—"I kinda threw the angel part in myself. You know, tying the boy in with being an angel added a little mystery to the lamp, Doc."

"And I also suppose increased the value of the lamp as well, Mr. Mason?"

Don is smiling. "It's all about business, Doc, and if you're interested in some quality merchandise, check out my inventory online. I'll give you a great deal."

"Thank you, Mr. Mason; I'll keep that in mind."

"You said you sold it to a lady. Do you have any information on where I might contact her?"

"I have her business card on file. Hold on, Doc, let me get it."

Don returns a short time later. "Her name is Melanie Jenkins of Jenkins Interior and Designs. She bought the lamp for her uncle's office. I don't know if she's still in business because I haven't heard any more from her since she bought the lamp. If you have a pen and paper to write on, I'll give you her phone number."

"Yes, I'm ready, Mr. Mason."

Don gives Dr. Nyondo Melanie's phone number.

"Hey, Doc, if you get a hold of her, tell her I said hello."

"I'll be sure to tell her that you asked about her, and thank you, Mr. Mason, you've been extremely helpful. One last thing, you wouldn't happen to know her uncle's name, would you?"

"Sure, I wrote his name on the back of her card. Let's see, his name is Jason Perkins. I think—"

"Thanks, Mr. Mason, for all your help. I must go now. Goodbye!"

Dr. Nyondo quickly hangs up the phone, and Don looks at his phone because of the abrupt ending.

"What in the hell got into him?"

———————

Dr. Nyondo hurries down the hallway. Ralu is walking toward the room, and when he sees Ralu, he begins speaking hysterically. "Ralu! Ralu!"

"Dad, what's all of the excitement about?"

"I think I found out who the person was that got rid of the lamp!"

"Who, Father? Who?"

"Doesn't matter right now until I can confirm a few things. I want to first speak with the original owner of the lamp. He's an attorney who lives in Stone Ridge, Virginia. He may help me put the pieces together about the mystery behind the lamp. I also need to contact Melanie Jenkins, who gave the lamp to her uncle, Jason Perkins. You said that Mr. Perkins is the person who the chartered boat manager claimed to have lost the bag containing the lamp. Ms. Jenkins may have information about its disappearance. Let me do more research, and I'll get back with you later."

CHAPTER 24

The Discovery

Dr. Nyondo surfs through Ralu's laptop and Google's Attorney Ryan Henning. He comes across the law firm of Lawson, Snyder, and Henning, located in Stone Ridge, Virginia. He writes down the phone number and dials it on his mobile phone. Diane, the receptionist, answers the phone.

"The law offices of Lawson, Snyder, and Henning. This is Diane speaking. How may I help you?"

"Good morning, Diane. My name is Dr. Kendall Nyondo, and I'm calling to speak with Attorney Ryan Henning concerning a personal matter."

"Is Attorney Henning expecting your call, Dr. Nyondo?"

"No, he isn't. This is the first time I have called his office, but tell him I won't take up much of his time."

"Hold on, Dr. Nyondo, and I'll see if he's available."

Diane puts Dr. Nyondo on hold and rings Ryan's extension, and he picks up.

"Yes, Diane."

"Attorney Henning, there's a Dr. Nyondo on the phone for you. He says he'd like to speak with you and won't take up much of your time."

"Dr. Nyondo. Never heard of him. Put him on."

Diane takes Dr. Nyondo off hold and tells him she's going to transfer him, and after a couple of seconds of silence, Ryan answers the phone.

"Attorney Henning speaking. How may I help you, Dr. Nyondo?"

"Thank you for taking my call, Attorney Henning. I just spoke with Mr. Mason, the owner of Don's Treasure Chest in Grosse Pointe,

Michigan, about a lamp that I received as a gift. He told me he'd purchased the lamp from you about four years ago."

"You got to be kidding me. How's ole Don doing?"

"He seems to be okay, full of jokes."

Ryan is laughing. "Still ole Don. I haven't seen that lamp since I sold it to Don, so why are you contacting me?"

"My son is an oceanographer and professional scuba diver and found the lamp a couple of days ago along the Florida coast, submerged on the ocean floor. The lamp was in a nylon bag wrapped in plastic, and there were four bricks weighing it down. Someone was obviously trying to get rid of the lamp. Do you have any idea why someone would want to dispose of such a lamp, Attorney Henning?"

Ryan pauses and takes a deep breath before answering.

"Dr. Nyondo, I'll be free around eight o'clock this evening. Give me a number where I can call you back."

"Certainly, Attorney Henning."

Ryan writes down the number, and the two of them hang up. Dr. Nyondo lies back in his chair as Ralu walks into the room.

"Hey, Dad, the guys are back and want us to join them for dinner at the Seafood House. Have any luck finding information about the lamp?"

"Yes, I did, Son. The original owner, who sold it to Don's Treasure Chest, is going to call me back at eight o'clock this evening."

"Great news, Dad. Come on, let's go and eat. We'll be back before then."

The two of them exit the room, and Ralu closes the door behind him.

Dr. Nyondo has reserved a room of his own at the hotel and sits back in the recliner waiting for Ryan to call, and at eight-fifteen, Dr. Nyondo's cell phone rings.

"Hello."

"Hello, Dr. Nyondo, this is Attorney Henning calling you back."

"Thank you, Attorney Henning, I appreciate the callback."

"You know, Dr. Nyondo, I've been thinking about our earlier conversation because I often wondered what happened to that lamp."

"Why is that, Attorney Henning? Is there more about the lamp that hasn't been told? The description on Mr. Mason's website says the lamp belonged to a homeless boy who gave it to a shelter as a gift for allowing him to stay there. It also stated that the boy was an angel." Dr. Nyondo chuckles as he continues, "Mr. Mason admitted that he added the part about the angel."

"Why doesn't that surprise me? The part about the boy living in a shelter was true. Dr. Nyondo, this is like déjà vu all over again. I remember telling this story to ole Don Mason four years ago when I sold him the lamp. My father was given the lamp as a birthday gift from a coworker named Ruben Polanski in the early nineties. Mr. Polanski's son gave him the lamp. His son, Joey, stayed in a homeless shelter at the time, and a boy he met there gave it to the shelter as a gift for allowing him to stay there. Joey said the woman who managed the shelter discarded the lamp into the dumpster behind the building, and he fished it out and took it home to his father."

"Interesting, Attorney Henning, but why was Mr. Polanski's son in a shelter?"

"Joey had been on drugs and slept in and out of shelters and abandoned houses and wanted his father to have the lamp, so he gave it to him. Mr. Polanski was skeptical about taking it because he thought it might have been stolen, but later found out that Joey had told the truth about how he acquired the lamp, and later Mr. Polanski gave it to my father as a birthday present. The young boy who made the lamp disappeared and was never seen or heard from again, and because of the mystery surrounding the lamp, my father kept it stored away."

"Wow, that's quite a story. Is there anything else that you can remember about the lamp?"

"About four and a half years ago, my mother-in-law was diagnosed with brain cancer and was given just a few months to live. You're a doctor, what do you know about brain cancer?"

"I know it's a terrible thing to have with a low survival rate. I'm a general practitioner and have worked in hospital emergency rooms most of my career and have diagnosed several patients who have had early stages of brain tumors."

"Then you know, Dr. Nyondo, that brain tumors don't just disappear overnight."

"No, Attorney Henning, they don't."

"Well, it did in the case of my mother-in-law, and that brings me back to the lamp. The morning that my mother-in-law's brain tumor miraculously disappeared, at about two o'clock that morning, I heard voices coming from her room. When I went to check on her, I saw a light glowing beneath her bedroom door, and when I opened it, she was fast asleep, and the light had extinguished."

"Interesting, Attorney Henning, but what does this have to do with the lamp?"

"The lamp was in my son's room. I had given it to him as a gift after his grandfather died. In fact, I had given it to him the day before my mother-in-law made a full recovery. A few days after things had quieted down, my son wanted to get rid of the lamp."

"Yes, go on, Attorney Henning."

"My son, Luke, told me that he also heard voices coming from his grandmother's room that same morning and said that the lamp in his room was off. Immediately after the voices stopped, the base of his lamp started glowing, and the lamp came back on. He was afraid to tell me because he thought I wouldn't believe him. I became upset with him when he didn't want to keep his grandfather's lamp, and that's when he told me what happened and that he didn't want the lamp anymore."

"Do you believe the lamp had something to do with your mother-in-law's recovery?"

"Over the past four years, I wondered that myself, Dr. Nyondo, and to be truthful, I just don't know, and maybe that's the way I'd like to leave it."

"I understand, and thank you for sharing that information with me."

"You're welcome, Dr. Nyondo, so what's your next move?"

"Well, Attorney Henning, I found the original owner of the lamp, which is you. Now I want to speak with the person who purchased the lamp from Mr. Mason, a Ms. Melanie Jenkins."

"Now that you know where the lamp came from, why do you need to speak with her?"

"The lady who purchased the lamp took it to Fishers, Indiana, to her mother's health care facility. That's where all that mysterious healing took place. It was The Gold Diamond Health Care Facility. I need to know if there was a connection with the lamp and the miraculous events that took place there."

"If my memory serves me correctly, Dr. Nyondo, I believe the conclusion was that it was just a prank, a publicity stunt. So why are you so concerned about what happened over four years ago, and if it took place, it apparently hasn't happened again, so what's your point?"

"That may be the case, Attorney Henning, but why would the lamp end up buried on the ocean floor off the coast of Florida, and I can hear it in your voice that you believe the lamp may have played a part in the disappearance of your mother-in-law's brain tumor. I also believe that someone discovered the connection between the lamp and the healings and tried to get rid of it, and if so, I need to find out why."

"Do you really think there's a connection?"

"You had the lamp when your mother-in-law made a miraculous recovery, and I believe that the health care facility in Fishers possessed the lamp when their patients made a supernatural recovery. I just have to prove it. Attorney Henning, I'm a hospital administrator in a third-world country, and my hospital is flooded with hundreds of new patients every day. If this lamp has the power of healing, it is from God and should be used to heal the sick and afflicted, not only in my hospital but in hospitals around the world."

"That would be quite incredible. Excuse me, Dr. Nyondo, but my wife is calling me on the other line, so I must be going. I wish you the best of luck. Let me know how things turn out."

"I will, Attorney Henning, and thanks for all your help. Goodbye."

"Goodbye, Dr. Nyondo."

There's a knock on the door, and. Dr. Nyondo opens it and sees Ralu standing there.

"Come on in, Son."

"I can't stay long, Dad. Arnold wants to meet with the group in about ten minutes to go over tomorrow's assignments. Did you get in contact with the original owner?"

"Yes, I did, Son, but I'll fill you in on more of the details in the morning after I've spoken with Ms. Jenkins. For now, you have a meeting to attend, and I'm tired, so I'll say goodnight, Son."

Ralu tells his father goodnight and leaves the room.

CHAPTER 25

The Discovery

T he following morning, Dr. Nyondo and Ralu finish eating breakfast in the hotel restaurant, and Dr. Nyondo returns to his room to call Melanie Jenkins on his mobile phone. He sits down at the table and dials the number that Don gave him yesterday, and Ashley, Melanie's receptionist, answers the phone.

"Jenkins Interior and Designs."

"Good morning, my name is Dr. Kendall Nyondo, and I'd like to speak with Ms. Melanie Jenkins."

"Certainly, Dr. Nyondo. I'll see if she's available."

Melanie's voice is heard on the other end of the phone while sitting at her desk. "Hello Dr. Nyondo, this is Melanie. We can arrange a beautiful setting for your office that will be aesthetically pleasing and comfortable for your patients."

"Nice introduction, and I'm sold, Ms. Jenkins. If I ever need to upgrade my office, I'll be sure to contact you."

"Oh, so this isn't a business call?"

"Not today, but tomorrow it could very well be."

Both are slightly chuckling.

"Ms. Jenkins, I received a gift from my son. It was a lamp that may have once been in your possession. I spoke with Don Mason, the owner of a resale shop in Grosse Pointe, Michigan, and he told me that you'd purchased it from him about four years ago."

"You said a lamp, Dr. Nyondo? I've purchased hundreds of items over the years, and you expect me to remember the purchase of a lamp?"

"This was a unique lamp, Ms. Jenkins. It had an image of an angel engraved on it."

Melanie is pondering her thoughts for a moment.

"An angel, yes, I do remember. I purchased it about four or five years ago. I bought it as a gift for my uncle, and the lamp was destroyed in a fire."

"A fire, you say, Ms. Jenkins?"

"Yes, Dr. Nyondo. It was a desk lamp in my uncle's office. One afternoon while we were having lunch together in the cafeteria, my cousin's cat was left in the office and knocked over the candle on his desk, causing a fire. The lamp was destroyed, so why are you asking me about a lamp that no longer exist?"

"Ms. Jenkins, what if I told you I had such a lamp in my possession?"

"I'd say you're wasting my time. There must be other lamps made with the image of an angel on them."

"But only one was sold at Don's Treasure Chest, and it was sold to you. It had a QR code label on the base of the lamp. That's how I was able to trace it back to Don's Treasure Chest."

"That's impossible. I saw the lamp after the fire, and it was badly burnt."

"When you say badly burnt, Ms. Jenkins, was it completely consumed?"

"I can't remember, but the insurance company gave me full replacement value."

"How was the lamp disposed?"

"My uncle disposed of the lamp, or what was left of it. You may have heard of my uncle; he's been in the news all week. He just returned from Boston, after launching the opening of our fifteenth Gold Diamond Health Care Facility."

"Would that be Mr. Perkins, Ms. Jenkins?"

"Yes, Dr. Nyondo, Mr. Jason Perkins."

"Where is your uncle's office located?"

"In Fishers, Indiana, at our first facility, where it all started. Do you know my uncle?"

"No, but I plan to, and thank you for your time."

"You're quite welcome, and don't forget me when it's time to up-grade your office."

"I won't, Ms. Jenkins, and goodbye."

"Goodbye, Dr. Nyondo."

Dr. Nyondo scrolls down his contact list until he sees the name Azilia Kreta. Azilia has a distinctive South African accent and is a tall, slender woman, in her mid-twenties, with a dark brown complexion. She's a travel agent at Malawi Grand Tours in Lilongwe and exuberantly answers the phone when she recognizes that Dr. Nyondo is calling.

"Dr. Nyondo, how are you? When are you coming back home? We miss you."

"Soon, I hope, and I miss everyone as well. I just have a couple of business matters to complete. Azilia, I need you to schedule me a flight out to the Indianapolis International Airport in Indiana from Sarasota, Bradenton International Airport, here in Florida. I need a flight out early tomorrow morning."

"Okay, Dr. Nyondo, I'll schedule the flight when we hang up, and I'll give you a callback. Will there be anything else?"

"Yes, I'll also be needing a rental car when I get to Indianapolis. I'll be traveling alone, so a smaller car will be just fine."

"Sounds good, Dr. Nyondo, you'll be hearing back from me shortly."

Dr. Nyondo knocks on Ralu's door, and he opens it.

"Hey, Dad, any new developments?"

"Ralu, I'm going to fly out to Indiana. I have all the pieces in place, and I've located Mr. Jason Perkins. He holds the key to the entire mys-tery of the lamp. He's also the administrator of the facility in Fishers, where all those miraculous healings took place."

"Dad, I thought you told me just a couple of days ago that it was probably just a hoax?"

"According to the news and media reports, that's what their concluding arguments were, but as I began putting the final pieces together, I'm convinced that this has been just one big cover-up, and I think I can prove it."

"You better be careful, Dad. Do you want me to go with you?"

"No, Ralu, you're here on a contractual assignment. I'll be okay. Just wait to hear from me. I've contacted Azilia, and she's booking me a flight out in the morning, so let me get back to my room and wait for her call."

Dr. Nyondo exits Ralu's room and heads down the hallway. He opens the door to his room and sits back in his recliner, and his phone rings.

"Yes, Azilia."

"Dr. Nyondo, you're all set. Your flight leaves at nine fifteen tomorrow morning, and you'll arrive in Indianapolis at eleven forty-five. You'll be on United Airlines Flight 274, and you can go to the will call window to pick up your ticket. When you arrive in Indianapolis, go to Budget Car Rental to pick up your vehicle. Is there anything else?"

"No, no, Azilia, that is everything. You're always on top of things, and thanks. By the way, I'll be calling you from Indiana in a day or two to book me a flight back to Kamuzu International Airport."

"Very good, Dr. Nyondo. I'll be here waiting for your call. Goodbye, Dr. Nyondo, and have a safe and pleasant trip."

"Goodbye, Azilia, and thank you."

They hang up, and Dr. Nyondo lies back in his recliner, takes a deep breath, and closes his eyes.

———————

Dr. Nyondo has boarded Flight 274 and has a window seat three rows back from the front. The Fasten Seat Belt sign has just gone off, and an announcement made that food and beverages are available for purchase. As passengers unfasten their seatbelts, the captain makes this announcement. "Good morning, everyone. This is Captain Melvin Stein speaking. I want to welcome you aboard Flight 274 to Indianapolis, Indiana. We're currently cruising at an altitude of 33,000 feet and at an airspeed of 400 miles per hour. The time is nine twenty-seven a.m., and the weather looks good. We're expecting to land at Indiana International Airport at approximately eleven forty-five a.m. as scheduled. Enjoy the flight, and thank you for choosing United Airlines."

Dr. Nyondo notices that a middle-aged man sitting in the aisle seat to his left is quite talkative and extremely annoying. The woman seated in the middle between them doesn't seem quite interested in his conversation but humors him with small talk, obviously hoping that it will get him to quiet down. To make matters worse, he orders three bottles of whiskey from the stewardess's beverage cart, but when Dr. Nyondo tries to tune him out, the conversation becomes quite interesting.

"My name is Bob Shorter. I hope I'm not annoying you too much, madam. My wife says I talk too much, but I always do when I get a little nervous. I've never been to Indianapolis, or Indiana, for that matter. That's why I'm a little on edge. I must attend a business meeting in downtown Indianapolis later this afternoon. I lived in Florida all my life and was born in Miami. How about you?"

The woman, in her mid-fifties, reluctantly replies, "I'm from Fishers, Indiana."

Dr. Nyondo slowly opens his eyes and focuses his attention on the conversation.

"Let's see Fishers, Fishers. Why does Fishers sound familiar to me? Oh, I know! About five years ago, there was a health care facility in Fishers where people were supposedly healed. It was all on the news and the Internet. So your city became famous because of that incident, Ms. hmm . . ."

The subject seems to spark the woman's attention, and she speaks more openly to Bob's comments. "Ms. Shaw, Mr. Shorter, and, yes, that incident did bring the city a great deal of attention."

"Was all of that true, Ms. Shaw; I never heard any more about it?"

"I can't say for sure, Mr. Shorter, but if it was true, it only happened to a few people, and that was the end of it. A friend of my mother claims that her beautician's cousin was amongst that group, but she never saw her cousin again, after the commotion had died down."

"So she doesn't know whether her cousin made a full recovery or not?"

"I guess not. The word was that all the people involved were moved out of the state and paid to keep quiet. Imagine that, Mr. Shorter."

"What do you mean, Ms. Shaw?"

"Those people were already wealthy, so if they were healed, they got their health back, became wealthier, and are now living *The Life of Riley* on some luxurious island. We, on the other hand, are stuck out here financially challenged, hurting and in the middle of nowhere. It just doesn't seem quite fair."

Speaking in a calmer, more settled voice, Bob says, "I see what you mean, Ms. Shaw, and I agree."

The thought of such a scenario being real seems to calm Bob down, and he quietly sits back in his seat. It's apparent he's disturbed by the notion that he doesn't belong to that elite group. Not that he had any health issues to be concerned about, but to belong in the category of the wealthy is what he wanted most. As the conversation ends, Dr. Nyondo lies back in his seat, closes his eyes, and thinks to himself, *Well, Ms. Shaw, you just gave me another piece to the puzzle. All of the people have been conveniently relocated, out of sight, out of mind.*

CHAPTER 26

The Discovery

D r. Nyondo sits in his rental car and types in The Gold Diamond Health Care Facility's destination address on the car's navigation system. The route indicates that it will take him about forty-five minutes to drive to the facility, making his destination arrival time at about one forty p.m. He begins heading northeast on Colonel H. Weir Cook Memorial Drive and quickly merges into a sea of commuting traffic, heading to and from Indianapolis International Airport. After experiencing a couple of traffic delays, Dr. Nyondo drives up to the facility's front gate. He focuses his attention on the well-designed marque sign on the front of the building reading, *The Gold Diamond Health Care Facility / Fishers, Indiana*. A young woman sits in the security guard booth and motions for him to stop.

"Hello, sir, who are you here to see?"

"My name is Dr. Kendall Nyondo, and I'm here to see Mr. Jason Perkins."

"Is Mr. Perkins expecting you?"

Dr. Nyondo looks intently into the security guard's eyes.

"Yes, I believe so."

The security guard pauses for a moment and stares at Dr. Nyondo before speaking.

"Sign your name here on the visitor's login sheet and park your car over there in the parking lot. When you enter the facility, you must check-in at the front desk."

Dr. Nyondo nods his head and smiles. "Thank you."

Dr. Nyondo, carrying a small white gift bag, enters the facility and walks up to the front desk. A woman in her late forties is sitting behind the counter and greets him. "Good afternoon, sir. How may I help you?"

"My name is Dr. Kendall Nyondo, and I'm here to see Mr. Jason Perkins."

"Certainly, Dr. Nyondo. Do you have an appointment with Mr. Perkins?"

"No, I don't, but I have some important information that he'll want to hear."

"I'm sorry, Dr. Nymble."

Dr. Nyondo politely corrects her. "It's Dr. Nyondo."

"Well, like I said, Doctor, unless you have an appointment—" The attendant quickly stops talking as Jason walks past the information counter.

"Excuse me, Mr. Perkins!"

Jason walks over to the information desk.

"Mr. Perkins, the doctor here is wanting to speak with you."

"Mr. Perkins, my name is Dr. Kendall Nyondo."

"Dr. Nyondo, I don't recall ever meeting or speaking with you before."

"No, Mr. Perkins, we've never met."

"Well, Dr. Nyondo, it's two fifteen. If we had a two o'clock appointment, you're late. On the other hand, if we didn't, you must be lobbying for one of your patients to live in one of our health care facilities. If that's the case, you're late again. All our facilities are filled, including our newest facility in Boston. So with that said, Dr. Nyondo, if you have any more to discuss, have the front desk connect you to my secretary to schedule an appointment."

"I don't need an appointment, Mr. Perkins, for what I'm about to say."

"Is that so?"

"What do you know about a lamp with the image of an angel on it, Mr. Perkins?"

Jason pauses a moment before answering. "I don't, Dr. Nyondo."

"Didn't your niece, Melanie, give you such a lamp about four years ago?"

"Since you know so much, Dr. Nyondo, you should also know that the lamp was consumed in a fire."

Jason motions toward James, his security guard, standing about five feet away.

"James, please escort Dr. Nyondo to the exit doors and make sure that he's not allowed on the property anymore."

"Yes, sir, Mr. Perkins."

Jason turns toward Dr. Nyondo. "Enjoy the rest of your day, Doctor."

Dr. Nyondo stares into Jason's eyes and speaks before the guard has time to escort him out.

"You ever charter a boat off the coast of Bradenton, Florida, Mr. Perkins? Victor said you did, about four years ago. You know Victor, Mr. Perkins. He's the man who manages your friend's charter boat company in Bradenton, Florida."

Jason pauses and motions to James to let him pass through. Looking nervously at Dr. Nyondo, Jason walks up to him. "Follow me, Dr. Nyondo."

Jason escorts Dr. Nyondo to his office and shuts the door behind him, and locks it. He tells Dr. Nyondo to sit on the opposite side of his desk. He picks up the phone and dials a three-digit number.

"Jennifer, don't send any calls through to my office until I instruct you otherwise."

Jason sits down in his chair, opens the bottom right drawer of his desk, and takes out a brown-colored prescription bottle, a drinking glass, and a bottle of water. Dr. Nyondo watches as Jason pours water from the bottle into the drinking glass and removes two pills from the prescription bottle. Jason puts the pills into his mouth with a sip of water and swallows them. Jason takes a bottle of brandy from his drawer along with a shot glass and fills the glass with brandy. He chugs down the alcohol as Dr. Nyondo picks up the prescription bottle and examines the label.

"Xanax and alcohol, Mr. Perkins, are bad combinations."

"Pain and suffering are bad combinations, Dr. Nyondo, but they exist."

"Just as true is the lamp that exists which you claimed was destroyed in a fire."

"Are you prepared to provide proof of your accusation, Doctor?"

Dr. Nyondo reaches into the white bag sitting on the floor next to him and takes out a black nylon bag.

"Do you recognize this bag, Mr. Perkins?"

Jason looks frantically at the bag and is visibly upset, and begins to stutter.

"I don't know. I mean, I can't say that I do."

"Sure you do, Mr. Perkins. It's the same bag that you lost, remember? You told Victor that you had a new rod and reel inside of the bag, and when you returned without it, you said the bag had accidentally fallen overboard. Shall I go on?"

Jason begins to stutter more profoundly in his speech, with his head turned down.

"I, I don't know what to say."

"My son found the bag on the ocean floor a few miles off Bradenton, Florida, weighed down with bricks."

Jason looks at Dr. Nyondo in disbelief.

"And you know what was in the bag, Mr. Perkins?"

Jason looks at Dr. Nyondo with an intense but calm stare as Dr. Nyondo takes out his cell phone and shows an image of the lamp to Jason. Dr. Nyondo is speaking in a loud, stern tone of voice.

"This lamp, Mr. Perkins! The lamp you threw into the ocean and tried to destroy!"

Jason places his left forearm on his head and puts his head down on the desk as Dr. Nyondo continues.

"You found out that it had the power of God to heal the sick and afflicted, but instead of sharing it with the world as God intended, you tried to destroy it for your own personal gain!"

Jason looks up as if in a daze at the ceiling's left corner as tears begin rolling down his face. Jason's voice trembles, recalling the events of his actions.

"Yes, Dr. Nyondo, I dumped the lamp into the ocean. I had no choice."

"No choice, Mr. Perkins!"

"People would have fought each other to control the power of the lamp, and it just wouldn't work out!"

"How did you discover that the power was in the lamp, Mr. Perkins?"

Still looking off in the distance, reliving the scene in his head, Jason continues recalling the events to Dr. Nyondo.

"When the second group arrived, everyone was on alert. I had planned to stay at the facility the entire evening of their first overnight stay. The only light in my office was that of the lamp which was on my desk. Around two a.m. that morning, I had fallen asleep in my chair and was awakened by the lamp because the base of it was glowing, and then it went out. I inspected the lamp with a flashlight, thinking that the bulb must have blown out, but when I looked at it, I noticed that the image of the angel on the lamp was gone."

"What did you do then, Mr. Perkins?"

"I ran upstairs to check the residents on the second floor, and when I arrived, the nursing staff and I heard voices from the residents' rooms, and we saw a light shining beneath their bedroom doors. I returned to my office, only to find out that the lamp was back on, and the angel had reappeared on the lamp. I knew then that the power was in the lamp."

Dr. Nyondo stands up from his chair and leans over the desk addressing Jason. "So, Mr. Perkins, by getting rid of the lamp, the healing ceased, and your facilities have flourished. Those people who were healed have conveniently disappeared, probably living on some private island, courtesy of the corporation."

"I knew the public would anticipate it happening again, which would allow us unlimited growth."

Dr. Nyondo leans over the desk again to address Jason. "You ought to be ashamed of yourself, Mr. Perkins! You need to ask God for forgiveness!"

Jason looks up at Dr. Nyondo and begins crying profusely and speaking louder. "God has already punished me! I lost my daughter, my ten-year-old daughter, Celeste, two years ago!"

"I'm sorry to hear about your daughter, Mr. Perkins."

Jason continues crying and speaking uncontrollably. "She had brain cancer! And I got rid of the only thing that could have saved her!"

Jason picks up the picture on his desk and brings it firmly into his face. His crying is louder, attracting James, the security guard, and causing staff members to knock on the door to gain entrance. Dr. Nyondo walks over to the door and opens it, and James rushes in with his gun drawn. He looks at Dr. Nyondo and then over at Jason.

"What's going on, Mr. Perkins, are you all right?"

Dr. Nyondo calmly addresses James and the staff, "Mr. Perkins will be just fine, but for the moment, he's releasing a lot of guilt."

CHAPTER 27

The Discovery

D r. Nyondo hurries past the crowd and exits the building to the parking lot. He gets into his car and takes out his cell phone, and places a call. Azilia's voice comes echoing through his Bluetooth car speakers.

"Hi, Dr. Nyondo."

"Hello Azilia, I need you to book me on the next flight back to Malawi from Indianapolis International Airport."

"Oh, Dr. Nyondo, you're returning home, how nice."

"Yes, Azilia, and I'm so excited to be getting back."

"Very good, Dr. Nyondo. I'll check on the international flights leaving out of Indianapolis to Malawi and get right back with you."

"Fine, Azilia. I'll be waiting on your call."

Azilia hangs up, and Dr. Nyondo immediately takes a white writing tablet from the glove box and an ink pen out of his jacket pocket. He writes on the pad, *Call Nurse Zane, to make a mandatory meeting for everyone ASAP*. He drives out of the parking lot and heads back out to the airport.

After a forty-minute drive, Dr. Nyondo pulls into the Crowne Plaza Hotel parking lot, located at the Indianapolis Airport, and parks the car. Seconds later, his cell phone rings and activates the car's Bluetooth.

"Yes, Azilia."

"Dr. Nyondo, I booked you on American Airlines Flight 3326, leaving tomorrow morning, at seven fifty a.m. You'll arrive at Kamuzu International Airport on Friday morning at one forty-five p.m., and I'll have Akachi pick you up from the airport. Have a safe trip, Dr. Nyondo."

"Excellent, thanks, Azilia, and let's both pray for a safe return."

Dr. Nyondo enters the lobby of the hotel. Once checked in, he walks to his hotel room and slides his key into the slot to open the door. Dr. Nyondo places his luggage and the nylon bag onto the floor next to his bed. He takes the lamp out and puts it onto the table, and then calls his son. Ralu sits on the side of his bed and answers his cell phone.

"Hello, Dad!"

"Yes, Ralu, it's me. I made it here safely, and I found out all I needed to know about the lamp. I'm going back to Malawi in the morning, and I'm taking the lamp with me."

"Dad, what did you find out?"

"It's the lamp, Ralu! God has given it the power to heal, and I'm taking it back to the hospital."

"Dad, are you sure? What if it doesn't work?"

"Ralu, listen to me! It will work! Trust me! Jason Perkins tried to destroy the lamp, but because God has a purpose for it, he allowed you to find it. I have a hospital in Lilongwe, where hundreds of people are dying daily. I know that God wants me to take the lamp there so He can be glorified through the power of the Holy Spirit, by healing them all. Don't worry, Son; everything will be all right. I'll get back in touch with you once I return home."

"Okay, Father, but be careful!"

"I will, Son, and I'll talk with you soon."

They hang up, and Dr. Nyondo places a call to the Kamuzu Central Hospital in Lilongwe, Malawi. Nurse Zane Bella answers a tall, dark-skinned woman in her late thirties, wearing a white nursing hat and a white-and-red nursing uniform, sitting at the front desk. She's relieving the hospital phone attendant for a dinner break. Patients are moaning throughout the hospital ward while the footsteps of doctors and nurses scurry past the counter.

"Kamuzu Central Hospital."

"Hello, Nurse Zane, Dr. Nyondo."

"Oh, Dr. Nyondo! How are you, and when are you returning?"

"I'm fine. I'll be returning home on Friday afternoon, and I want you to have Nurse Ada set up a meeting with the entire staff shortly after I arrive. The meeting will be at three o'clock, and everyone must be there. This meeting is critical. In fact, it's the most important meeting of our entire lives. Do you understand?"

She looks puzzled. "Yes, Dr. Nyondo, I understand, and I will tell her."

"Fine, I'll see you on Friday. Goodbye, Nurse Zane."

"Goodbye, Dr. Nyondo."

The two of them hang up.

Dr. Nyondo has picked up his luggage and walks out in front of the Kamuzu International Airport in Lilongwe, Malawi. Akachi Balewa, Dr. Nyondo's aide, is sitting outside in a two-seated, old, uncovered Jeep when Dr. Nyondo walks up to him. Akachi is a tall, muscular man with a dark complexion, in his middle thirties and dressed in jungle fatigues. He's wearing a red ascot around his neck and a green beret on his head. They greet each other, and Akachi puts his bags into the Jeep, and they drive off toward the hospital. The paved street quickly turns into a rural road that is full of potholes that Akachi must avoid. Keeping his eyes on the road and speaking loud enough to overcome the engine's noise and the clattering of the Jeep over the rugged terrain, Akachi addresses Dr. Nyondo. "So, Dr. Nyondo, how was your trip?"

"It was a long and difficult journey, Akachi, but well worth it."

"Dr. Nyondo, have you brought back new medicine that will make our people well?"

Dr. Nyondo looks over at Akachi and smiles. "I did much better than that, Akachi; I brought back the medicine man himself, the Holy Spirit."

They continue down the road for another forty-five minutes before arriving at Kamuzu Central Hospital in the capital city of Lilongwe.

It's a four-story, one thousand-bed, public tertiary hospital that serves a population of nearly four million people. Dr. Nyondo and Akachi exit the Jeep, while the sounds of crying babies bellow from a couple of open windows. The smoldering heat of the mid-summer sun makes it difficult for them to keep the sweat from pouring down their faces. Dr. Nyondo instructs Akachi to grab his luggage, and he picks up the nylon bag containing the lamp.

Dr. Nyondo and Akachi enter the hospital, and staff members, immediately surround Dr. Nyondo, including about twelve doctors and twenty nurses. Nurses Zane and Ada rush up to Dr. Nyondo and hug him. Nurse Ada Awolowo is the head nurse. She's in her mid-forties, about five feet, four inches tall, stockily built with a light brown complexion, and is the first to address Dr. Nyondo.

"Dr. Nyondo, how are you, and how was your trip?"

"Extraordinary and well worth the trip."

A puzzled look comes across Nurse Ada's face.

Dr. Nyondo clarifies, "I mean in a good and fantastic way. Have you got things set up for the meeting?"

"Oh, yes, Dr. Nyondo. I have everyone attending. Everyone, including myself, is wondering what's going on?"

"You'll find out at the meeting, Nurse Ada. I'm going to my office, and I'll see everyone at three."

Dr. Nyondo unlocks his office door, takes the lamp out of the bag, places it under his desk, and waits for the arrival of his staff. Staff members begin filing outside of his office at three o'clock, and the hallway becomes exceedingly crowded. Dr. Nyondo instructs everyone to stand and remain silent as he proceeds to conduct the meeting. Dr. Nyondo slowly walks up to Nurse Ada.

"Nurse Ada, how many patients do we have now in the hospital?"

"We have twelve hundred and seventy-two patients."

"And how many patients do you anticipate won't live through the night?"

"I'd say around seventy-five patients, Dr. Nyondo."

"I want everyone to listen very carefully. I know we're understaffed, and everyone is working extremely hard. I'm going to give specific instructions that you must follow exactly as I state them. For those of you who will be working at one a.m. tomorrow morning, I want all of you to stand out front until I instruct you to come inside. The only two people that I want in the hospital are Nurses Ada and Zane. Even if you disagree with what I'm about to say, you must follow my instructions to a T."

Everyone has a puzzled look on their faces and begins silently speaking amongst themselves.

Dr. Nyondo continues, "Any patient, and I mean any patient that dies this evening is not to be moved until I tell you to do so."

The group becomes outraged and starts complaining. Nurse Ada replies, "Dr. Nyondo, you can't be serious. The bodies must be removed immediately!"

"Quiet! You must do exactly as I say."

"But, Dr. Nyondo, why are we doing this? It makes no sense!"

"You must trust me! I assure you, it will all make sense to you in the morning. When you're allowed to come back into the hospital, all the patients will be sleeping, and the hospital will be quiet, so don't be alarmed. I want everyone else back here at six a.m. tomorrow morning, and I will give you further instructions then. Let's all pray for our patients' speedy recovery."

Dr. Nyondo quickly turns around, walks into his office, and closes the door as the group becomes noisier and more confused.

Nurse Zane shakes her head. "Pray for their speedy recovery, has Dr. Nyondo lost his mind?"

Nurse Ada clasps her hands together. "Something has happened to Dr. Nyondo since he's been gone. He is not the same."

CHAPTER 28

The Discovery

D r. Nyondo sits at his desk, and he reaches down, picks up the lamp, and places it onto his desk. He plugs it into the electrical socket and turns it on. After staring at the angel for a moment, he slowly gets up from his chair and walks down to the hospital ward. Dr. Nyondo walks through and surveys the patients in each area. Many of them will die before sunrise, while others hang on, hoping to live another day. Moaning and crying from the pain of illnesses resonates throughout the complex, while dead bodies lay side by side covered with sheets. The stench of dead bodies is almost unbearable as Dr. Nyondo continues surveying the hospital ward.

Dr. Nyondo offers a kind word of encouragement to each patient he encounters before moving on to the next area. Nurses, Zane and Ada look at each other, shaking their heads, carefully observing Dr. Nyondo. He notices them watching and slowly walks over in their direction, and they quickly turn their heads as if they weren't paying him any attention.

"Well, ladies, I know you may think I'm crazy, but believe me, I am not."

As Dr. Nyondo walks away, they look at each other for a second time, shaking their heads again. Dr. Nyondo returns to his office, sits down in his chair, and stares at the lamp as he closes his eyes, bows his head, and begins speaking softly. "Dear Heavenly Father, I know you have brought this lamp to me to heal your people so that your name can be glorified. You have manifested your power into this lamp through the power of the Holy Spirit. I thank you, oh gracious God, for your Son,

Jesus Christ; our Lord and Savior, Who has died for our sins and has provided salvation to all who believe in Him. Amen."

Dr. Nyondo lies back in his chair and falls asleep. He wakes up after a long nap and takes a Bible out of his desk drawer. He begins silently reading a few scriptures before returning to the hospital ward for a final visit.

Dr. Nyondo greets Nurses Ada and Zane and addresses them. "What's the patient status, Nurse Ada?"

"Thirty-two patients have already died, Dr. Nyondo."

Nurse Zane speaks to Dr. Nyondo with a voice of disappointment. "Dr. Nyondo, we thought you'd bring back more medicine that—"

Nurse Zane's conversation is interrupted by voices at the far end of the ward. They look down toward that direction as light shines brightly on the far end of the hospital ward. Nurses Ada and Zane begin to walk in that direction when Dr. Nyondo stops them. Nurse Ada becomes frightened. "Dr. Nyondo, what is happening?"

"Come with me, ladies. Let's go outside and join the others."

They walk out of the hospital and join the other staff members who are standing outside talking. When they see them coming, everyone becomes silent, and Dr. Nyondo addresses the group. "How is everyone?"

The group hesitantly nods their heads.

"It's good that everyone is okay. When you return to the hospital, I want you to make sure that there is enough food prepared to feed everyone once they awake. As I stated earlier, everyone will be asleep, so don't be alarmed."

A young nurse assistant speaks out. "Dr. Nyondo, what do we do with the bodies of those who are dead?"

"When they awake and are hungry, feed them."

The group becomes outraged, claiming that Dr. Nyondo has lost his mind. Many of them are saying he's insane, while others stand in a state of shock.

Dr. Nyondo is speaking in a loud voice. "If any of you have faith in the power of the Holy Spirit, then stay! For those of you who do not, then you're free to leave! I'll be in my office, and we will come together after sunrise. Until then, stay calm and work together for the benefit of the patients. For that has always been our mission."

Dr. Nyondo leaves to go back to his office, with the group in an uproar. When he arrives back, he sees that the lamp is off and discovers that the image of the angel is gone. Dr. Nyondo smiles while silently saying to himself, "Praise the name of Jesus," and sits back in his chair and falls asleep.

Nurses Ada and Zane walk cautiously around the ward, observing the patients as they sleep, and Nurse Zane says, "Nurse Ada, everyone is still sleeping just as Dr. Nyondo said. I'm afraid. What has happened here?"

"I don't know, but we must wait until daylight as Dr. Nyondo instructed us to do. Maybe then we will know what is happening."

The light of the lamp awakens Dr. Nyondo as it comes back on, and he sees that the image of the angel has returned. He joyfully smiles but is still tired, so he closes his eyes and falls back to sleep.

As the sun begins shining through his office window, he wakes up to exuberant screaming and yelling. Loud voices scream out while frantic knocking is heard at his door as Nurse Ada comes rushing in, screaming and talking uncontrollably.

"Dr. Nyondo, come quickly! It's a miracle! Those who were sick are well! And those who were dead are alive!"

Dr. Nyondo rushes out of his office, running behind Nurse Ada, and when they get to the hospital ward, men, women, and children are dancing and joyfully celebrating—all giving praises to God. A couple of nurse assistants who temporarily passed out because of the events that have taken place stand up and join the celebration. Dr. Nyondo stands in the middle of the floor with tears running down his face as men, women, and children are everywhere, running up and down the aisleways. They're screaming and yelling. "To God give the glory!"

Dr. Nyondo falls to his knees as tears continue running down his face, and he looks up toward the ceiling. "Yes! Yes! For God has healed them all!" He continues to speak slowly and silently as he bows his head and says, "Amen."

Akachi pulls up in his Jeep after performing hospital errands, stopping directly in front of the hospital, and all the floors are visible from his vantage point. He hears and sees all the commotion and excitement through the windows of every story. He can tell from the loud outburst of exuberance that a glorious event has taken place.

He graciously smiles and looks up at the heavens and says, "My God! My God! What has happened here? Has the Holy Spirit truly arrived?"

As he continues looking, tears begin running down his face, and he becomes filled with overwhelming joy. He slowly bows his head and says, "I thank God for being God. Amen."

The End

EPILOGUE

S in is the corruption of the mind that penetrates the heart and soul, but love is a gift from God that dwells within all believers' hearts in Christ Jesus. The power of the Holy Spirit that dwells within me inspired me to write this book. We're all mesmerized by watching fantasy movies of all kinds. Movies like *Star Wars*, *Lord of the Rings*, *Harry Potter*, *The Hobbit*, and the list goes on. The films produced in Hollywood continue to dominate the fantasized imagination of people worldwide.

Everyone wants to take a journey into the unknown and experience the magical mystery that it possesses. The Holy Scripture is the ultimate source for us to journey into the realm of mystery and intrigue. Still, it's not a fantasy novel; the Bible is God's written word, documenting actual events that occurred. What could be more dramatic and sensational than the parting of the Red Sea, a river changed into a sea of blood, and the resurrection of the dead?

God could use a lamp to perform miracles, allowing it to travel from place to place to heal the sick and afflicted if that is His will. I hope this book has lifted your spirits and inspired you in a way that only God can do because, with God, All Things Are Possible. **May God Bless You All.**

 Derwyn Golden, a native of Detroit, Michigan, is a senior citizen and disabled veteran who spent ten plus years in the United States Air Force. He worked five years as a film director for a Fox Affiliate in Dayton, Ohio, and four years as sales director for the Best Western Hotel at Detroit Metropolitan Airport (DTW).